THE LOST SOUL ATLAS

PRAISE FOR

The BONe SPaRROW

'A contender for the children's book of the year . . .
a heartrending tale about how our stories make us,
and also an angry polemic, vividly convincing in
its detailed description of what it means for your home
to be a tent in the dust behind a guarded fence'
THE SUNDAY TIMES

'The story of Subhi, sensitively told and immensely moving,
gives us a glimpse of what a homeless, imprisoned
existence life feels like . . . and how the hope invested in a
vision of a better future can end up being the difference
between making it out, and surrendering to despair'
THE BIG ISSUE

'This is a tragic, beautifully crafted and wonderful
book whose chirpy, stoic hero shames us all.
I urge you to read it'
THE INDEPENDENT

'*THE BONE SPARROW* is one of those rare, special
books that will break your heart with its honesty and
beauty, but is ultimately hopeful and uplifting'
BOOKTRUST

'A profoundly poignant novel about
what it means to live as a refugee'
METRO

'The writing is beautiful and the message
of survival and bravery a universal one'
THE BOOKSELLER

THE LOST SOUL ATLAS

ZANA FRAILLON

Orion

ORION CHILDREN'S BOOKS

First published in Great Britain in 2020 by Hodder & Stoughton

1 3 5 7 9 10 8 6 4 2

A CIP catalogue record for this book
is available from the British Library.

ISBN 978 1 510 10682 6

Typeset in Sabon by Avon DataSet Ltd, Alcester, Warwickshire

Printed and bound in Great Britain by Clays Ltd, Elcograf S.p.A.

The paper and board used in this book
are made from wood from responsible sources.

Orion Children's Books
An imprint of Hachette Children's Group
Part of Hodder & Stoughton
Carmelite House
50 Victoria Embankment
London, EC4Y 0DZ

An Hachette UK Company
www.hachette.co.uk

www.hachettechildrens.co.uk

To Jugs, Luca, Mischa and Mani,
for showing me how to fly.

The struggle of man against power is the struggle of memory against forgetting.

Milan Kundera, *The Book of Laughter and Forgetting*

LESSER BAY OF NIGHTS:

UNDEREALM

OUTER WILDERLANDS

THE RI...

SOUTHERN DARKLANDS

S

Prologue
The Beginning

In the beginning, the Gods were bored. There was nothing to do any more. They had made their world and their creatures. They had played and built things and flooded things and dried things. And now they were bored.

The souls of the people weren't bored. They had memories to hold on to and stories to tell. They had loved ones to watch over and places to haunt. They quite enjoyed being dead.

But Gods can be jealous beasts, for why should people have all the fun?

And so the Gods decreed that when souls arrived in the Afterlife, they would enter a state of blissful unknowing. They would forget their time on earth. Memories were banished to the edges of the Afterlife.

And so it was.

It was the God of Winter Mornings who suggested they should all try a memory or two. Just to see what the fuss was about . . . The memories entered their beings, fed them smells and sights and sounds and feelings. For

1

a small time, the Gods existed purely within those small snatches of life. But once tried, the Gods wanted more. They wanted bigger, stronger memories. Memories to make them feel . . . alive.

The Gods took matters into their own hands. With just a flick of their heavenly fingers, they could create all the memories they needed. Destruction was rained down upon on the earth. Wars were waged. Walls were built. The earth was mined and torn and sundered. Seas rose and fires ravaged. Everything got a little hotter. Memories got a lot stronger. Souls arrived more quickly. Their memories horded more readily. The Gods feasted.

And so, it was.

Chapter 1

The End

And so, it was. This was it. The end. Twig couldn't look at those eyes. Or the arm aiming. It didn't tremble, that arm. Not even a bit. Neither did Twig. 'Go on. Do it then. I dare you.'

And the whole world exploded.

Wherever he was, it was dark. Deep dark. The thick, heavy dark that claws at your throat and scratches at your eyes. The kind of dark that picks you up and tosses you around and holds you close and whispers promises and pulls you apart. And just as Twig no longer knew if he even still existed, a neon sign burst into life and stilled him in its light.

WELCOME TO THE AFTERLIFE!

'Oh.'

That was the only word he could think of for quite some time.

The sign was broken. It made that fizzing, static sound that a loose connection makes, and the bulbs behind some of the letters flickered, spat and gave up. Without the bulbs, the sign now read

WE COME TO   LIFE!

Twig shuddered and gave the sign a cautious poke. A whole string of lights blossomed around him, glittering and twinkling along the edges of an old cobblestoned path that stretched and twisted into the darkness. They made Twig think of the time they had all wrapped fairy lights along the graves between the shacks and bought fish and chips and—

> *And the crows dive in for the chips and*
> *'Here's to us! We're the Beasts of the City*
> *Wilds!' and we all race to the top of the*
> *gargoyle tomb so we can look out over*
> *everything that's ours . . .*

The memory was like a snatch of dream, refusing to stand still. The more Twig tried to grab hold, the more his thoughts dimmed and fuzzed at the edges. He rubbed at his arms and wished he was in more than just his shorts and T-shirt. It wasn't the warmth he wanted, but the security of being wrapped tight. He peered into the dark stretching from the path. It was a forest, Twig

4

decided, a very thick, very dark, very foresty forest. Every so often, a branch would shuffle in the breeze and a leaf would catch in the twinkle of the lights. Twig imagined he could hear the rustle of branches being pushed aside, the snuffle of something lurking.

His head throbbed. What was it that had happened, exactly? He reached around to rub the pain from the back of his head and his hand came away bloodied. There had been something . . . It was silver and pointing and he'd known how dangerous it was, to be pointed at like that with . . . what was it? Twig could remember the laugh, cold and iced and hollow, that had sent shivers down his spine. The eyes he couldn't look at. The *clap. clap. clap.*

Another light fizzed into life, its bright red arrow pointing forward. 'OK. This way it is,' Twig said out loud, and was surprised by the dullness of his voice. Like he was being quietened. Everything seemed quietened. Even his footsteps along the path were just the whisper of a step.

There were more signs now. Twig slowed to read each one and to touch the letters. He liked the feel of something real and solid under his fingertips.

BE WELCOMED AT OUR WELCOME CENTRE! 2 MILES

KEEP TO THE PATH!

YOU ARE SAFE AND HAPPY!

GOLDEN GATES AHEAD!

LEAVE YOUR TROUBLES BEHIND!

EVERYTHING IS FINE!

STAY ON THE PATH!

**EMOTIONAL BAGGAGE DROP-OFF POINT
– ALL BAGS TO BE LEFT HERE**

FOREST TRAIL CLOSED – ENTRY PROHIBITED

DO NOT FEED THE BANSHEES

IT IS ALL SO LOVELY HERE. JUST PERFECT.

Some signs were nailed on to wooden stumps, others lit in bright lights like the signs down the High Street and casinos where Twig and the Beasts would scout for dropped coins and open pockets—

> *'Watch it!' and hands are reaching and
> someone is yelling and the coppers are
> pointing and . . .*

But the memory was like seeing something underwater, all vague and choppy and not quite there.

6

It made him a bit panicky, not being able to remember, but as soon as he thought that, another feeling washed over him, whispering through his mind, *Everything is so lovely here. Keep walking. You have nothing to worry about.*

'I have nothing to worry about,' Twig said, and kept walking. The further he walked, the lighter the sky became, like he was walking his way to morning. He focused on walking towards the light, and with each step, he felt his spirits lift, as if the light from the sky was seeping inside him. By the time he reached the **WELCOME CENTRE – 1.5 MILES** sign, it seemed that nothing really mattered any more. Even the forest didn't seem so sinister. Twig paused to admire the brilliant swirling green of a leaf, fallen on the path, and watched as a line of tiny stick-figure people weaved their way across the cobbled stones and into the forest. They were like little drawings come to life. They hummed a happy sort of tune as they walked, and each one carried an assortment of bits and pieces on its head or back. Buttons, a ring, an ancient-looking bell. One had tied a string to an old rusted **MEETING SPOT** sign and was heaving it along the ground, inching its way slowly forward. The smallest of the figures turned to Twig and waved a little stick-figure wave. The kind of wave one gives an old friend.

That was when the *thing* saw Twig. Flying overhead, a darkened patch against the light blue of the sky. It had been looking for the boy. Searching. And now it had him in its sights, it would not lose him again. It circled, closer and closer. And just as Twig started to walk again along the path, the thing clicked its beak and swooped.

Chapter 2

After Life

The thing dropped from the sky, landing hard and sharp on Twig's shoulder.

Twig yelped, grabbing at the thing and flinging it away. It clattered to the path in an explosion of bones, and the stick figures wailed and ran in every direction.

Twig's breath came in short, sharp gasps. Had he killed it? Whatever *it* was? Could something even *be* killed in the Afterlife? And what was a boned *thing* doing attacking him when everything was so lovely and . . . and . . . oh.

The bones began to shake. Wobbling and wriggling. Dragging themselves along the ground. Piecing their bits back together. One. Bone. At. A. Time. First came the clawed foot bones. Then the legs. Then all eight rib bones clattered together at once. Then the curved neck, and the particularly sharp beak, and finally the bones of both wings clicked together, screwed their skull firmly in place, then folded themselves rather angrily across their chest. Twig found himself trapped in the glare of a

9

skeleton bird. If a skeleton can be said to glare, which, Twig decided, it definitely could.

'Well, now,' the bird said, one clawed foot tapping in displeasure. 'That wasn't the kind of warm greetin' I was expectin'. It's lucky for you I'm not one to hold grudges, me.' The skeleton hopped closer to Twig. 'But I'm well glad I found you. I thought I'd gone and lost you, didn't I? What'd you go and leave the Meetin' Spot for? Didn't you read the sign? It's a spot for *meetin'*. The clue is in the name, see? I mean, I know I was a little on the late side, like, but it was only a minute, five at most, ten maybe, but re-aaaa-lly!'

'Sorry. I didn't see a sign at the meeting spot.' Twig glanced at where the stick figures had dragged the rusty sign into the shadows.

'Anywhatsit, all's well that ends well. Now, where was we? Oh yes. I'm your Guardian. Krruk's the name and how de do and shake hands and we'll be home for break-fast.'

'Hi, Krruk.'

'No. Krruk. Krruk. Copy me now. Krruk.'

'Krruk.'

'Kr . . . never mind. That will do. I tell you now, you are lucky you got me. I'm the best Guardian of the lot, I am. You won't remember all those times durin' your alive years that you saw a raven guidin' you through the trials and tribulations of livin' because of the Forgettin' that happens once you're . . . well . . . dead, like. But, if

10

I do say, I was quite magnificent.' The raven nodded at Twig and twirled proudly. 'And it was probably me them times when you thought it was a crow lookin' over you and all, because people are always gettin' us confused, don't ask me why, we don't even look similar.'

Twig looked at the skeleton bobbing up and down. 'So it was your job to keep me . . . alive?'

'Exactly!'

'But, I'm . . . dead, right?'

'That you are. Oh. Right. Well. I see what you're gettin' at.' The raven hopped awkwardly from foot to foot. 'But what it is is, the mortal world can get more than a tad bo-rin', you know. It's all so teeeeeeedious. I was well bored. Was you bored? I figured you was bored . . .' He looked at Twig, then pulled a black feather out from the empty space between his ribs. 'Here. Have a feather. Raven's feathers are good luck, you know. That should make you happy. Anywhatsit, yous are in a much better place here. Once we walk through them Golden Gates you'll see. There's a train. And gardens. And lots of people playin' bridge. I hear they've yoga on a Tuesday too.' The raven glanced at Twig. 'And congratulations on the dyin'. Not many people die well nowadays but yours was a good 'n.'

'Was it? I can't really remember . . .' His thoughts were all so thick and sludgy . . . there was—

'Go on.'

and—

11

That arm. And that laugh. And those eyes.
Someone is whispering to run. Run rabbit,
run rabbit, run run run. But running is so
very tiring. Everything is so very tiring.
There is only one thing left to say.
'Do it then.'

The niggle of memory faded. 'Why can't I remember? I want to remem—'

'Oh now. Don't be daft. That life is done and dusted. No one remembers a thing here. By order of the decreewhatsit. Complete and blissful unknowin' – that's what's waitin' for you once you pass through them Golden Gates. You won't even know you've anythin' *to* remember in a bit. Isn't that great? Never have to worry about a thing.'

Twig didn't think that sounded great at all. It sounded . . . devastating. The loss tugged at his chest. Knowing that he had once felt something that he would never feel again. All those things that made him who he was . . .

He let out a small sigh, full of longing and sadness and want. The sigh was so small his Guardian didn't even hear it. But the wind picked it up, cradled it, bustled it higher and higher, then released it over the tops of the trees where it drifted gently into the forest below.

The creature dwelling in the shadows of the forest heard the sigh and nodded. She pulled the black hood over her head. 'The boy,' she hissed, and her clawed hands clapped and clasped at the bones scattered on the forest floor. 'The boy is here,' she whispered, and the forest erupted into howls.

Chapter 3

The Calling

'Righteo then, best keep walkin'.' Krruk nudged Twig with his skull. 'We've a train to catch! They've a lovely welcome pack waitin' and all, with a dressin' gown and lush fluffy-bunny slippers.'

'A train . . . yes . . . slippers . . .'

'Hang on a minute.' Krruk stopped and glared at the line of stick figures marching past. 'Is that my wing bone?'

Two of the larger stick figures were stealthily rolling a thin hollow bone along the ground.

'Oi! Give that back, you thievin' little blighters!' Krruk pecked dangerously close to the one who had wrapped its arms protectively around the bone.

The tiny figures abandoned their line, arms thrashing the air as they ran in frenzied circles, keening, 'MEEEEEEP! MEEEEEEEEP!' and trying hopelessly to escape. The littlest one turned and dashed towards Twig.

'Don't eat them!' Twig cried. They looked so helpless.

Krruk popped his wing bone back into place. 'But

14

meeples are proper pests they are, terrible thieves. I lost my best pocket watch to a roving pack of meeples once. And they is quite tasty. Sort of peppery in flavour . . .'

The littlest one was holding tight to Twig's foot, gnashing its little stick teeth in fear. Twig held his hand out for it, and it climbed shakily on.

'But if you insist,' Krruk huffed and clicked his beak and the few remaining meeples disappeared into the dark. 'Come on. We don't want to be late, like. Them Gods appreciate punctuality. They like the memories nice and fresh, they do.'

Twig placed the meeple on the very edge of the path. 'Good luck,' he whispered, then paused. There was just the faintest tune, carrying softly on the wind. It was a tune of yearning, and complete comfort. It held stories and songs and cold winter nights and hot milk with honey, and warm arms wrapping tight. 'I know that song . . .' Twig scrabbled to find the memory. 'Krruk? Did you hear that?'

'Krruk, not Krruk. You've to roll the tongue like—'

'It's coming from the forest.' Twig took a step towards the sound.

'Get back on to the path, would you?' Krruk flapped at Twig and herded him back. 'Didn't you read the sign? STAY ON THE PATH!'

'But I heard—'

'Just the wind, wasn't it.'

The song came again, louder this time, wisping

closer. A tangled memory cracked through the sludge of forgetting and Twig knew the sound for what it was. A tin whistle. Just like the one his da used to play and—

'This is the song of our people. Passed down
through time. This whistle is older than you.
Older than me even. My da used to tell
me that it was older than him and older
than his da. One day, this whistle
will be yours . . .'

'Da!' Twig turned to Krruk. 'He's in the forest! Da!'

'Don't be daft. And not being funny, but if we don't get a move on, they'll send the Officials to come lookin', and then we'll both be in a whole realm of trouble. We're already runnin' behind schedule due to the fact that *someone* left the meetin' spot. Listen, presh, you'll love it here. It's all so lovely, don't you think?'

Twig looked at the skeleton bird. The feeling of calm washed over him again. 'It *is* lovely,' he agreed. What was it they had been talking about? It felt important, but . . . ah well. 'It's perfect, isn't it, Krruk?'

The raven smiled. 'Krruk. Say it with me. Krruk. Come now, the train is waitin'.'

'I like trains. Ow!' Twig yelped. The little meeple sank his needle teeth deeper into Twig's ankle. 'Oww!' The meeple spat once, wiped his tongue, then beckoned towards the forest, tugging at Twig's leg with his little stick hands.

'Get lost, would you!' Krruk snapped his beak. 'I told

you they was pests! Can I eat just this one? Chopsy little blighter he is.'

And now the song came again. Louder and clearer—
'One day, my darling'
Twig didn't wait for the forgetting to overcome him again. His da was calling for him. He picked up the meeple and ran into the forest, focusing on the music.

And in that instant, Twig existed purely inside the notes. He became the soft wind of breath flowing through tin, spinning and twirling, tripping higher and higher on the wind.

And he is smaller now, and he is in a tree, and his da is playing his whistle and the notes are wrapping him safe and whispering him stories and promises of things to come. His da holds out his arms, *Jump!* and somewhere, far away, something is calling to Twig, trying to drag him back, but all Twig wants now is to know the strong safety of those arms again.

'Da!' Twig closes his eyes and lets the music take him where it will.

Chapter 4
Fruit of the Gods

'Da!'

'Get down, you monkey. You'll fall.' But Da's smiling, his arms held wide and I know he'll catch me. 'Jump!' And I'm in his arms and he's spinning me so the trees and birds smudge together in the twirl of light, and my ears fill with all the secrets of the world, whispering too fast for me to catch.

We sit under the tree and watch the rabbits feeding behind the bushes. 'Run rabbit, run rabbit, run run run,' Da sings. 'Don't give the farmer his fun fun fun. He'll get by, without his rabbit pie, so run rabbit, run rabbit, run run run.' And Da plays the song on his whistle and gets me to keep time on a rock, and when I get too fast for him to keep up, he laughs and laughs and it's like the whole world laughs with him.

Da leans back against the tree and rests his hand on my head, heavy and warm. 'I almost forgot. I've got something for you. A secret,' he says and takes a small package from his coat pocket, brown paper holding the

18

treasure tight, and his voice drops low even though there's no one around but the birds. 'This, my love' – and he looks over his shoulder to make sure we're alone, and I roll my eyes at his pretending – 'is the Fruit of the Gods. One taste and you will know the taste of Heaven.'

'Fruit,' I echo, and already my mouth is watering. I wonder how he got it. I can't remember the last time I had fruit. Da told me that when he was a kid, fruit was everywhere. They used to say *a fruit a day keeps the doctor away* and kids wouldn't eat an apple if it was just a little bit bruised or wormed. Da says when I was little, we used to have a bowl in the kitchen, just for fruit, but I can't remember that bowl. Or that fruit.

Da unwraps the paper slowly, and all the birds in the trees shuffle closer on their branches and lean in to get a better look.

But it's not an apple. Or an orange even. It's dark red and hard and heavy in my hand. 'Fruit of the Gods,' I whisper and my tongue edges the skin. It's waxed like the candle we light for Mum in the church with the story windows and where the kid with the red bandana is. Sometimes I leave things behind a loose stone in the church wall for that kid and they're gone the next time we come. And sometimes there are different things left there for me. Like one time I left a toy car I'd found and whispered as loud as I could in the church, 'I've left it for you, kid!', and the next time there was a little stone dragon waiting for me which is much better than a car.

And another time, there was a watch that was broken, so I fixed it and put it back in the wall. It's a game that neither of us knows for sure we're playing. Sometimes I think that kid is following us too, because sometimes when we work the cars stopped at the bridge, I'll see a flash of red darting in and out of the people on the footpath, and I can feel eyes pushing into my back. At first, I thought we were playing some kind of tag or something, but now I think we're just being followed. I bet that kid's never tasted Fruit of the Gods before.

'Where did you get it from, Da?'

But Da just looks up at the skies. 'I told you, from the Gods. I nicked it fresh from those Heavenly trees, just for you.' But I wish he'd tell me for real where he got it from. I know it's from wherever he goes at night when he thinks I'm asleep and he stalks dead quiet out the door. He thinks I don't see.

I crack open the skin with my teeth. 'Good, hey?' Da whispers and the taste on my tongue is new and full of a thousand and one brightnesses. 'Like a mouthful of stars,' he says. 'Now finish the juice and save the jewels for later. They'll keep. You don't want to waste it, now.'

Next time I sit with Da on the rooftop and we wish on the stars, I'll wish for a whole bag of these fruit. We could eat all of them at once until our stomachs ache and burst and we wouldn't have to think about saving. I add it to my list of wishes. That list is getting quite long now.

'Da?'

He is looking out at the fence, to where a woman is watching us and holding her spade and wondering what we are doing here out in the plots with our cart stacked high with bags for selling. She's wondering if we've been thieving her vegetables and wondering if she should chase us off herself or call the coppers. She's not thinking that maybe we just like sitting here among the bees and the birds under the shade of a tree to break up the walk, and there's no harm in sitting, is there? But then Da's hand squeezes mine and I forget all about the woman with the spade.

'Where do you really go when you go out at night? Why can't you tell me?'

'I did tell you. I go to Heaven. I follow the gargoyles. You have to wait for a Gargoyle Moon of course. But if you wait and watch you'll see them crack free from their rock skin, called out by the moon. They dance and spin and hunt in the moonlight, and if you're not careful you'll get caught up in their dance and you might just end up a gargoyle yourself. But . . .' And Da leans in close, his hands weaving the air in front of him. 'If you're careful, if you're mouse-quiet and fox-clever, you can follow them. They know all the ins and outs between the worlds . . .'

I shake my head and turn away so he knows *I* know it's just a story, even though it is quite a good story really.

'Oh ho, you don't believe me? Are you too big all of a sudden?'

But it isn't all of a sudden. Da just still thinks of me as little. That's why he won't tell me where he goes. He thinks he can't trust me. But he can. I keep showing him he can. He just doesn't see.

Da nudges me. 'Well then, Mr Non-Believer. If I don't follow those gargoyles, how is it that my old coat here has the smell of the Heavens on it? The smell of rock skin and night wind and secret tunnels that weave through stars?' Da raises an eyebrow at me, and I smell his coat. It's stupid, but Da's coat does smell like old rusted rock dust and cold night winds. It's what Da smells like too.

Da laughs and squeezes me to him and calls me his little one and that's when I think it. My plan. And at first it's just the whisper of a thought. A small voice scratching and hissing – *fine then*. If Da won't tell me where he goes, I'll just have to see for myself and prove to him that I'm not a 'little one' who'll be fooled by any old story any more. Maybe then he'll let me leave off school and I can work with him always and not just in the holidays. And even though that scratchy voice is the one that always gets me into trouble, I'm so caught up in imagining, that I pretend it's a good idea this time. I pretend that this time, nothing could go wrong.

The voice in my head laughs.

Chapter 5

Thieves and Rogues

It takes for ever to walk back along the rails. There's a faster way, cutting through the Factory Estates, but Da says there are too many windows to see from and mouths to whisper and not worth the risk. Da points out things along the way – 'That flower there is the Queen of the Night. She only ever blooms in the dark, isn't that amazing?' – and gives me maths problems and tells me about the earth and stars and moon and tides, and tests my spelling, because he reckons the whole world's a school if you've got someone teaching.

I try not to think about how far the walk is because Da hates it when I complain, even if it is just a sigh which I can't help, and which technically isn't complaining. I try not to think how each step nags at the cut on my heel from where I sliced it climbing through a broken window when Da told me specifically that empty flats are not for exploring, but all the kids were and everyone knows the empties are the best for finding treasure and if I didn't then the others would rag me for being a do-gooder baby, so what choice did I have?

And I try not to think about the kids from Riverside crew who follow when we pass too close to their camp, calling out things and throwing rocks. Da doesn't get bothered. He just puts his hand on my shoulder to stop me turning and says, 'Crew kids. Thieves and rogues, that's all they are, and not worth our time. We stay away from them.'

I look back and they're laughing, those kids, all with their torn-up trousers and shirts hanging in scraps, and the snotty-nosed little ones digging in the mud looking for treasures and picking through bin bags and fighting the rats for the good bits. I don't think their world is a school. Still, it might be nice living with your grannies and grampas and aunts and uncles. I'd like that more than the Tower flat we have to share with the Collinses and Old Man Tipper whose wife is dead but he keeps her ashes in a jar that he whispers to all day and night like she's still alive and gossiping.

One day, Da says, we'll make enough money buying and selling stuff to move into a flat all of our very own, just like when he was a kid, but until then, we share with as many people as that flat can fit. I don't know anyone that has their own flat though. How would the city hold everyone? It wouldn't be so bad to be sharing with your own family like they do next door. That would be nice. Even though there must be about fifteen of them in that flat, I hear them through the wall and they laugh all the time. We don't have any other family though. Just me and Da.

I've been thinking while we've been walking, and I reckon I've figured where Da must go at night. It must be the black markets. I've heard about them from the bigger kids. The black markets are where you go to buy and sell things which aren't *exactly* legal, or have been thieved and sold on the cheap. Where else would Da find Fruit of the Gods?

He must reckon it's too dangerous for me to come, but I'll show him. I think he forgets I'm almost eleven. It's like he still sees the little six-year-old me skipping along behind. He never notices how I fix the cart on my own to stop the dodgy wheel rolling off and check the tyres *every* morning for pumping and patching. Or how I bargain with the sellers to get the best price for the stuff we fix up, or push the price up when I'm the one doing the selling. I can fix just about anything and make it good as new or better even. But Da never notices. Maybe, if I can prove that I'm old enough, then we can be proper partners buying and fixing and selling things all over the city. Maybe then he won't look at me and shake his head in that frustrated way he does sometimes when I've asked a stupid question or messed something up.

We're not far from the Towers when Da stops to restrap the cart. That's when I see the red of the bandana, like a flag waving. I knew that kid was following us.

'Da.' But he's busy scribbling words into his book.

I look again at the kid poking through the rubbish, dipping into the bag and out again, keeping watch for any coppers coming along with their sticks and their boots and their whistles. Coppers always go for bin rats because no one wants their bins gone through, do they?

'Da, look. That's the kid I was telling about. The one following us. That bin rat.'

Da stops writing. His eyes turn thin and sharp and his chin lifts and for a moment I think it's me he's angry with, for disturbing his thinking. But then he turns, his body pulled straight and tall and puffed so suddenly he is two, three times bigger. The kid has their back to us, but even so they can feel Da looking and they stop moving, their whole body turned to stone like when a cat runs in front of a car at night and just stands, waiting to be hit.

'That little squirt of a thing?' The edge in Da's look turns soft and he sighs and shrinks back to his normal person size. 'Perhaps there's no one else to follow, hey?' And Da kisses the top of my head like when I was little.

'Da?'

But he's walking again, pushing the cart and looking at his watch, his steps getting faster. 'And don't call people bin rats, Twiggy. We're all just people. Come on. We're late.'

But those words about the kid are still pecking at my thinking and my feet dance up and down on the spot, not knowing if they should be walking or standing. 'Perhaps there is no one else to follow,' I whisper. I look at the kid again, that hair chopped all ragged under the bandana and trousers so big the cuffs are turned up almost all the way to the knees, and more bracelets jangling on those wrists than a jewellery shop – but no boots or shoes. Not even in this cold.

'Come on!' Da doesn't like it when I lag.

The kid has darted into the shadows of the building, squeezed in behind the bags of rubbish, just a toe poking out into the sun. I take the saved fruit from my pocket. 'Hey, kid! Hey, squirt!' But nothing. That toe doesn't even wriggle. 'This is a taste of Heaven. A mouthful of stars. Fruit from the Gods. Hurry, it's for you, squirt!' But even that doesn't do it. I lift the brown paper from the fruit and my tongue flicks just one more small taste of Heaven, then I wrap it back up and lay it gentle on the grass, and run to catch up with Da. That kid can have it. I'll be getting more tonight when I follow Da to the markets.

'Come on, love. It'll be dark soon,' Da says and I jump up and on to the cart and wait for him to push me back off again, but he just *oof*s in pretend surprise, then starts whistling and tapping his hands on the handle and up here I am the king of the world.

'Look there,' Da says and stops to point to an old car parked on the street. 'You know what that is, don't you? It's an old DeLorean. They only ever made a handful. That one there would be worth a fortune. Look at those doors, do you know what they do?' And Da tells me all about the car from an old movie with doors that open up like wings and I wonder if red-bandana kid has anyone to tell them about old cars and movies and wings.

I look back, but the kid has gone. So has the parcel. And even though I can't see that kid or anyone else paying us any attention, I get that feeling of hair raising on the back of my neck, like someone is watching and following. It gives me the shivers, like my body is calling me to pay attention, warning me. And that feeling, it doesn't go away.

Chapter 6
The Hoblin

Da and me are on the roof. From up here, you can see right across to the city walls. Sometimes, when there's no smog, you can see even further, stretching out to the swamplands even.

We watch the lights go out one by one for curfew, like someone is switching off the city. 'When I was a kid,' Da says, 'the lights in the city buildings would stay on all night. Like they do at Christmas now,' and I think how pretty that must've been.

I lean closer to Da. The roof always makes me feel weird. 'You're shaking. You're not still scared up here, are you?' Da laughs, and I tell him it's just the cold is all. 'Ah. Of course.' Da takes off his coat and wraps me in it and holds me tight against him, and my shaking stops and we look up at the stars. It isn't often you get a wind strong enough to push away the smoke that wraps the city so you can see the stars clearly. 'Can you see her?' Da says and I look for the brightest star in the sky, the one with the three little stars wriggling around it.

'There she is, Da. That's her, right?'

'Sure it is. Say hello to your mum and your baby brothers, love,' Da says and I look up at the stars and say 'hello' and wonder if they are my big brothers, being born before me, or if I'm their big brother because they never grew past being babies. I try to imagine what it would be like to have three big brothers looking out for me for real, and a mum that didn't only show up when the wind was strong.

'Have you got a wish for your mum?' Da asks.

I think of everything on my list, but instead I just wish that Da would see I'm not a little kid any more. Then I think that maybe wishing is only a thing little kids do, so I stop.

Da turns quiet and I think he is talking to Mum and my brothers and he always looks so peaceful talking to them. I don't think he ever looks like that talking to me. But then he squeezes me to him and I listen to his heart beating and his stomach gurgling and I feel peaceful too. He runs his finger over a long scratch from the cat I tried to make mine because it would be nice to have a cat. That stupid cat. If it had stayed with me I would have looked after it and those Riverside boys never would have cornered it and . . . it was a stupid cat anyway.

'That's nasty looking. How did you get it?' Da asks. I shrug. Da always tells me not to play with the street cats. 'It wasn't from a bear, was it? Or a . . . a devil bear even?' he whispers and I sigh loudly and try not to smile.

'I told you about the time I came up against the devil bear, didn't I? When I was just a little fella and learnt to howl my wild wolf howl? And how I was saved by the King of Wolves himself?' Da rubs his hands together. He knows he has told me this story a thousand times over, but I snuggle in to listen again.

'Spit dripped from his teeth and his roar was straight from hell's fires. He took a step towards me. My legs were shaking, weak as jelly' – and Da looks at me with his bright wide eyes – 'like your legs when I taught you to swim, remember? *No, Da, it's too cold, it's too dark!*' And Da squeaks his voice high and laughs.

I remember. I remember Da telling me that fear is the hardest fight, but the most important win, because people will always try to scare you out of doing. '*To know yourself you must be strong,*' he said, then threw me in the river to get out on my own. I hate that river. I still have nightmares, of water dark and flaming black, dragging me down, down, deeper and deeper into nothing . . .

'But' – Da taps his chest and keeps on with his story – 'we Galliots have warrior blood running through our veins. We never give up. I couldn't fight him with my hands, so I fought him with my heart. I opened my heart and howled every true thing I knew, right at that devil bear. And from out of the forest came a pack of the wildest wolves this world has ever seen, called by my howls. Must be they could understand the language of the heart, because the King of Wolves, he stood before the bear and joined in my howl, and the bear roared in fury and took off back to the gates of Hell.' Da howls into the night and gives me a nudge.

I try out a howl of my own and Da laughs. 'You think that's a wild wolf howl? Ah, you've got to be careful. You've got to make sure your howl is *true* to call the wolves. Not any old howl will do. The wrong sort of howl could bring down all sorts of trouble. You could howl down banshees.' He pretends to look for approaching banshees, and I howl again, louder into the night. 'Oh no!' he says, 'you could howl down fairies of the very worst kind!' He puts his finger to my lips, and whispers, 'You could howl down a *Hoblin* even . . .' And the hair on the back of my neck spikes in warning again . . .

'A Hoblin?'

'A Hoblin is the worst of them all. They look like beautiful women, dressed in fine robes and jewels, but that is just a skin they wear. Inside they are the beasts from your very worst nightmares. All they need is a single piece of hair and then they can steal your soul and make you do anything. A mother would eat her own baby with only a flick of a Hoblin's finger. But no one lives for long without a soul. Your body just turns to dust, puff! No one can stop a Hoblin. No one . . . RAH!' Da tries to make me jump.

I laugh to show I'm not even a bit scared and Da laughs with me and pulls out his whistle and plays for a bit and it's just about the most perfect night in the whole world.

'Right then, down we go and into bed. It's well late now.'

'Are you going out tonight?' I ask softly. 'To buy things from the black markets? That's where you go, isn't it? Can't I come with you? I can help.'

Da looks at me and I think he's going to try to bluff me about gargoyles and Heaven again. But then he sighs. 'Listen, love. Those markets aren't for little ones. They're dangerous. I wouldn't go if I didn't have to. But sometimes customers ask me for stuff, you know? Stuff they can't get. Like medicines that are too expensive or that you can't buy here. Or fruit or . . . well, lots of things. I'm sorry. But with you here, I know you're safe from all the devil bears—'

And suddenly I'm angry and hot and I wonder if maybe the cat had rabies because it was a fairly angry cat, and I've never been angry with Da before. Not this fast and furious anger that swells up from nowhere and takes me by surprise. 'There are no bears! This is not your forest!' I spit out the words, hiss them like the cat hissed at me and I think how stupid his story is. How stupid all his stories are. 'I'm not a *little one* any more. I'm too old for your stupid stories. Why can't you see that?'

Da looks away. I stop. I hate myself for saying any of it, and I start shaking even more than before, my teeth chattering and my bones trembling.

'Ah, love. There are more bears in this city than in all the forests of the world. And these city bears, they're twice as dangerous.' He kisses my head and brushes my hair back with his hand.

'I'm sorry, Da.' And Da waves my sorry away like I never said a thing against him.

'To bed, hey? Get you out of this cold.'

He tucks me up on the mattress with the other kids and kisses me goodnight, curling his coat over me. 'So you can dream of the stars. In the morning, you can draw us your dreams, OK, love? Make my heart sing.' He moves my shoebox of pictures closer to my head – all the pictures I've drawn from Da's stories, of elf trails and troll towns and far-off mountain kingdoms, and my hand rests on top like they'll feed my dreams.

And everything is so perfect again, and so right, that I almost decide not to follow him after all, because I have everything that matters right here. I almost curl up in his coat and just dream.

Almost.

Chapter 7
City Bears

I'd make an excellent spy. No one has spotted me. Not even anyone in the flat except for Old Man Tipper but he just glared and whispered to his jar. The other kids thought I'd chicken out. Franky Collins said I wouldn't get as far as Main Road without turning tail and running back. I'll show him. When I come back with arms full of Fruit of the Gods, that Franky Collins will have to beg me to get a share.

I'm out of the Tower now, my da's coat flowing behind me like a cape. I can see Da just about to turn the corner at the clock tower. I follow him past the Lion's Head pub, and past the playground that's all gated up because it's too late even for swings. Past the old post office where the pigeons have cracked through the window, and I imagine them all nested in with the letters and parcels people never picked up. There must be loads worth selling in there. It wouldn't be stealing neither, because the post office is closed for good now and the stuff is only going to waste. But just as I'm about to race past, I see that red-bandana kid again, jiggling something in the lock. The door swings open and the kid turns and sees me.

'Hey! Squirt!' the kid calls to me and smiles, and they're the squirt, not me. I called them that first, and I'm bigger than they are. Don't they even know what squirt means? But before I can yell back, the kid steps into the post office, and that kid'll take all the good stuff for sure. I shake my head and start back off after Da.

He turns again, and again, and now we've twisted so far down the mazes of streets and alleys I've no idea where I am.

It's like the whole world has squeezed into these streets. There's music playing and bells ringing and people parading up and down in colours and feathers and laughing louder than anyone should ever laugh. Great big torches burn bright and lanterns hang from doorways, choking black smoke into the sky. The way the torchlight flickers turns the gargoyles on the buildings to life and I swear I see their rock skin crack and their shadows shift and follow me along the streets. And there are so many people, all in their coloured clothes, flapping and flowing and stepping in and over and around me, and shoving me this way and that, that I almost lose track of Da in the crowd. I see him though, turning down an alleyway, and I wait just a little to make sure I'm not too close behind.

But I shouldn't have done that. A proper spy wouldn't

have done that. Because when I turn the corner, Da isn't in the alley. It's like he's just disappeared. Like the big grey stones of the road have swallowed him whole. I think of Da's face when he comes back and finds me gone. I think, what if I never see my da again?

I curl up behind the bins, my fist in my mouth to stop the moan leaking out because spies definitely don't moan but to be honest I'm beginning to rethink the whole spy business anyway. That's when I see the bag from the cake shop Da likes. And somehow, holding that bag makes me feel like everything will be OK. Like maybe it's Da's bag. Like maybe he'll come back for it. But there is no cake in the bag. There is something though. A package wrapped tight in silver and plastic and—

And then hands are grabbing me, lifting me high, slamming me against the bricks of the building so I can't breathe. Faces are pushed into mine, voices yelling, fingers twisting, laughing, poking, their teeth black holes in their mouths.

'You stealing from us?'

'That what you doing, boy? You stealing our bag?'

'You crazy?'

I'm trying to tell them no, but my voice won't work, and now they are talking to each other, 'how much you reckon we get for a fish this big?'

and their fingers are in my mouth, pressing up my lips

37

'good teeth, that helps'
and they're twisting my body and holding my arms
above my head
'healthy 'nough'
'nice and young, this one'
'what d'you think?'
and I see who these men are.
These are the city bears.

Chapter 8

The Wrong Sort of Howl

Da's right. These city bears *are* worse. But I am a Galliot. I have warrior blood running through my veins. And so I fight. I bite and tear and rip, and pretend it is *me* that is the King of the Wolves and that I wear the crown, and I will not be tamed.

My mouth fills with blood and my ears fill with the sound of a grown man screaming and my arm fills with sharp pain as they twist it behind my back and I'm slammed into the stones of the street and my face is squashed flat with a boot and my hair is pulled tight and my neck stretches back further and my eyes are wide enough that I see the man I bit vomit and the other men laugh.

'He's a fighter! Even better, hey?'

'There's them cage fights down the way . . .'

Then my da is there. Come to save me. He drops his bag and all the special things for all his special customers that he bought from the black markets roll into the gutter.

And those city bears turn fiercer and dangerouser than Da ever told. They have him on the ground. They are attacking, ripping, shredding, tearing him to pieces and I open my mouth and I howl.

Da's own howl breaks free, and we both open our hearts and howl every true thing in the world to each other. The wind picks up our howls and cracks through the city, and runs in the river, and splits open the earth and tears down the skies, and all them people wrapped up tight in their beds, and all them others out on the street dancing and singing and parading, they stop and shiver and hold their arms tight wondering at that sound, never knowing that these are the howls of the wildest wolves, and that these are the howls of truth.

No King Wolf comes to save us though. No pack comes to scare those bears back to the gates of Hell. Our howls call something else instead.

She steps from the shadows. A lady, all dressed in fine clothes and jewels. *The wrong sort of howl could bring down all sorts of trouble . . . banshees . . . fairies . . . a Hoblin even . . .* Those men take one look at that lady, and their eyes turn bug-big and white-scared and they drop me and Da and they run, helter-skelter, back to their caves.

Da's looking more scared and beaten now than when those bears had him. And that angry cat scratch fills me white-hot and burning again because, what? Is he scared by his own stupid made-up story? Hoblins. What rubbish. Da said we never give up, but he isn't fighting at all. He's not doing a thing, just staying crumpled and beaten at the feet of some stupid lady and he's pathetic and weak and I'm yelling at my da to come on and go home and get up and you said you're a warrior so do something and why won't you make it stop. Why won't you even try—

Now bigger, harder, rougher hands have me and I'm looking up at a man the size of a giant. The lady leans down to Da. 'Ah, Mr Galliot,' she says, and her voice is the voice of death. 'I didn't think I would see *you* again.' She looks at me and nods – 'Such a pretty, pretty boy' – and walks slowly round me in circles. 'What is your name, Little Mouse?' And she brushes the hair from my eyes and even though the giant has me held tight, I snap my King Wolf teeth and growl my King Wolf growl because Da may have given up but I haven't, and see, Da? I'm not scared.

The man pushes his knee into my back and squeezes my jaw open and my teeth are aching to tear skin and taste blood and chew bone, and he hisses to 'play nice'.

The lady turns back to Da. 'After everything you did . . .'

Da looks at her. He won't look at me. 'Let the boy go,' he says, his voice so quiet, I almost can't hear it. The lady looks at the giant and he lets me go.

'Come here, Little Mouse,' the lady says, but then Da

pulls himself up. Bigger and taller and huger than the giant even.

'Run! Run NOW!' And I run.

I turn, just the once. I see my da, shrunk down to normal size again, smaller even than before, kneeling before that lady.

I turn away and run harder. My feet pound faster. My breathing is torn and shredded and the trees shake and crackle like fire around me and the branches twist and snap and the wind whips the shadows from the ground and sucks the lights from the torches and my howls break free again and crack the skies apart and all the Gods waiting for us in Heaven with fruit in their arms start crying great big tears that leak from the sky and drown us in their waves and all I can do is run rabbit, run rabbit, run run run.

Chapter 9

The Gatherer

Twig opened his eyes, the shadowed memory of his howl still echoing on his lips as he ran through the dark of the forest—

'Run! Run NOW!'

And the music from the tin whistle was still playing, and Twig was still following the tune weaving through the leaves. 'Da! I'm coming.'

'Come back, boyo! This is rid-ic-u-lous!' Krruk crashed through the trees behind him. 'We have to STAY ON THE PATH! Are you listening to me? Agh, scrimpkins!'

Twig kept running. Branches scratched his face and tugged at his skin. There was some small part of him that whispered if he stopped running, he might forget what he was running for. Who he was running for. If he stopped running, he might forget who he was altogether. He let the notes guide him. As long as the music didn't stop, he'd be fine . . .

The music stopped.

'Da?' But there was only silence, deep and empty.

The shadowed trees of the forest leaned close. In the dim light, Twig could make out a sign: *MEEPLE MOUND – EXTREME DANGER*, sticking out from a rocked knoll. A long line of meeples made its way into the mound through a large opening in the rock, dragging a length of fairy lights behind them. The little meeple waved his arms wildly, leaping from Twig's arm and running into the mound. Twig leaned forward, peering into the entrance – there was just a hint of song still hanging inside the mound, like it had been trapped within the rock walls.

'Da's in the mound!'

'It's just the meeples, presh! You can't go in there – those mounds twist for ever under the ground. Like a labryinthwhatsit. You go in, you'll never come out. If we don't get you out of here and on that train, the Gods will send the Officials!'

Twig didn't stop to think, just crawled through the narrow opening, the rock pressing against his shoulders, squeezing the air from his lungs and squashing at his ribs. Tiny candles burned bright on the tunnel walls, lighting up pictures of meeples painted in muted colours that trembled at the edge of his vision. The tunnel twisted and grew, breaking off into smaller darker tunnels, larger tunnels, tunnels that weaved and wound back on themselves. Twig followed the trail of candles, concentrating only on reaching the next flame as he crawled deeper and deeper, until finally the tunnel opened up into a large cavern. Great crystal stalactites hung from the roof, and the ground was scattered with hundreds and thousands of stone-white bones.

'Krruk?' Twig breathed. There was a sudden gust of warm wind, like the cave was sighing, and every single candle went out.

'Well. I told you, didn't I?' Krruk thumped on to Twig's shoulder. 'There is nothin' and no one here, and now we is both up the proverbial creek without a paddlewhatsit. I do wish you'd listen. I am your Guardian, like, and I do know a thing or two. I mean—'

'*Here we come a-gathering . . .*' The voice sang through the dark. Cracked and ancient, slipping through the rock and seeping inside Twig's head as if it were his own thoughts, directionless, and somehow distant and close at the same time.

Krruk's claws tightened on Twig's shoulder. 'Agh, scrimpkins! I don't believe it. Of all the grottos in all the realms, you have to find your way into *her* grotto. And she's singin'. Oh nonono. That isn't good. If it's you she's singin' after, there's no escape . . .'

'Her?' Fear bloomed across Twig's skin.

'She's one of the *Olds*. Been around as long as the Gods, maybe more, and some say those Olds know a fair bit more about the ways of things than those Gods do. I wouldn't say such a thing mind, but the thing with Olds is, they is ver-ry set in their ways, like. Stubborn. And a little scary. This one is called the Gatherer, and she's proper fierce. Completely unpredictable. Maybe we can just back down this tunnel . . . Maybe it isn't us she is singin' after anyway . . .'

The voice cackled, closer now, and a light blossomed in the darkness in front of them. *'Here we come a-gathering and look what we have found . . . fresh bones for the baskets, and fresh blood for the hounds . . .'* An eldered woman stood hunched in a hooded cloak, her hands clawed in front of her, the light spreading from her palms in a glowing ember of amber sun. 'I heard your sigh, boy . . .' she whispered. 'I have been waiting for you . . .' She was as old and cracked as her voice, her hair wild and white, and her skin deep wrinkled and furred with a light covering of grey. A jangle of brass keys hung from her neck, and a small silver bundle swung from a rope around her waist. She peered at Twig, sucking on a bone that Twig felt looked decidedly human.

A crowd of meeples crawled along her skin, watching warily. But these were not the meeples from the path. These meeples stalked on hands and feet, baring sharp teeth and sniffing at the air. These meeples made Twig afraid.

The old woman tipped her head and howled and the cave came alive with the howls of a hundred wolves; all of them crept up out of the tunnels, their shadows turning them to giants on the walls.

The Gatherer circled Twig and the wolves edged closer. 'I know you,' she breathed, and a clawed finger scraped across his face. Twig couldn't move. Couldn't breathe. His cheek burned hot where her nail had touched, and he tried to still the shake in his legs. Krruk pecked at the finger. The Gatherer pulled her hand back and curled her lip at the raven.

'Now listen here,' Krruk snapped. 'This boy isn't one of your Lost Souls. He's mine and we are on our way to the Golden Gates. We just got a little side-tracked was all, so just leave us be. Find someone else to bother, would you?'

The Gatherer growled, 'Foolish bird!' and suddenly she was tight with beast fury, her muscles quivering and tense. From the blurred darkness at the edge of the cave, the wolves crouched low. 'I gather that which will otherwise be lost for ever. I did not find the boy. He found me. His ache was so strong, it called for *me*.'

Twig remembered again the tightness in his chest at the thought of forgetting, the small sigh of longing that had fallen from his lips . . . The Gatherer reached inside her cloak and pulled out an old book. Its pages were yellowed and warped and stacked full of scraps and oddments. And emerging from the book was an old tin whistle. Older than Twig. Older than his da. Older than his da's da . . .

47

'No! It's a trap!' Krruk hissed.

But Twig was already reaching for the whistle.

Chapter 10

The Lost Soul Atlas

'Leave it! Don't be fooled!' Krruk pecked at Twig's ear. 'We can still make the train! You love trains! Yoga! Bridge! Leave your troubles behind!'

The Gatherer cackled again and her laugh shook at Twig's bones. She held the book out to him, his da's whistle wedged between the pages, and he took it, trembling, from her fingers. He wiped the dirt from the cover. *The Lost Soul Atlas*. His fingers ran over ragged holes where the pages were bound by a thin leather strap. He breathed in its musked smell and heard the shadow of a voice in his memory—

'With a map anything is possible . . .'

He opened the atlas.

THE LOST SOUL ATLAS OF THE AFTERLIFE
A GUIDE TO THE OUTER WILDERLANDS AND S'ROUNDS
WITHE CROSSINGS NEW'LY DISCOV'R'D AND SET FORTHE
FORE KEEP'RS OF THE KNOWINGS

Twig read, feeling the heaviness of each word on his tongue. He turned to the page with the tin whistle. There was a map on that page full of mountains and trees and a tall tower that had been circled in gold, which shone from the cracked paper. In the margin, etched in silvered, spidered writing that Twig knew better than his own, were the words: *To know yourself you must be strong. Fight the forgetting, right the wrong.*

'That's Da's writing! Where is he?'

The old woman looked at Twig with iced blue eyes. Her nose quivered and she licked at the air. 'He was a Keeper, for a time. He hoped you would be a Keeper too. To carry the atlas forward.'

'Don't listen. She's nothin' but trou-ble,' Krruk clicked in his ear.

Twig blinked. 'So Da's here? He's in the Afterlife?'

'Yes. He waits . . .' the Gatherer hissed, and the darkness around them quivered and the shadows leaned closer to listen. 'I can show you where. But first—'

'Agh, nonono!' Krruk wailed.

The Gatherer unclasped one of the brass keys from around her neck. 'The Gods have almost got your soul locked tight. They have almost stolen all your memories to feed on for themselves. *All* your memories – those wild shadows that whisper to *who you are*. Do you feel the tightness in your chest? The ache? The loss? If you walk through their Golden Gates, you will no longer even remember yourself.'

Twig hated this feeling that everything he had ever known was floating away from him. He wanted his memories back. He wanted to know himself again. And as though hearing his thoughts, the Gatherer smiled. 'I can help you unlock your soul. I can help you call the memories back.'

'He won't be a part of it!' Krruk flapped and pecked angrily at the Gatherer.

'I will,' Twig said, and the meeples meeped and the wolves howled and the rock walls trembled with noise.

The Gatherer stepped closer, dangling the key from her fingers. 'This is a skeleton key. It can open any lock, even the ones laid down by the Gods. Put it on and it will keep your soul unlocked and open to those memories that are part of you. Of all of us. Of everything that ever was, and everything that ever will be. Do you know why you ache for the lost memories? Because memories are never just your own. They are the stories and the *knowings* of everyone who has come before. It is what you feel without thinking. All those song lines, story lines that run wild and deep between us all – the power of those memories is stronger than any *God* could ever be.' She spat the word 'God' and curled her lip to reveal sharp, yellowed canine teeth. 'The key will stop you forgetting. Use the key to set you free! Our stories are the maps for how we can be. Key, maps, map key, see yourself and be set free!' the Gatherer sang and screeched and spun another circle in the dirt.

'Listennnn . . .' And the air in the cave hung heavy. 'Can you hear them? Your wild shadows? They are coming. They are waiting for you to beckon them back. You almost lost them all, you know. You almost forgot *everything* . . .' And the words were so full of sadness it tore at Twig's heart.

'If I unlock my soul, will I get to be with Da?'

'It is not just your soul that must be opened . . .'

Twig nodded. 'Tell me then. Whatever it is, I'll do it,' he said, ignoring the pain of Krruk's claws scraping at his skin and the hissing of the bird's warnings in his ear.

The Gatherer clapped her clawed hands and cackled. 'There are places between the Afterlife and the mortal world where the boundaries between them are thin. Places that can be *crossed*. These *Crossings* have been used since before time to pass on all those knowings that dwell in our memories and dreams. They are the places where the ghosts of those dead can whisper to those left living.

'But' – and now the Gatherer drew close to Twig, her clawed fingers grasping at his hands – 'since the Gods took away their memories, the souls have forgotten they have knowings to pass on. They've forgotten about the Crossings, and now those boundaries have closed over. If the Crossings are not used soon, they will stay closed. They will *cease* to exist. All those living will be left alone and detached, with no idea of what they have lost . . .' The old woman gnashed her teeth and an iced wind blew through the cave and howled a wolf howl all of its own.

The Gatherer stared at Twig. 'When every Crossing is reopened, all the memories hoarded by the Gods will be released. Every soul will again remember, and they will be free to become the ancestors they have forgotten to be.' She held Twig's face in her clawed hands, and whispered, 'Open the Crossings. Release the memories, and you can have your heart's true wish.'

The cave hushed and every meeple, every wolf, every eye turned to look at Twig. 'I—', but before he could answer, the earth beneath them trembled, and a voice boomed through the tunnels.

Krruk's eyes rolled in fear, the Gatherer screeched, the wolves howled and the meeples meeped and wailed and swarmed in frenzied circles.

The voice spoke again, and Twig was chilled to the bone.

Chapter 11
The Gods

'GREETINGS,' the voice boomed. 'THIS IS YOUR GODS SPEAKING.' The voice was the voice of a thousand beings, like the buzzing of an enormous hive of bees, a thrumming, beating susurrus, surrounding Twig in a wave of noise that ate into his ears, into his skull, into his mind, and every part of him crawled with an unbearable itch.

'Oh, scrimpkins! Nonono!' Krruk wailed and tried to flap away the voice.

The Gatherer crouched low, growling and baring her teeth as around her the wolves prowled.

'YOU APPEAR TO BE LOST,' the voice continued. 'DON'T WORRY. WE WILL FIND YOU. WE ALWAYS FIND LOST SOULS.' This last part didn't sound reassuring. Twig heard himself whimper.

'THE OFFICIALS HAVE BEEN SENT FOR. POINT YOUR FINGER TO THE SKY ABOVE YOU AND A FLARE WILL BE RELEASED. *ALL* WILL BE WELL. ALL WILL BE FORGOTTEN. YOU WILL NOT

REMAIN LOST. WE ARE THE GODS. WE ARE ALL-SEEING AND ALL-KNOWING. AND WE ARE COMING FOR YOU . . .'

Twig curled himself into a ball on the floor of the cave. He waited for more, but the voice had stopped.

'I told you not to go into the forest, didn't I? But would you listen? No. Of course not. No one ev-er listens.' Krruk crossed his wings across his chest and shook his head. 'Look at the mess you've got us into now, like. The Gods didn't sound best pleased.'

'Have they gone?' Twig whispered.

'Yes, I think—'

'THAT SHOULD DO IT. WHAT? OH. HOW DO I TURN IT OFF? THE BLUE BUTTON? AGH! WHOOPS. BLAST IT. NO, NOT LITERALLY – AH, TOO LATE. SORRY! WELL, THE VAQUITA PORPOISE WAS A RIDICULOUS ANIMAL ANYWAY. IT WAS *NOT* ALL MY FAULT! YOU SAID TO PRESS THE BLUE BUTTON! THAT ONE? I WOULD SAY IT IS MORE PURPLE THAN BLUE . . .'

The voice of the Gods faded, and the itch slowly lessened. Twig waited.

'Now they've gone.' Krruk wriggled a claw into his ear and shook his head.

The Gatherer turned back to Twig. She looked at him, waiting, and Twig felt she was looking into his deepest thoughts.

He looked at the atlas, old and worn. It felt good in

his hands. *Fore Keep'rs of the Knowings*. His da had been a Keeper. He had believed this was important.

'How do I open the Crossings?'

'Now wait on!' Krruk pecked at Twig's ear. 'Did you not hear the Gods? They are comin' for you! It is not a good idea to go around openin' things which the Gods want closed! Let sleepin' Gods lie and all that. They will obliterate you into a million and one pieces if they catch you messin' about with all that nonsense. What will the Gods feast on if you release those memories? It would be tomfoolery and foolhardery and hardtommery and—'

The Gatherer snapped her jaws and Krruk fell backwards off Twig's shoulder. She growled low in her throat, then tugged at the bundle tied to her waist. 'In here are the Bones of Lost Wonders. They carry the whispers and memories and stories and knowings that will soon be lost to the mortal world for ever. You must carry a single bone through each Crossing and leave it in the mortal world so it can be found by those whose eyes look for whispers, and whose ears are wonder-wide . . . they will carry the knowings forward.'

Twig looked inside the bundle, at the six white bones cluttered inside.

'There is only this bundle left. The rest have already been carried through all the other Crossings. We are so close to releasing the banished memories. *A single bone, a single soul, open the Crossings, awaken them all!*' the Gatherer sang and spun, arms raised and clapping, and her wild meeples danced and clapped too. 'But it will not be easy.' And now her face darkened, and Twig felt a chill of fear creep across his skin. 'There are Sentries at each Crossing who must be appeased. And to open a Crossing, you must *enter* the Crossing. Not all who cross over remember to cross back. It is easy to get carried away by your memories and forget. You must fight the forgetting. Here *and* in the mortal world. Do you understand, boy?'

The woman wrapped Twig's hand tight around the skeleton key. Krruk tried to flap her away. 'Do not forget who you are.' And this last whisper was so soft in Twig's ears that he wondered if she had said the words at all.

Twig nodded. He wanted to be with his da. No matter what it took. The Gatherer pointed to the atlas open in Twig's hand and flicked to the next page – *Map of the Wilderforest*. She pointed her boned finger at the parchment. '*Where you see a key, a Crossing will be,*' she sang. Twig looked closely at the map. The map was covered in trees and twisting plants and hiding beasts, and there, under a small hill, was a symbol of a key. It looked just like the skeleton key in Twig's hand.

'A circle around the key means the Crossing has been opened by a Keeper that came before – like your father . . .'

Twig thought of the tower circled on the map he had seen before. Of his da's handwriting looping beneath.

'What happened to them? The Keepers that came before? Why did they stop?'

The Gatherer pulled back her lip in a half snarl. 'Those Keepers have come to the end of their journeys. They are done. They can cross over no more. Time is running out, boy. We have been waiting for so very, very long for one that sighs . . . If you do not succeed . . .' The Gatherer stopped, her head tilted to the side as if listening, and when she spoke it was faster, more urgent than before. 'Open the Crossings. Release the memories. Only you can do it now. There will be no time to wait for another. And you have already started on your journey.' The Gatherer tapped again at the map, at the symbol of the key under the hill. 'This is where we are. You are here already!' she crowed. 'You found the first uncircled Crossing on your own. *Where you see the key, a Crossing will be*,' the Gatherer sang. '*Wear the skeleton key! Call to every memory! Call with your ache like you called to me! They are waiting for you to set them free!*' Her eyes sparked with wild energy. 'The Crossing is through there.' She pointed down a thin tunnel surrounded by meeples. 'The Sentry will be waiting. Don't forget to use the atlas.' And as quickly as she had appeared, she turned and ran, wind-fast on her crooked, clawed feet, back into the tunnels, in a sea of howling wolves.

Twig let his lips brush across the atlas in a sort of promise, feeling the trace of his da in those pages, and a voice inside him whispered *now, before it is too late . . . before you forget . . .*

'Don't do it, boyo. She was speakin' through her hat was all. Full of conspiracy theories that one . . .'

'I'm sorry, Krruk.' Twig lifted the skeleton key and hung it around his neck.

Chapter 12

Unbecoming

Twig gasped, all the air pushed from his body and then – he knew himself again. He could remember. He felt as if he had emerged from a fever, and realised how empty he had been before, a dried husk of himself.

'Agh, scrimpkins! Now you've gone and done it, like.' Krruk clicked his beak and paced up and down, moaning and muttering 'nonono' under his breath. 'The Gods say, "send up a flare", but you go and fight the forgettin' instead. The Gods say, "don't worry, we'll find you" and you go on the run. You're a rebel now and there's no foolin' anyone.'

'I'm sorry, Krruk. But—'

'Krruk! Get it right!'

'I don't want you to get in trouble. You should go back . . . tell the Officials you never found me, or—'

'Agh, no, it's too late for that. I already logged you in, like, didn't I? They know we're together. They'll obliterate us both. Oh well. I'm a rebel now too. An unwillin' bystander, it's true, pulled into your mess by no doin' of mine own, but a rebel all's the same. On your head be it, boyo.'

'I'm sorry.'

'I should hope so.' Krruk pecked Twig affectionately on the ear, ruffled his bones and nestled into his shoulder.

'So the Crossing is through there?' Twig peered into the dark of the tunnel. He wondered how he would even fit.

'Now listen, boyo. She only told you half of it when she said that bit about gettin' carried away by your memories and forgettin' to come back. And I'm not tryin' to change your mind or nothin', I can see you are as stubborn as she is, but I wouldn't be a Guardian if I didn't warn you properly, like.'

'Warn me?'

'It's all ver-ry technical, but the thing of it is, souls that get carried away by their memories become lost in them, and they don't *ever* come out. You start fadin'. The more time you dwell in your memories the less you are *here*, in *this* moment. You would last for a time in the shadows of your memories, but then' – Krruk shook his head softly – 'then you simply *unbecome*. Your memories no longer exist and it's like you never, ever were.'

'Unbecome?' Twig thought of what that would mean, to never have existed. To never have known or be known.

'Any old soul can open a Crossin', but it takes a proper strong mind to claw itself back. It won't be easy.

It will be near impossible if you ask me.'

'Impossible,' Twig whispered, and had a flash of memory—

> *'Impossible is just what they say when they don't want you to try.'*

'I'll come out though, Krruk. I've got you. You won't let me get carried away and lost. I know you won't.' Twig smiled at Krruk. 'So what did she mean, about appeasing the Sentries? Who are they?' Twig didn't want to imagine what could be waiting for him at the end of the tunnel.

'Oh, they is the absolute worst, they is. They thinks they're clev-er, but really they are terrible bores. All with their silly little riddle-whatsits and all *oh, I am so wise, if you don't answer right, I gets to eat you so answer care-fully*. When has threatenin' someone with becomin' lunch ever helped the brain? If they was really smart they'd know that. Ridiculous, the lot of them.'

'Riddles? Eat you? Lunch?'

'Are you feelin' all right, boyo?' Krruk turned his head to peer with one eye at Twig. 'I warned you, I did. Yous are the one who went and put that silly skeleton key on.'

Twig took a deep breath. 'So, what do I do? What if I don't know the answer?'

'How am I to know? I admit I am ver-ry wise and a fount of all knowledge, but this is outside my area of expertise, like. She said to use the atlas, so . . . oh!

I know, I know! I've got it!'

Twig leaned forward.

'When you see the Sentry, don't wait for the riddle. Just say, "Hello, nice Sentry, I have brought you a present, I have", and then bring out the atlas and whack them over the head with it. Might need a few goings over, dependin' on size and that, but you've a good arm on you, you'll be fine.' Krruk took a closer look at Twig's arms. 'Well, you'll give it a good go anyhow.'

'I'm not sure that's what she meant . . .' Twig turned back to the Map of the Wilderforest. There must be something in the atlas to help him. Some clue . . .

Twig ran his fingers across the parchment. Trees towered and beasts stalked across the page. Arrows pointed off the map in every direction. *To Central Station; To the Sea of Finality; North lies the Silver Mountains; Here flows the Lake of Everwonder* . . . And scrawled across the map in varying pens and languages and scripts were notes and snatches of advice.

Through the Golden Gates is an eternity of forgetting. Ignore the signs;

It's not only the beasts that lurk in the forest. Eyes and Ears are everywhere;

Follow the trail of little people, but keep hold of your valuables;

63

But then the word had faded and Twig couldn't make out the rest.

Never enter a Crossing without someone to call you back.

Twig paused at the next note. It was written outside the meeple mound, by the uncircled symbol of the key. *To the brave souls who went in, and unbecame.* Next to it was a small pressed blue flower. A forget-me-not. Twig touched it gently and thought how they had been his da's favourite flower.

'You'll come with me, right? To help?'

Krruk looked up from where he was scratching a picture of himself on to the cave wall and writing BIRD BIG GOD under it. 'What's that then? Oh sure. I'll be with you, I'm your Guardian. I'm always with you. But I won't be helpin'. I hate riddles, me. Hurts the head. You'll have to figure thems out on your own.'

Twig sighed. He took a deep breath and squeezed himself into the tunnel.

Chapter 13

The First Crossing

Twig pulled himself along the tunnel on his stomach. Krruk flapped behind, telling him to 'hurry up, would you' and pecking unhelpfully at his ankle. The meeples led the way, humming happily, small flames lit on their torches. They stopped as the tunnel opened up into a small chamber.

Twig peered into the dark. He wasn't sure what he was expecting. A monster maybe, or someone like the Gatherer. But the Sentry wasn't like that at all. 'Is *that* the Sentry?' Twig whispered, and wished he had been able to read the faded note in the atlas.

Krruk moaned. 'Oh, not a bloomin' garden gnome.' He rolled his eyes. 'Trust me and give him a whack with the atlas quickly like . . . we'll be here all day otherwise. They talk soooo slow it drives you round the bend.'

The Sentry wasn't at all scary. He looked nice, with his green hat and little jacket and walking stick. He didn't even move. Twig wasn't quite sure if he was alive, or actually just a painted lump of concrete. 'Um. Hello?'

The gnome turned slowly. Suddenly he wasn't so friendly looking. He smiled at Twig, his sharp teeth shining in the torch light. 'Ahh . . .' he said, his voice crackling. 'I was just thinking . . .' The words dripped from his mouth. '. . . that I could do . . . with a little . . . something before tea . . . a little something . . . to snack on . . . and look . . . a snack crawls through my tunnel. They always do . . . sooner . . . or . . . later.' The gnome's eyes grew wide and he licked his lips with a yellowed forked tongue. 'Tell me, Snack. Do you know . . . what a sloth's favourite meal . . . is?'

Twig began to panic. He didn't know anything about sloths. He looked at the atlas, but there was nothing there that seemed to be able to help either. Maybe the Gatherer *had* meant for him to use the atlas as a weapon . . .

'Wait on a minute.' Krruk hopped in front of Twig and peered at the gnome. 'I know what game yous is playin'. Yous is a trick-sy one yous is. Tell me – is that the riddle or what?'

The gnome frowned. 'Riddle? Of course . . . not. I was just interested.'

'Well, enough about sloths! We wants the proper riddle because this here boy is a proper Keeper and needs to go through that there Crossin', so let's to's it and hurry up, will you?'

The gnome seemed to shrink a little. 'You don't . . . want . . . to talk about sloths?'

'No.'

'Oh.' A tear fell slowly down the gnome's face. 'No one ever . . . does.'

'I'm sorry,' Twig said. 'But we haven't much time. Maybe later?'

The gnome thought about this. 'Before . . . I eat you?'

Twig shrugged.

'All right then, snack. Here is the . . . riddle. Answer me right and you may . . . cross. Answer me wrong and I . . . may feast.'

Twig nodded. The gnome took the hat from his head and began to sprinkle dirt and ash into it, dancing slowly around it in a circle, waving his stick and chanting as though casting a spell.

> *'Lobster claws and devil's hand,*
> *Hang with corpses, rise from sand,*
> *Snap at dragons, follow the sun,*
> *Be morning glory,*
> *and Queen when day is done.*
> *Take me for your own –*
> *be warned, for soon I will but fade.*
> *But leave me when you're journeying,*
> *And your memory will be made.'*

Twig repeated the words to himself, trying to remember them all. *Lobster claws and devil's hand.* There was something . . . a connection that he couldn't quite get. *Queen when day is done* . . . Something he couldn't quite remember . . .

The gnome took a step closer, his tongue lolling, drool slowly dribbling from the side of his mouth.

'Wait!' Twig said. 'I need time to think!'

'You said . . .' The gnome smiled and took another step. '. . . you didn't have much time . . . tick . . . tock . . .'

'Come on, boyo! Think! Look at those teeth! They aren't messin' about teeth!' Krruk hissed.

'Tick . . . tock . . .'

The littlest meeple nudged Twig's hand gently with his head. The meeples were all digging at the earth, tiny little meeple shovels making a line of miniature holes in the tunnel floor. It looked as though they were planting something. Twig looked back at the atlas. At the forget-me-not dried and pressed on to the parchment. *Your memory will be made.* Forget-me-not.

He smiled. 'I've got it.'

'Good one,' Krruk whispered. 'Now hit him hard. That head will take a good hit, you'll need to be hard and fast.'

'No. I know the answer.'

The gnome stopped walking. He glared at Twig. 'Really? What . . . is it . . . then?'

'I think they are all names of flowers. Snapdragons, lobster claws, devil's hands, hanging corpse flowers . . .' Twig paused. He wasn't actually sure any of these *were* flowers except he thought snapdragons were. The gnome was still watching him, not convinced, but not approaching either. Twig kept going. 'Morning glory, and Queen of the Night.' He remembered his da teaching him and smiled. 'They're a kind of flower that only opens in the dark. And when you take flowers for your own, they fade, but if you leave them for someone when you go away, then you will be remembered. That's why people plant forget-me-nots . . .'

'That . . . is a . . . long . . . answer. I need but one word . . .'

Twig paused. There was nothing else it could be. 'Flowers.'

The gnome slumped on the floor and crossed his arms sulkily. 'It's because I'm a . . . garden gnome, isn't it. People always . . . think of flowers. I've tried to vary my interests . . . but flowers are just so . . . interesting . . . Hurry . . . up then. Do your crossing.' He turned and faced the corner, still grumbling to himself about sloths and monkey face flowers and carnations and tulips.

Krruk clicked his beak. 'I still think you should have whacked him.'

Twig was about to ask what to do now, when suddenly he just knew. He sat on the cave floor and reached into the Gatherer's bundle, pulling out a small bone. He held it up to the light of the meeples' torches. It seemed to shimmer almost, and he thought he felt just the slightest tremor coming from deep within the bone. His fist closed tight around it, and he was squeezing a part of *himself* into its core. He wondered how many secrets and stories and wonders were carried in its marrow. And without thinking, without a moment's hesitation, Twig tipped his head back and howled into the darkness, a keen of longing and wishing and dreaming and wondering.

Slowly, the memories came. A wild pack of shadows creeping through tunnels and across walls. The meeples cheered and climbed high on the rolling black cloud, arms waving, toppling and tumbling, and the cave was suddenly full of tiny moments of living, dust specks of existence flitting and fluttering around Twig, darting and dipping and circling, coming harder and faster—

the cold slap of river water in winter, and there's
something in the water,
scratched, scarred hands
leaves brushing sticks scratching
smiling hands held blue sky winter
the clatter of a ladder,
'Run! Run NOW!'
gripping tight and those eyes –
'Twiggy!' And those eyes are screaming for help and
the Hoblin is laughing and
'Go on. Do it then . . .'

And suddenly there is a bright, white speck of pure light and it is engulfing, consuming, squeezing all the air from

Twig's lungs from his blood from his bones and just when he understands that he has been swallowed whole – the shadows pull him down, down, down and he feels so wonderfully, perfectly free . . .

Outside the tunnel, outside the mound, dancing across the leaves of the Wilderforest, the wind heard Twig's howl, watched the shadows race across the forest floor towards him. She picked up the echo of his howl and held it to her chest. She twirled and bustled, moving in and out of branches, swirling through caves and tiptoeing across the tops of mountains. And as she moved, small droplets of the howl fell from her fingers like falling stars, drifting on to the ground and leaving a trail of the brightest silver glinting across the countryside.

But neither the boy nor his Guardian would notice. Not until it was too late.

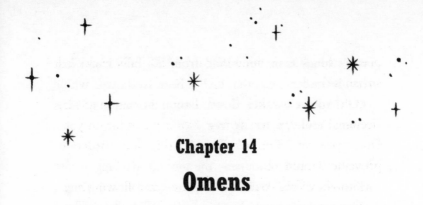

Chapter 14
Omens

It's morning. I can tell by the sounds of the streets waking and the light leaking through my closed eyes. I keep them patched tight together so I don't have to see what's real and can keep pretending.

I pretend I didn't follow Da. I pretend I'm safe in the flats and that nothing has changed and that I'm not sleeping on Da's coat between two bins down some alley. I pretend I can fix everything, just like always.

Da'll be worrying about where I am. I don't even know where I am. I ran too far last night. My legs pumped so hard and I didn't stop until my lungs screamed and burned and there was nothing I could do but curl between the bins and try not to think.

'Hey, squirt!'

My eyes pop open, but I squeeze them shut again before the kid sees I'm not really sleeping.

'Twiggykid! Wake up!' And this time my ribs are poked, hard, with a bony finger. Twice.

I open my eyes and the red-bandana kid's face is

peering so close to mine that my head pulls back and smashes the bin.

'Oh, you're awake? Good. I thought you might be sleeping. You sure are skinny. Not a bit of fat on you. Don't you eat?' I'm poked again, this time harder to prove how thin I am.

'Stop it, would you? And why are you following me?'

'Am not following.' The kid sniffs. 'Why do they call you Twiggy anyway?'

I shrug. Why is anyone called anything?

'Is it because you're skinny as a twig? Or because you were born under a tree? Or is it because you like to eat those twiggy stick things they sell down the markets? Is Twiggy even a proper name?'

This kid talks a million miles an hour. It makes me tired listening. 'I've just always been called Twig.'

'Oh. That's boring. I'm Flea.'

I don't point out that Flea isn't much of a proper name either.

I look at Flea's face and clothes and hair and bracelets. 'So, are you a boy?'

Flea shrugs. 'Sometimes. And sometimes I'm a girl. And sometimes I'm both at the same time or neither. Mostly I'm just somewhere in between. Anyway, I was thinking we should go into business together. What with how good I am at getting into places and how good you are at fixing things – I've watched you down the markets fixing things back to working – we'd make good

73

partners. I can steal it, you can fix it and we can split the difference 70/30, deal? OK, OK. 60/40.'

All I can do is blink and shrug and hope Flea knows that means *no way, never in a million years* and *I don't want to end up in jail thanks very much*.

'Don't worry. I never get caught. I'm the best thief this city's got to offer. Some were born for greatness, I was born to thieve. It's a gift, it is. I've lighter fingers than the wind!' And Flea's fingers wave in the air to prove it. 'I'm the one who can steal the hat off of your head without you even knowing. I'm the one who can fool grown men into thinking they can win at picking the shell that hides the pea. I'm the one who people leave behind, thinking they've managed the better end of a dodgy deal, only to find there's nothing left in their pockets when they get home. I never get caught. Not never.'

'I don't—' I start, but Flea starts talking again like I hadn't said a word.

'Right. I've come to tell your fortune.'

I try not to laugh. Flea looks at me with a sharp glare. 'Make fun if you like, but it's in my blood. I have the *Sight*. Here. Tell me what you see when you look through this. It's a seeing stone. If you're special like me, you'll be able to see all the magic in the world.' Flea pulls a rock with a hole in it from one of their hundreds of pockets and peers through at me. 'Huh. Why didn't you tell me you had wings?'

'What?'

Flea glares at me like I'm fooling around, then looks at me again through the stone. 'Great big white ones. They could probably do with a wash, they're looking a little mangy if I'm being honest. What? Don't tell me you haven't even flown on them yet? What a waste.'

And all of a sudden my shoulders ache with wanting wings for real, and for a minute, I let myself pretend I can feel them, pushing clean through my shirt and shivering against my back.

'And you should know there are an awful lot of troll tracks around here. They're probably planning an ambush,' Flea says, and I think of Da and his stories of trolls and my breathing goes funny.

I take the rock and look through. There are no troll tracks. No wings. No magic at all. The world is just the same, only a bit blurry from squinting. 'It's only a rock with a hole in it.'

'Yep.' Flea nods as though that proves everything. 'You haven't got the Sight. Now, your fortune.' Flea pulls out a Magic 8 ball from another pocket and starts shaking it violently from side to side.

'Is that your crystal ball?' And now I am laughing.

'These things are proper powerful for people who know what they're doing. Shush. I'm listening . . .'

I listen too, but the only sound is the rumble of the passing rubbish truck.

'I have a message coming through from a G . . . Gisella

maybe. Do you know any Gisella? Ga . . . Gail? Anyone whose name starts with G . . . ? She says the river holds the cake . . . no wait . . . the knee. The tree? The river holds the . . . k . . . nope. She's gone. To be honest, I don't think that message was meant for you.' Flea pauses. 'I know what your question is. You want to know how to fix the mess you're in.'

How does this kid know about my mess?

'But you aren't asking the right question,' Flea goes on. 'The right question is, will you find what you're looking for?'

'What I'm looking for?'

Flea turns the ball three times and gives it a gentle shake. 'Not what. Who. You'll find *who* you're looking for, when you find yourself,' Flea says softly, looking into the ball, at the *It Is Certain* message bobbing into view. 'It's just a matter of listening to the whisper of your soul.'

Flea looks at me then, and suddenly those words seem more true than anything. I try to listen to what it is my soul is whispering, but all I hear is that small scratchy voice that gets me in trouble, sniggering like all this was its plan in the first place.

'So, did your father dump you then?' Flea says. 'Did you do something wrong? Or have you decided to become a street sleeper now? Run away? Are the coppers after you? Is your father after you? Some fathers are the worst. Yours looked kinda nice, but

76

looks can be tricksters.'

'What? No, he . . . I . . .' But I don't want to talk to this kid about things that are only mine to think about, this bin rat who doesn't know anything and pretends to know everything. 'My da would never . . . I need to get home now. I'm already late for work. Da takes me with him every day when there's no school, and we were even thinking about setting up as proper partners.'

Flea nods and gets up. 'Sure. I was going to say you could come and grab a feed if you're hungry, but if you're late you'd better not. By the way. There was something else in the Magic 8 ball . . .'

But the dark noise is starting up behind my eyes. 'It's rubbish. It's just a stupid toy.' I turn so Flea can't see my face.

'If you say so. But if it were me who was in *Grave Danger*, I'd want to know *when*, or at least *how*, so I could try to dodge it, you know. And if you don't believe *me*, listen to the raven up there.' Flea points to a scrawny old bird watching us from the metal staircase. 'They're messengers of the Gods, don't you know? If you listen right, they reveal omens and foretell the future.'

I look at the bird and shake my head at them both. 'Go away and stop following me, would you.' I hope Flea doesn't hear the way my voice is shaking.

'OK, squirt, see ya, wouldn't want to be ya.' And Flea walks away, leaving a brown paper package at my feet. Inside is half a hot dog. Still a little bit warm.

77

'You're the squirt, not me! And I don't like mustard!' But Flea has already gone.

I breathe in the smell of the hot dog and wonder if I'd rather know *when* I was going to die, or *how* I was going to die.

The bird looks at me then, and croaks in a way that sounds almost like words. 'Krrrrrruuuk. Kru. Krruk. Krrrrraaaa.'

'Rubbish,' I tell it back. 'Like a stupid Magic 8 ball knows anything.'

The bird clicks its beak and stares harder.

'Rubbish,' I say again. I try my hardest to believe it.

Chapter 15
Walking the Dead

Da told me once that every little action changes the world. We're all bound together like dominos lined up and ready to topple. Like if a butterfly lands on a flower instead of flying on by, that can set off a whole bunch of events that change everything. I wonder if you can change everything back again. I wonder if once everything is changed, it can ever be fixed.

It takes me hours to find my way back to the Towers. The whole time I'm thinking about how Da will be worried and scared at where I am and disappointed at how I'd followed him, and how the others will all be tutting, and how Franky Collins will be laughing and saying he told me so.

I wish I'd been faster. I wish I hadn't been the butterfly that landed on the flower and toppled everything.

I know before I even get to the Towers what has happened. I know by the mutterings and mumblings of everyone gathered outside, and by the bonfire of clothes and furniture and blankets and books, all smoking into

79

the sky. I know by the long line of bright red buses that I can see turning down the street and on to the freeway.

Border Protection. They don't care how long you've lived in a place, or how old you are or if you go to school or work or anything. If you can't show Border Protection your City ID, then they stick you on the bus and take you away and lock you up and sometimes they send you to some other country so you can't ever come back. Franky Collins said they don't even bother sending you to another country, and that that's just what they tell people. He reckons they just lock you up in these great big hidden camps and just leave you there to die from sickness and sadness. I don't know if you can die from sadness though, can you? Anyway, Franky Collins is full of it.

Da told me that if Border Protection ever come looking, I'm to run and hide. Da said I'm to leave a message with Charlie on the corner newspaper stand so he can get the message to Da. But I can't run and hide. Not again. I have to find Da. Da doesn't have a City ID.

I jump the barrier, taking the stairs three at a time. Then I'm at our door. I'm hammering on the wood and yelling and screaming, because our door is locked, and our door is never locked. Never.

'Da? Da?' Where is he? He wouldn't have got on the bus without me. Not in a million years. Not even if they dragged him. Not even if—

'What, are you trying to walk the dead with all that

80

banging? They took everyone, squirt, don't you know? On the bus. No one's got ID around here. All you're going to do with that racket is get yourself locked up and how would we go into business then?'

Flea is leaning against the wall watching me, spinning a pocket watch on a chain around and around and I wonder who that watch was stolen from.

'I said stop following me,' I yell. 'We're not going into business. I'm not a thief. My da's in there. He must be. And it's *wake* the dead, not *walk* the dead, and why are you even here? And—'

'All right, all right. Keep your tail feathers on. Move over, will you.' And then Flea pulls something out of an inside pocket and starts fiddling it in the lock. 'These are my sister's lock picks. With these, I can open any lock in the world. Just like Houdini. Are you sure it's *wake* the dead? I'm pretty certain it's *walk* the dead.' The door swings open. Flea smiles at me and bows like a doorman at a fancy hotel. 'Your room, good sir.'

But the flat is empty. Old Man Tipper's wife is all over the floor, her jar smashed, and there are fingerscrapes in her ashes like someone has tried to pick her up. There are broken plates and a photo of Franky Collins trampled on the floor. My tin of pictures is under a pile of broken glass. I brush it clean with my sleeve and put it in Da's coat pocket. Da would hate it if I lost these. My pictures make Da's heart sing . . .

'Is there a note? He always leaves notes. Where's his

note?' My voice has gone all high and cracky.

There are footsteps then, strong and fast along the hall, and it's Da coming back for me and he'll scoop me in his arms and hold me tight and everything will be better and I don't care if he thinks I'm little and—

But it's not Da. It's a man with a black beard and blue eyes and an orange council jacket and he's yelling at me to get from the flat *now*. When I don't move, he grabs me by my shirt and throws me on the floor so I'm covered in Old Mrs Tipper. A piece of broken glass sticks into my hand and makes it bleed. I stare at that blood and wonder if dead-woman dust is in that cut, does that mean I will now be part Old Mrs Tipper?

Then Flea is yelling, fists waving in the air. 'May a dirty crow peck out your eyes by their roots and leave your brain for the maggots, you piece of rotting cow flesh. You leave him alone. Does it make you feel like a tough man to throw around a scrawny little kid like him?'

I guess the man doesn't know what to do with someone like Flea yelling at him because he just shakes his head and starts talking into his radio. 'There are more of them. Like rats crawling from a drain. You'd better send another bus.' He turns to us then and takes our photo with his phone.

Flea pulls me from the floor and out of the flat and slams the door on the man's hand, and he yells and swears and Flea is laughing and telling me, 'Run faster, do you want to get bussed out and locked up and never see the city again?'

'I have your faces!' the man yells after us. 'We've got you. You're listed! Do you hear me? You come back here again, and it'll be the last time! Do you hear me?'

And when we are far enough away that there's no risk of being caught, Flea sits down on a wall and looks at the cut on my hand. 'Spit is the best medicine, that's why dogs lick their wounds,' Flea says, wiping the blood from my hand and spitting on my cut. 'And, don't you know, when a hero comes to save someone, the least the someone can do is say thank you. Well?'

I wipe my hand and spit on the cut myself.

'You told that man I'm scrawny. I'm not scrawny. Or little. And you didn't save me because I was just about to save myself, and—' And then I stop. None of that matters. The only thing that matters is finding Da. 'I need to go to Charlie. I think Da said Charlie. It's hard to remember. We hadn't talked about Border Protection for ages. But Da will have left a message with Charlie. That's our plan. I think. We had a plan for everything.' Except this is nothing like the way we thought it would go.

Flea looks at me for a bit without saying anything, just muttering and nodding like I'm some kind of puzzle that needs figuring, and maybe Flea is thinking of a proper plan. I lean forward.

'I'm pretty sure,' Flea says slowly, 'that it's *walk* the

83

dead. Like zombies, you know?' Then Flea sighs and nods. 'All right then. Let's go find this Charlie.'

And the scratchy voice in my head laughs and laughs and whispers *you are the butterfly that toppled them all. Let's see you fix this now . . .*

Chapter 16
We Are All Made of Stardust

There is no message. Charlie hasn't seen Da. No one has. I've gone to the newspaper stand every day for a week now and every day Charlie just looks at me and shakes his head and says, 'Sorry, kid' and I try not to let that swallow me whole.

'Don't worry, Twig, it'll get easier, every day,' Flea says. Flea's stayed with me almost the whole time. Sometimes Flea goes for a bit and I think maybe their home is nearby. It's lonely without them nattering at me a hundred miles an hour though.

'How long do you think it will take for Da to come back?' I ask, but Flea just shrugs and takes out a slingshot and points to a tree.

'What will you give me if I can hit that tree?'

There is no way Flea will be able to hit that tree. But before I can answer Flea has cocked a rock in the band and fired. We see the bark fly and can make out the mark it leaves from here. 'Do you want me to show you how? It's easy.'

I take the slingshot and hold it steady. I aim and let fly. The rock falls at my feet and the rubber band snaps my fingers and the wood of the slingshot cracks in two. Flea glares and grabs the broken slingshot. 'That was my best one!'

'Sorry. I'll make you another.' But Flea waves me away.

'I don't have my parents either, you know. They're both dead, and my sister too, so if we're keeping score, I win,' Flea says and nods at a man in a suit reading his paper with his lunch all laid out on the park bench.

'What?' I say, but Flea just walks behind the man and steals his sandwich right out from under his nose.

'It'll always ache a little. But every day the ache gets deeper so you don't feel it so much, you know?' Flea keeps walking and hands me half the sandwich. 'Mmm. Schnitzel and coleslaw. My favourite.'

'But my da's coming back.'

'You would have liked my sister a lot,' Flea says. 'Almost as much as me. Do you know what her very last words to me were? *Why did the chicken go to the séance?*'

'What's a séance?'

'It's a place you go to try and talk to the dead.'

And it's not funny because Flea's sister *is* dead and they are the worst last words ever, but I can't help laughing. Flea laughs too and then I'm laughing so hard I can hardly get the air in, and I'm gasping and crying and choking on the sandwich and telling how angry I was with Da and telling all the things I screamed and why didn't he run with me and away from that Hoblin woman? Why didn't he fight?

'Don't be ridiculous,' Flea says. 'Don't tell me you believe in Hoblins? What are you? A baby?'

I don't say how that voice in my head whispers that Da hasn't come back yet because he was glad when those buses came. That he didn't tell me to run to save myself, but that he told me to run because he didn't want to see me any more.

Flea sits down on the grass with me and starts singing then, in a voice that doesn't sound anything like Flea's talking voice, and in words I've not ever heard before. I'm not crying when it's finished.

'What was that song?'

'It's in the old tongue, not spoken any more. My mamma used to sing it to me, and her mamma sang to her and so on since the very beginning of time. It says' – and Flea's nose scrunches trying to twist the words into ones I know – 'we are all connected. To each other. To this world. To everything that ever was, and everything that ever will be. So whoever you are, and wherever you are, you are never alone. Because we are all made of stardust.'

'Is that true?'

'Of course. Everything in the old tongue is true. The same dust that made the stars is in us. In our blood, in our bones. And when you die, that dust from the stars floats back up on the wind and becomes a new star.'

I think about my mum and my brothers and the way me and Da would watch for them in the sky, looking down on us. Listening to our wishes. I think about Da and wonder if he can see the stars from wherever he is.

'Look. There's a storm coming.' Flea points to the pine cones on the ground. 'When they close like that, it means a storm is on its way. I'm not spending another night in the park, not in a storm. And neither are you. Especially now those coppers are doing their rounds through here. Have you ever woken up to a face full of pepper spray before? It's not the nicest way to wake. Come on, you can stay with me.' And without waiting for me to answer, Flea takes my arm and starts to walk me away. 'If we were to rob a bank, what would you do with the money?'

'I don't want to rob a bank.' I look at Flea and think of the lock picking pins.

'Think what we'd do with it! We could go anywhere and do anything. We could journey all over the whole world and visit every single place that exists. I bet no one's done that before. We'd be famous. We should make a list so we don't miss some places by mistake.'

'But we're not robbing a bank, right?'

'But before we go, we should make sure that everyone gets a share of the money. Everyone that needs it anyway.'

'Everyone? That would be impossible.'

'Pft. Impossible is just what they say when they don't want you to try. It would be easy. We can go into the tent city down the canal, the stations, Riverside, even the drain towns,' Flea says. 'We'll come at night, all quiet and secret and leave it next to people so they'll wake in the morning and just find it there. Wouldn't that be amazing? If you woke up and there's a pile of money waiting for you?'

'Like Robin Hood,' I say. 'But there is no actual bank robbery, right?'

'Who's Robin Hood?'

'You don't know Robin Hood? What are you? A baby?'

Flea shoves me, and I shove back and we walk all the way up to the top of the hill and into Miner's Park. There's a boy being pushed on the swing by his mum. She's trying to take a photo with her phone but the boy isn't even smiling. It's because she isn't pushing him high enough.

Flea pulls me over to a wall edging the park where someone has dumped piles of rubbish. 'Twig! Look. There's loads here. An old frame, a broken chair, a tin of paint! It's still half full!' Flea waves the tin at me and I shrug.

Half the wall has crumbled to rubble, leaving a gap through to the other side where the hill starts off grass then has turned to cliff and drops away sharp like the ground just gave up. I look down to where the river runs

89

dark and deep beneath the cliff. It makes me shiver just looking at that water. I pull Da's coat tight around me, and step back from the wall.

Flea smiles and steps through the gap like the cliff doesn't even exist. 'Come here,' Flea says. 'I can show you what you can't see.'

'What are you on about?'

Flea points to the broken wall and the cliff dropping down to the river. 'You've got wings. You just don't know it. But I can show you.'

I try to laugh, but Flea won't have it. For a moment, I imagine my wings thrumming bright white and brilliant and then I see myself falling, faster and harder, down and into the dark of the river and it's so real it's like a kind of memory and my legs start to shake.

'Twig,' Flea says again. 'Come with me. I can show you how to fly.'

Chapter 17
Learning to Fly

I look out over the cliff.

Flea doesn't smile. There is no joking about it. 'Do you trust me?'

And I do. I really do.

'Come on.' Flea reaches for my hand. 'Don't be a baby. There's loads of room. There's at least two metres of grass before it drops.'

It's not two metres. It's maybe one metre. I take a deep breath and let myself be pushed up against the wall. 'Of course, who knows how sure this ground is . . .' Flea stomps hard on the earth and smiles.

'That's not funny. We could fall.'

'Course we could. But we won't. All you're doing is standing against a wall. What does the drop matter?'

I put my hands against the bricks, gripping with my fingers and trying not to look over the edge. Flea dips their hands into the tin of paint and presses hard against the bricks next to my shoulders, over and over, leaving handprints rising up along the wall.

'You can't see your wings because you're not clever like me,' Flea says, 'but that doesn't mean you can't learn to see, to believe. That doesn't mean you can't learn to fly.'

I turn my head and watch my wings appear on those bricks, brilliant white wings, growing hand over hand on the wall. And suddenly, I'm not so scared any more.

I move from the wall, carefully, because I'm not silly like Flea, and dip my own hands in the cold of the paint, wrinkling my nose at the smell, and we print more and more hands, growing those wings big and bright, and the drips from our hands turn to specks of stardust that catch the sun and water our eyes.

Flea runs back into the park and spins circles on the grass, arms wide, paint flicking and raining down, and shouts, 'Don't you know? We are all connected! Whoever you are, and wherever you are, you are never alone. Because we are all made of stardust!' And the little boy giggles and laughs and raises his hands to catch the specks of white paint and the woman rushes from the park, her phone forgotten on the slide.

'Quick!' Flea pushes me back in front of the wings. 'Close your eyes. You're flying, Twig. You have to let yourself believe.' I close my eyes and breathe in deep and for just the smallest second, I think I can almost feel the wind pushing me higher, I think I can almost feel my wings beating hard against the sky. For a moment, I think I almost do believe. Almost.

There is the click of a camera and I open my eyes. There I am on the woman's phone, arms stretched, wings skeleton-white and blurred as though they were trembling, as though I had actually circled the skies. 'It really does look like I was flying.'

'That's because you really were, stupid. One day, you and me, we're going to fly ourselves higher and higher. We'll take to the skies and we'll fly anywhere we want, and do anything we want, bank money or not. With wings you can do anything, can't you. You and me, OK?' And Flea smiles and looks at me with eyes the colour of the setting sun, only deeper and more wonderful than any sun could ever be. 'OK,' I say, and wonder at how true it feels.

When the woman comes back for her phone, it's on the slide again, white fingerprints wiped clean, and she looks through the gap at us, sitting on the grass, our backs against the wall, the wings rising up above us.

'Flea? That joke that your sister told. What's the answer?'

'I don't know. Maybe my sister made it up. Maybe she's the only one that knows.'

'I'll find the answer for you. Even if I have to kidnap a clown and drag it out of him.'

'You promise?' Flea looks at me, all serious even though it's a stupid promise and where would I even find a clown?

But I nod. 'I promise.'

Then Flea grabs my finger and dips it into the paint, and pushes my finger back and forth along the bricks. I try not to complain about the scraping of my skin and the crunching of my nail on the brick. I watch as TWIG AND FLEA appear in wobbly white on the wall. 'There. So everyone knows we made this. Before there was nothing. Now, there is something *real*. And we made it. Twig and Flea.' Flea's hand rests on my chest and leaves a handprint white on my black shirt. 'For always.'

And the wind whips up the white specked dirt and swirls it in the sky and all around us the stardust falls like rain, hard and sweet, and we are the only things in the whole world that exist.

I wished it could last for ever, that feeling. I should know by now that wishes are for nothing. I should know by now, that wishing for something just calls attention to it. Makes it an easier target to destroy. I should know by now, that if I really cared for Flea, I should never have wished at all.

Chapter 18

The Boneyard

'Come on,' Flea says. 'I want you to see the place before dark.' Flea leads the way, down alleys, over fences, along the river, through gardens and all the way up the hill that runs from the old city gates. I've never been this way before. 'Where are we going?'

'Just across Kingswood Road.' Flea points and I look across the road at the huge oaks guarding the cemetery, the heads of stone angels barely visible, peering over the old stone fence.

'You live in the graveyard?'

'Sure. Isn't it great?'

I try not to think of the stories Da told of the ghosts and ghouls that haunt graveyards at night.

'What's wrong, Twiggy? You aren't scared of the dead, are you? The dead are no bother . . . mostly. I think they quite like having us stay. I mean, most of the graves were already cracked and broken and growing vines even, so I'm pretty sure the dead would appreciate what we've done with the place. Without us there, it'd be dead boring just lying there all day. We probably give them something to chat about. And the best part is, even the coppers leave us alone in there. We never get woken up by their boots and sticks and spray and told to get like the street sleepers, because if you annoy the spirits they suck your brains out right through your nose. Not even coppers want to risk having their brains sucked.'

And why does Flea keep saying 'us' and 'we'?

'You'll love it, Twig. There's this old carving over by the gate that says something like "Here, so the dead and the living may find peace together". I can't remember who worked out the words, might have been Preacher. Squizzy said he could read it because he's had learning, but then he said they were old-fashioned letters and hard to read. I reckon he just hasn't had as much learning as he'd like us believe. Come on. I'll introduce you to the crew.'

Flea's words stick in the air and hang between us and Da's voice whispers in my head, *Crew kids. Thieves and rogues, that's all they are, and not worth our time. We stay away from them.*

'You've a crew?'

'Of course. Everyone needs family, right?'

I try to steady the hammering in my chest. I should go now, before the others see me. A crew? 'Actually, maybe I should stay closer to the Towers. So Da can find—'

'Don't be stupid, squirt. I asked the Magic 8 ball if you'd stay. It said *Outlook Good*, so you have to now.

There's no arguing with the ball.'

A raven perched on the gate looks at me with its white eyes and croaks, 'Krrrrruuuuk,' and I try not to imagine what omen it is warning or future it is foretelling.

'Come on.' Flea grabs my hand and pulls me across the road and through the old iron gate. 'Welcome to the Boneyard!' Flea smiles, arms spread wide, and I stop and stare.

I've never seen anything like it. It's like a town all of its own. There are shacks built up between every grave, huddled in clumps and leaning into each other. Kids are jumping between headstones and babies scream and suck muddied fingers and crawl in and out of doors. There are shops, and lights strung between shacks and along posts, and a rainbow of washing, breezing from ropes between trees. Everywhere people are eating and smoking and drinking and talking and laughing, and around one of the fire pits, a group is playing on their guitars and tambours and harmonicas, and an old fella starts dancing, tapping out the rhythm with his shoes.

A kid, no older than six, tugs at my coat and offers to sell us a pack of cigarettes, 'I'll give you a good price? Two for one?' and Flea pushes him away.

'Watch your pockets,' Flea says to me. 'They're terrible thieves, the lot of them. Especially when there's new blood around.' Flea grabs my arm and we walk past a circle of women shrieking and laughing at their card game and a girl not much older than us stares at me, bouncing a grizzling babe on her hip. She sees me look, and turns and climbs back inside a shack.

'Who's this then, Flea?' A little bug of a kid pops his head out from behind an old broken-up motorbike with no wheels. He's holding a spanner and is covered over in oil and dirt, his hair so knotted that no amount of brushing could ever fix it.

'It's my friend, Twiggy. He's brilliant at fixing stuff. He could help you fix that bike up even.'

The kid beams and looks at me like I'm some kind of hero. 'Can you really help me with my bike?'

'Not now, Silas. Later.' Flea pulls me away. 'Here we are. Home.' Flea stops next to a crumbling tomb room with a cracked, winged gargoyle perched on top. There's a line of shacks, the first one leaning into its wall, stacked together with tyres and bits of wood and broken bricks and a plastic sheet tied tight with bright blue rope. 'Pretty nice, hey? I built it myself. Look inside.'

From the outside, it looks like the only thing holding up the shack is luck, but on the inside, it's like crawling into a magic tent that grows and stretches up around me. Every single wall is covered in maps. Old maps and new maps and half-drawn maps and maps torn from books. The one on the roof is *A Map to Fairyland*. It has all the places marked from stories I remember from an old fairy tale book I used to have, and a whole lot more places marked from stories I've not yet heard. There is *Avalon* and *The Valley of Time* and

Scheherazade's Palace and *Ferryman's Cove*. I touch my finger to each one. I could lie and look at that map for ever, remembering those stories, imagining new ones. It makes them seem proper and real somehow.

'Do you like it?' Flea asks.

'It's amazing. And here – *Robin Hood's Hideout*, see? I told you he was real. Where did you get them all from?'

'I collect them. With a map anything is possible. Maps are like a promise, you know?' Flea smooths out a curling corner. 'These are all the places we can go, Twiggy.' Flea smiles. 'One day, hey?' Their fingers run across words burning bright on one of the maps. *'To journey is to follow the promise of footprints down paths not yet taken.* That's what we'll do. One day. We'll see all there is to see and smell all there is to smell, and follow the promise of our footprints down every path in the world and—'

'Flea! Flea!' There are faces at the door, dirt-covered and ash-drawn and one kid has a tattoo in bright blue across their forehead. 'Who's this then?'

'What have you brought?'

'Where'd you find him?'

'Is he new? Is he staying?'

'What's he called?'

'How old is he? Hey, boy, how old are you? What's your name? Where d'you come from?'

'Come on.' Flea pulls me out of the shack and walks me down to a fire pit, the crowd growing behind us as we walk.

A bunch of kids playing dice in the dirt and eating chicken and rice with their fingers stop and stare. 'Right, you lot. This here is Twiggy. Be nice, will you? He's staying with us while he waits for his dad. Isn't that right, Twig?' Flea leans over the fire to warm up.

I shrug and look at the ground and try to pretend that the others aren't looking at me like foxes watching a mouse. *Thieves and rogues* . . . I shove my hands in my pockets so no one sees how they shake.

'Fetch us some rice, would you?' Flea nudges a little one and the kid scampers and comes back with a bowl for each of us. 'You should have been here last week. We had fresh lemon sole fish. My favourite. I get bored of rice. And chicken.'

'Is this who you were telling us about?' a tall kid, even skinnier than me, says, and I try not to think that his eyes look thin and mean.

He's springing cards between his hands and I wonder how he doesn't drop a single one. 'The one you were saying? The one you said whose dad was taken by the Hoblin?'

And the world stops spinning and goes dead quiet, and my breath catches in my throat and I think of our howls and my da, knelt down before that lady. But Flea said Hoblins weren't real. Flea said it was all rubbish.

Flea looks at me and turns away.

Chapter 19
Beasts of the City Wilds

'A Hoblin? What's a Hoblin?' a little one asks. There's a whole crowd gathered now. The boy with the cards speaks in a voice iced to scare, and the little kids shuffle closer together, their fingers twisting each other's sleeves and holding tight.

'A Hoblin is the worst monster there is,' the kid says. 'They look just like regular people, but you can tell by their eyes. Like the eyes of a snake. There is no soul in a Hoblin's eyes, because they eat souls for breakfast and you can't eat souls and have one of your own. And if she's here, if she's looking for souls, do you know the first place she'll come?'

The little ones shake their heads, eyes wide and lips trembling. 'The gravvvvveyarrrrd,' the boy sings and looks over his shoulder. 'You'd better watch out . . . I can hear her . . . she's commmmming . . .' And the kids take a step backwards and then another, then scat away quick. I wish I could follow.

And even though there's no such thing as a Hoblin,

that voice in my head is poking and prodding and making me think that there is such a thing, that I knew it all along. And that voice in my head scratches that maybe Da hasn't come back, because maybe Da never got on that bus after all . . . maybe Da is dead. His soul sucked and his body puffed to nothing but ash on the ground. Just like Old Mrs Tipper.

'That's the stupidest thing you've ever said, Squizzy.' It's a little kid who says that, chewing on a stick and scratching at already-bleeding scabs growing in rashes up and down her arms. She's littler than Flea, but her face looks like an old woman's. There's an old burn across her cheek, all red and scarred, and the top of a knife sticking out from under her belt. I wouldn't mess with this kid, no matter how small she is. 'There's no such thing as a Hoblin.'

'There is so, Preacher. You've heard her whispering in those drains and you know it,' Squizzy says, and throws one of the cards, so it spins through the air and hits Preacher in the leg. But Preacher just spits bits of stick into the dirt and shakes her head.

'That was just the whispering of the drain folk. You dumb as a thumb.'

'I was only messin' about, Twig,' Flea whispers. 'There's no Hoblin.' But I'm not convinced.

'What did you even bring him here for?' Squizzy turns to me then.

'Leave him alone,' Flea says.

I pick at the rice and watch the chickens all ragged and scrawny pecking at the dirt, the street dogs wandering in and out, the rubbish piled up in the corner, and it makes me think of the Riverside crew and the way Da would shake his head every time we passed.

'If you're staying here, you've to pay.' Squizzy steps in front of me and spins his cap backwards on his head, his chest thumping mine. 'We're the Beasts of the City Wilds. We don't take no squatters and scabs. No money, no staying. I don't care what Flea told you, I'm in charge and what I say goes. You got that?'

The others all hoot and start laughing and kick rocks at Squizzy and the dogs start barking and nipping at our ankles, and Flea steps around him and grabs my arm.

'Don't listen. There is no "in charge".' Flea turns to Squizzy. 'Anyway, we'll be making money. Twig here is going to sell postcards, aren't you, Twig?'

'What?'

But Flea has already pulled my drawings from my pocket and is showing the others. A picture of the troll hill I drew for Da falls to the ground and Squizzy picks it up and smiles. It isn't a nice smile. It's the smile Franky Collins always had just before he mashed my head into the wall.

'Some of them are almost good,' Flea says. 'If you tried a bit harder and they were cheap and you smiled and looked pathetic enough, maybe people wouldn't look too close at the pictures.'

I don't say how my drawings are just for me and Da. How they're like a piece of me that I don't want anyone else seeing.

'And he can fix anything. Go on, give him something. He'll show you. He's already promised to fix up Silas's bike.'

'Anything, you reckon? How about your *money maker*? No one could fix that.' Preacher smiles and wipes her nose on her sleeve and now everyone's laughing.

Flea glares, but then walks into their shack and pulls out an old case. 'Ta da!' And there are more hoots and whistles.

'This, my friend, is my money maker. With this beauty, I'll be rich and famous.' Flea waits, wanting me to beg to see what's inside. But everyone's watching and waiting to see what I do. I'm not begging.

Flea's finger starts tapping. 'Well?'

'Well, what?'

'Don't you want to know what my money maker is?'

I do. I really do. I shrug and Preacher pats me on the back.

Flea mumbles something I can't hear, but looks so proud pulling the thing from the case that I can't bring myself not to ask.

'What is that?'

'Ha! That's what we all said!' Preacher crows.

'Don't you know? It's a piano accordion. Beautiful,

right? Best thing you've ever seen. Do you wish it was yours? Everyone does.'

I look at the tear in the fabric at the side and the handle that is hanging off. I can see at least three buttons missing. I used to have an accordion. It was Mum's. Da showed me how to play. 'It's in your bones, Twiggy. You make your spirit sing through that,' Da told me. I don't know what happened to it, but one night it was gone and Da never mentioned it again. But this one Flea's holding won't play for sure. It doesn't even look like an accordion any more.

'Did you find it in the bins?'

Everyone laughs even louder.

'I *bought* it. It came with the case and all. Well?'

I'm good at fixing, but there's no way I could fix this. I look at the others, and I'm about to say just what I think, but then I stop. 'It's amazing,' I say, and it *is* amazing, just not the kind of amazing Flea thinks, and now everyone's throwing rocks at me and calling me a suck and a scab, but they're not throwing the rocks hard and I think that means I'm OK.

'Thank you, Twiggy. When you fix it, maybe I'll even let you have a turn.' Flea places the accordion back in the case as if it's the most precious thing in the world. 'Come on. I'll help you build a shack.'

'Don't touch my bricks,' Squizzy says and everyone wanders away, back to their dice and card games and soon enough someone has called someone else a cheat and then they're wrestling in the dirt and throwing punches that sound hard enough to hurt and if Da could see me here . . .

'Hey. Tower boy. If you're staying, you'll need one of these.' Squizzy throws something at me. White and hard. I catch it before I realise what it is. A small skull, smiling up at me. 'Without a skull, the spirits will come for you,' he adds. 'We've seen it happen before. Last time someone tried to stay when they didn't belong. The spirits don't like outsiders. You'd better watch yourself.'

The wind picks up and swirls at the dirt, and I try not to think that the smell of the dirt in my nose is the smell of the dead. I close my eyes to the dark of night setting in thicker here than it ever was at the Towers. '*Da! Come find me. Please,*' I call, silent on the wind.

The wind pulls at me, twisting higher and faster. I let that dark take me where it will.

For a moment, Twig hovered between his memories and the Afterlife – he was everywhere and nowhere. He was the wind in the trees, the ash of a bonfire and the bark of a dog . . . he flitted from one being to another, flew across place and time. Everything felt so long ago and, at the same time, so far in the future, as though he had become entangled in memories, as if time was bending and curling back on itself so that the past, present and future were all existing at once.

When a flicker of curiosity called, he glanced briefly down to where a small child whose eyes looked for whispers and whose ears were wonder-wide searched through the mud on the river bank, bending, digging, seeking. Twig released the Bone of Lost Wonders, guided it towards the child's fingers until it was twisted free, slurped from the mud into the wet hands. The child stopped, eyes wide and stilled with the knowings trapped inside the bone. Twig warmed the mud beneath the child's feet, bloomed into the hollow of the bone itself, breathed wind into the child's lungs—

There was a roar of thunder and the call of a bird high on the wind. Twig remembered. He thought of Krruk. Focused on the call of the raven. On the key. The atlas. His da. He fought the pull to follow the child, to fall back into the shadows, and with one last great lunge, Twig hurled himself back into the meeple mound, the shadows swirling cloud-thick around him, spinning faster and faster, and then they were gone.

Chapter 20

Eyes and Ears

Twig and Krruk emerged from the tunnel and into the bright of day dripping through the canopy. The forest was no longer dark and haunting, but exquisitely, painfully beautiful. Twig reached out to touch the nearest tree. The bark swirled beneath his fingers, with colours so true they seemed almost unreal, and the leaves curled gently towards him as though responding to his touch. Every tree glowed blue and green and red, their branched arms whispering promises and dreams and twisting into shapes and creatures of their own.

Krruk dropped a stick at Twig's feet. 'Now where to's that atlas? Use this to mark off that Crossing we opened, like. Show everyone what we've done. That was close, you know. You were in there a long time. It's a bloomin' miracle you got out at all.' Krruk checked Twig over for signs of fading.

Twig used the stick to circle the symbol of the key by the meeple mound and watched as green ink flowed on to the page and shimmered in the light. It felt good, knowing that they'd opened a Crossing like those who had come before. He wondered how many Crossings his da had circled. And why he had stopped. 'Krruk. What did the Gatherer mean, about the other Keepers coming to the end of their journey? Did they all . . . fade? Did they unbecome?'

Krruk shook his head slowly. 'I wouldn't know, my boy. Perhaps.'

Twig was filled with a sudden desperation to see his da. He flipped through the maps, searching for something that could tell him where his da would be waiting. Monsters swam in seas of fire, dragons swooped with claws spread wide, beetles hovered in corners, and beasts, curious and strange, stalked through maps. There were seas of Forgotten Words. Archipelagos of Emotion where despair and hope swirled together across the land. There were Dream Maps and Cloud Maps and Star Maps and Bestiary Maps and Time Maps and Mood Maps and a Map of Imagination and a Map of Lost Wonders. There were maps that folded together – in and out in curious patterns, revealing secret routes and hidden messages. There were envelopes and pockets on pages that held compasses and talismans and drawings. There were maps that folded out like an accordion, showing incredible details of the larger map. Each map was full of added curiosities and scribbles in unknown scripts, like a field guide added to by many hands, and most maps already had the key symbol circled brightly and boldly.

The final map in the atlas folded out into a torn wedge, showing the Afterlife spread out and glorious. The words *Outer Wilderlands* were etched along one side. Twig's finger ran along the torn parchment, and he wondered what else lay just beyond the edge.

Flea would love this, Twig thought then, and his heart ached with not being able to share it. For a second he saw again those eyes calling, pleading, heard the laughing, saw the silver of . . . and . . . nothing.

'Krruk,' Twig said, his voice catching, 'I still can't remember how I died.'

'Of course not. Whad' you want to remember that for?'

'Isn't it important?'

'Important? Don't be rid-i-cul-ous. Dyin' is like an elevator trip. Takin' you from the mortal world to the Afterlife. You don't remember elevator trips, do you? Not even the music. Well, except for that slowed-down popcorn song they sometimes play. That's quite catchy that is. Listen, presh, the only deaths people remember are the really long, slow, painful ones. I knew a fella once— Well, maybe that's a tale for later.'

There was a gentle pop and a notice appeared, nailed to the tree in front of them.

MISSING: LOST SOUL

'Oh, scrimpkins. Would you look at that. Not being funny, boyo' – Krruk dropped his voice to a whisper – 'but we need to work out where we're to, because that looks to be your picture on that there notice.' Twig looked at the photo of himself. As he watched, the notice sank back into the bark of the tree, as though the tree was absorbing it.

'We need to get out of this forest,' Krruk hissed. 'These trees have communication systems that go for miles. All you need is one tree to try and score a few points by grassin' you up, and we won't have a chance against the Officials. They have bugles, they do. Bugles! But at least you are listed as MISSING and not WANTED. That means the Gods still think you might have just wandered off, like. It happens from time to time.'

A few trees away, the notice popped back into view again, before slowly disappearing back into the bark. Twig watched as the notice was passed from tree to tree and the leaves of all the trees turned slowly towards him. He shrank into the shadows, skimming through the atlas as quickly as he could, searching for another map with an uncircled key and trying to ignore the pop, pop, pop of the notice being passed through the forest. *Map of the Puddle of Tranquillity, Map of Sands of Time, Map of Gargoyle Rock, Map of the Hill of Depression.*

'Here. Map of Fish Mountain. There's an uncircled key here, at *Bus Stop 57*. It doesn't look too far . . . hang on. Are there buses?'

Out of nowhere, a thin vine reached out and wrapped itself around Twig's wrist. Krruk shrieked and snapped him free.

'Now, not to turn the cat in the pan, like, but do you hear that sound of the wind whisperin' in the leaves?'

Twig nodded.

'Well, it's not so much the wind whisperin' in the leaves as the leaves whisperin' *to* the wind. She's an awful gossip that wind. I won't lie to you, I'm not scared, not a bit, we Guardians don't feel fear we don't, but we need to be movin' on, proper quick, like. If the wind starts her gossipin', then it is a certainty that the Officials will be here in a minute, so we need to *not* be here, if you gets my meanin'. So, if you wouldn't mind, *which way*?'

'Ah . . . OK, here – it says *the Wilderforest lies to the south* – so that means we go north.'

'Right. North it is,' Krruk said and flew eastward.

'Krruk. This way. North.'

'Are you sure? We ravens have excellent senses of direction, but if you're sure . . .'

Twig pointed to the compass in the atlas. Krruk looked at it suspiciously, then took off in the direction of the arrow, nattering in Twig's ear to 'come on, boyo, run faster why can't you?' and the crowd of meeples on Twig's shoulders meeped encouragingly and waved their arms in the air.

Had Krruk and Twig been listening carefully, they may just have heard another sound hovering above the whisper of the wind. Had they been listening carefully, they may just have heard the faint sound of a bugle, heralding to all that the Officials were on the trail. And had they heard, they may have realised that the hunt was about to begin.

Chapter 21

Soul Music

They had been walking uphill for a very long time. 'Is it just me, like, or is this mountainthingy gettin' bigger?'

Twig stopped to let a school of giant fish pass, and watched as they weaved in and out between the shrubs and boulders dotting the mountainside. He looked again at the Map of Fish Mountain. 'One of the notes written here says *Follow the silver trail to reach the top. Ignore the arrows to get to the stop.* Can you see any silver trail?'

Paths of every colour grew out before them, snaking and turning on top of each other, skewed arrows pointing this way and that – but there were no silver paths.

Twig turned back to the notes scribbled in the atlas. Notes about not feeding the fish, and how to avoid *mountain madness* and another which simply said to *Lie down for direction.* He wished the previous Keepers could have been a little more specific. What did *L'sten to th' soul's songe sunge in sorrowe* even mean?

'Maybe they just liked a good tongue twister,' Krruk said, reading over Twig's shoulder. 'Try sayin' that ten times fast. *L'sten to th' soul's sunge songe* . . . no wait . . . *L'sten to the soul songe* . . .'

From inside Twig's pocket came a muffled meep. The meeples were leaping on to the ground in a swarm of waving arms and legs.

Twig knelt down on the ground. 'Krruk! Look! That's not it, is it?' The meeples were all excitedly pointing to a thin, silver snail trail.

Krruk tipped his head to the side and examined the trail with one eye. Then he tipped his head to the other side and examined it with the other eye. 'There is a trail. And it is silver. So, using my excellent skills of deductiwhatsit, I think we can safely say we have found *a* silver trail that *could* be the very same trail as mentioned on the map.'

The meeples took the lead, charging forward up the hill. And as Twig and Krruk followed, it felt to Twig as though the world around them was slowly growing. Or that they were slowly shrinking. The coloured pebbles that were scattered underfoot became huge rocks that they had to weave around and clamber over. The trail itself became a path the size of a road, and as they neared the top, the flowers became giant towers, swarming with bright rainbow-coloured bees.

'There! The bus stop,' Krruk cawed. 'I found it, I did! We're saved!'

An old cobwebbed street lamp flicked on as they approached, and a red metal flag with STOP 57 written on it hung from the post under the lamp, waving slightly on squeaky hinges above a wooden bench seat. A small snail making its way slowly up the lamp post paused and wiggled its antennae at them, then turned away.

Twig circled the bench seat, eyes wide for the Sentry. 'So where does the bus go? Could we catch it, do you think?'

'Bus? What bus? There's no bus up here, don't be daft.'

Twig was about to ask why there was a bus stop then, when a giant, flat, grey fish swam through the silvered sky towards them.

'Is that the Sentry?' Twig felt his breath catch in his throat. He thought of the scribbled *Don't feed the fish* message in the atlas and wondered if he would have a choice . . .

'That? Well now, the Great Big Fish variety of Sentry is not one I've come across myself. That's not to say—'

The fish began to sing. A mournful tune that erupted from its mouth in a sea of blue bubbles. '*Well I know now that the end days are coming, just as sure as the tide will fall and rise . . .*'

'Oh, for cryin' out loud. What noise! Get away would you, shoo. Back to the beach with you. We is waitin' for the Sentry, we is, and no one will come if you is botherin' us with that racket.' Krruk flapped at the fish.

'*And I feel now it's so hard to be happy, when you're nearing your sweet bye and byes . . .*' the fish warbled as it swam sadly away.

Twig sighed and sat down on the bench. 'Eugh. There's something sticky—'

But he didn't finish. The bench was suddenly engulfed by a heaving, slimy mass that sucked Twig deeper into its folds the more he struggled. The atlas fell from his fingers.

'Stay still!' Krruk called. 'And— oh my bones! Don't look up!'

Twig looked up. A jaw filled with thousands of tiny teeth hung open, and Twig could make out the excited antennae of a giant snail waving excitedly above him. There was a soft rumbling, like the sound of distant thunder, and the snail spat out a string of words that dangled in a long line, twisting and twirling on the wind like a kite string.

Krruk flapped in front of the words, tipping sideways to read them to Twig.

'*I erase all footsteps, I destroy castles tall.*
I never falter, yet often fall.
I never leave, yet go out night and day.
I have no wheels, yet roll away.

If I leave you now, I'll return to you soon.
My pulse beats true from the heart of the moon.'

'What?' Twig's mind was blank. If only he could reach the atlas, there must be a clue in there. 'Are you sure you're no good at riddles?' he whispered to Krruk, who was frantically flapping and trying to catch hold of the words between his claws.

'I never said *no good*. I just said they aren't my strongest point, like. Stupid snail, thinks he's so clev-er.'

The snail was now nibbling at Twig's hair, which made it rather hard to think. *L'sten to th' soul's songe sunge in sorrowe.* What song? What soul? The only song was from the fish, and—

'You should have been here last week. We
had fresh lemon sole fish. My favourite . . .'
Not a soul's song. A sole's song. Twig tried to remember the song, and suddenly everything became clear. *Back to the beach*, Krruk had said. 'Wait, I think I've got it.' He shook his hair free of the snail's teeth. '*I erase all footsteps, I destroy castles tall* – what if it's the sea at the beach? Footsteps on the beach get erased by the sea, sandcastles destroyed . . . what's next?'

The string of words was twisting madly now, and Twig struggled to read what was dangling in front of him. '*I never falter, yet often fall. I never leave, yet go out night and day* . . . Waves? They go in and out. They crash and fall, right?'

The snail smiled and his mouth opened wider. He covered the top of Twig's head with his jaw . . .

'No! That's not my answer! Krruk!'

'It's not waves!' Krruk screeched. 'Waves don't go in and out, they just get pulled out by the tide! Oh, scrimpkins, you're going to get eaten! EAT-EN!'

The tide . . . *I never falter, yet often fall* . . . 'That's it! That was the song – *just as sure as the tide will fall and rise!* Tides roll with no wheels! And the tide is controlled by the moon! Tide. The answer is TIDE.'

The snail stopped chewing. It huffed a small snail huff, then retreated into its shell, shrinking back down to normal snail size, and slowly crawling away.

'Krruk, you did it! You *are* good at riddles!'

'I did it? Me? Krruk? I solved the riddle? Well, I am quite the clever bird, but a rid-dle? Me?' He pranced on the ground, the meeples cheering around him. 'Well, come on, chop chop! No time to waste, boyo! Get crossin'! You take too long and he'll spit out another riddle to answer. But remember, don't stay in as long this time, right?'

Twig nodded and pulled a bone from the Gatherer's bundle. The meeples stopped dancing and circled Twig slowly, hands held, humming a low, toneless hum. Twig held the bone close to his chest and took a deep breath, breathing himself inside the bone. He closed his eyes, tipped his head back and howled, a long guttural keen that seemed to shake the mountain itself.

Then he waited. The memories came, creeping, twisting and swirling through the air and over the mountainside towards him. Twig felt completely at peace as he let himself drop deep into the swirling shadows of his memories.

Chapter 22
Spirits Singing

'Why did the one-armed giant cross the road? Hey, mister?' I can hear Flea from here. That voice sharp over the sound of taxis and buses and cars, their red bandana flashing in out of the traffic like a stop sign, trying to busk by telling jokes to people who don't want to hear any. 'To get to the second-hand shop. Get it?' But the drivers just flick Flea away. I snort a little bit at the joke. It isn't even funny.

'What do you call something with three legs, one eye, and that looks like a panda? A three-legged, one-eyed panda, of course! Hey! Listen, listen, what part of the car is the laziest?'

And now there's a kid hanging his body half out the window. 'What?' he asks, and Flea smiles because even though the kid's mum is shushing, that car is stuck in that bridge traffic now and won't be moving any time soon. Flea looks the woman right in her eyes and holds out a hand. She gives one coin and Flea waits for another.

'What?' the kid is shouting.

'The wheels, because they're always tired.'

The boy looks at his mum. 'I don't get it.' The window goes back up.

I worked out this morning that it's been over a year since I moved into the Boneyard. A whole year of terrible jokes and dodgy money-making schemes. A whole year and not a sign of Da. Every week I check with Charlie. Every week he shakes his head. Flea reckons Da's gone for good because others have come back from that bus ride but not Da. Flea even checked the Magic 8 ball. 'Will Twig's da come back for him?' *Outlook Doubtful*, it said. 'Is Twig's da dead?' I didn't look at that answer. There are lots of reasons he could be having trouble getting back. It takes time is all. But now Charlie's gone too, just vanished two weeks back, and that complicates everything. Now I need a new plan for getting word to Da.

A bus blares its horn, and I laugh at Flea's glare and start playing the accordion again. It took me months and months to find all the bits to fix it properly, and even still it sometimes breaks in the middle of a song and I have to stop to patch it up. When I showed Flea how I'd fixed it, they looked at it like it was magic. 'How d'you do it?'

'It was easy.' It wasn't. It was the hardest thing I've ever had to fix. Flea grabbed it out of my hands and tried to play and it was the sound of cats wailing and everyone booed and covered their ears. 'Sorry, squirt, it's still broken,' Flea said.

'Maybe you're broken.' I put my hands into the straps and played just the way Da showed me all those years back, and it was like I'd never stopped. Soon enough a crowd had gathered around the fire, and out came the fiddles and whistles and tambours and the Boneyard was full of music and laughing and dancing well into the night. Flea has never forgiven the accordion for that.

But Flea was right about this being a money maker. I could sit here all day if it weren't for the coppers who come past watching for kids who busk without a permit. If they catch you, they stuff your money in their own pocket and give you a whack with their sticks if you're not fast enough to dodge and run. And then the only thing for it is to double back and throw rocks at them to get even. But when I play the accordion, I feel something inside me beating and pushing, trying to get free, and if I close my eyes, the music takes me right back to when I was little, and I can feel Da, right there on the street with me. Sometimes I think if I sit here long enough, my da will walk past and think, *there's someone who plays an accordion like their spirit is singing*, and there I'll be, waiting.

I look over at Squizzy by the fountain, flicking cards across the top of a cardboard box, his smile and charm gathering a crowd before they even know what they're gathering for. 'Here's the easiest game that you'll ever see. Only these cards, a queen and two threes. The queen is flying from here to there, and when she lands you just say where. You pick a card, whichever you choose – if the queen you win, if not you lose.'

Squizzy tosses the cards back and forth along the box, teasing the crowd with glimpses of the queen. I can tell already which fella Squizzy has lined up to lose by choosing the wrong card. The trick is in letting the fella think he has the game worked out. Letting him think he has already won. Squizzy will let the fella win a bit of money first, and then, when he bets big, that's when he'll get it wrong. Any minute now, that fella is going to put a whole lot of money down on the table and lose it all.

Preacher whistles at me from across at the Town Hall. She gives me a nod and looks down the street at a woman clip-clopping down the footpath, talking so loud on her phone that the whole street can hear her say how 'money is no issue' and 'just get it done and be quick about it if they know what's good for them'. I nod back, and start playing more loudly, standing up and walking in time to my music.

The little kids go in for the woman first. Dirty hands out asking for money and offering to sell her all sorts. 'How about a bracelet, missus? I made them myself.' Flowers and smokes and drinks and dodgy watches. She holds tight to her handbag and brushes them away like flies, using her elbows to push through and hissing between her teeth at them like they're rats swarming.

Then it's my turn. Just as that woman is about to walk past, I jig right in front of her and she stops and glares and pushes me with her bag, tripping on another of the littlies. And she is so wrapped up in getting past *me*, she doesn't notice Preacher coming along the other way and just dipping a hand into her bag and liberating her purse. Liberating – that's what Preacher calls it. The woman keeps walking, and Preacher hands off the purse to a little one and the whole lot of them melt back into the shadows like they'd never been.

Works every time. We've rules for liberating though. We only ever go for them that can afford it, and never anyone with kids or who's old or looks like they're having a rough time. And if they stop and buy something from the little kids, or give off a coin or two, then the whole thing is called off and they can go on their way with their wallet safe in their pockets. It's like a test of good character, Preacher said. Turns out there just aren't that many good characters in this city.

Across the road one of the little ones starts banging his bin lid, and a warning whistle goes up along the street. There are two coppers, eyeing the crowd, listening to the radio buzzing in their ears. One of them looks right at me, pointing his stick, because someone must have told him that if you point a big stick at someone that makes them stop. It doesn't. This copper doesn't stand a chance. Not with that gut. And not with all the little ones ready to jump in front and trip him up if need be. I'm not a super-fast runner like Squizzy, but I can run faster than that copper, no question.

I smile at him, a great big smile. 'Come on then! Come get me, Doughnuts!' But before I can run, before I can do anything, my arms are grabbed from behind and a voice, harsh and thick, hisses in my ear.

'Gotcha!'

Chapter 23

Team of Thieves

Hands squeeze tight, twisting my skin, fingers digging into my arms. I turn my head to see the man from the shoe shop, his face red and sweaty, yelling, 'Here he is! This is the one been thieving wallets. I saw him just now,' while shoving me back and forth and waving my accordion in the air like a flag. We know this fella. He hates us hanging around. Says we're bad for business and that we scare away customers and shock the tourists who've come to see the city. He's been trying to move us on for months now.

And then Flea is there, fists flailing, and, 'You slimy snail brain piece of rotting cow. May a million hungry bees swarm inside your guts, you let him go, give us back our accordion!'

The coppers are on us now too. 'What did you call me back there, sonny? Say it again, I dare you.' And even though it wasn't Flea he was talking to, Flea tells him because they can never resist a dare, not ever. Not even when it gets me a jab in my ribs for the trouble. All the people on the streets are crowding now and trying to get a look and the shoe-shop man tugs my accordion by its strap and it sails up into the air, higher and higher, and the whole world slows to watch.

Flea and me are slammed up against the wall. 'Don't move!' I watch with my cheek pressed to the bricks and a police stick jamming my back as the accordion hits the road. There's a sound like a pop, and it explodes into a thousand and one beautiful pieces. Not even I can fix that. A truck blares its horn and runs right over it, and I think I hear it wheeze out just one last cry.

'Search him!' the fella yells, like we're all not standing next to him and can hear him just fine. His face is glowing red now and his eyes are buzzing and I bet he's thinking he's the hero of this story and is already imagining telling it down the pub.

The coppers empty our pockets of bits of string and tape for fixing and Flea's frame from their slingshot that can fire a marble faster than a bullet, and it's a good thing those police don't know what it is they're throwing on the ground or they'd arrest us for sure. I made Flea that shooter. From pipe that Squizzy nicked from a building site. I made us all one, but it's only Flea that can use it right.

The coppers pat us down to check we're not hiding anything under our shirts. They find where I keep my money and empty that pocket too, right into their own. 'Evidence,' Doughnuts says, his face pressed close to mine, and his breath smells like mouldy cheese. I see Preacher and Squizzy have climbed up on a statue to watch, Preacher sucking away at an icy pole and smiling ear to ear, waving the woman's purse in her hand.

'Well?' The fella is peering over the police and trying to get a look.

'Nothing. No wallet, no purse. No nothing, *sir*.' The coppers turn to the man, who isn't looking nearly as excited as he was a second ago.

The crowd have switched, and are mumbling to each other, 'Just little kids trying to make some money.' 'Leave them alone, why don't you.' 'Where's the harm in a bit of busking?' The people from the bakery have come out now and are swearing blind that we are the sweetest kids they've ever laid eyes on and politest bunch you'll meet and they vouch that we are certainly not pickpockets and thieves and how dare that man accuse us?

That's when the fella clocks Preacher, waving the purse. 'There! Over there! That's the kid! They're in it together. It's a whole team of thieves!' But by the time everyone turns, Preacher and Squizzy have already gone and the crowd glare at the fella and shake their heads and say they'll be buying their shoes elsewhere from now on. The police give us another shove against the wall for good measure and tell us to get from the streets, no begging no busking no loitering allowed, then start on the man about wasting police time, and the crowd go back to their phones and the bakery people bring us out a whole bag of cakes and pastries and tell us they're sorry about my accordion.

Flea sighs. 'It was a good money maker, but don't worry, squirt, you can come tell jokes with me instead. I'll teach you how to say them right so they sound funny.'

'It doesn't matter.' I try to sound certain and sure of myself. I pretend I don't care about the accordion. I pretend I'm talking to those film crews who come ask questions for their shows on *Children of the Streets*. They come and we stretch our mouths wide and try to show all our teeth in great big smiles and we answer their questions even though they're stupid questions, like, 'Do you like it here, living in the city?' And of course we do or why would we stay? And when we nod, they smile their sad smile that says they know so much more about this world than poor little us, but when their wheels get robbed right off their fancy cars, who knows about the world then? Especially when it's us doing the robbing.

When those film people ask something you don't want to talk about, you just pretend you're another kid with another name and another life and another head full of memories, and then the questions don't hurt and you can answer any way you want, knowing that when they go, they hand out money like it grows right there in their pockets.

So that's what I do now, I use all my skills to pretend

I'm another kid who doesn't care, and I try to ignore that scratchy voice in my head that whispers, *If Charlie has gone, and if you're not playing the accordion, then how will Da ever find you now? How will he know you even ever waited?*

Chapter 24

City of Beasts

'Here, you start.' Flea throws me the spray can and points at the brick wall.

'What are we doing again?' Preacher scratches her head and looks around the alley.

'A map of the city.'

'And why are we doing it?'

'So Twig's dad knows where to find him. We'll make a map, and write *Twig waits here* and then Twig will stop going on about it and driving us all nuts.'

'Twig, your dad isn't coming back. He's either dead or shipped out or locked up. Or maybe he's got some new family now. Who cares? We're not wasting this wall on a map for someone who isn't coming.'

Flea glares at Squizzy. 'It's not only for Twig. It's for all of us. To tell everyone that *we* are here too. That this is *our* city. City of Beasts!'

And now everyone is talking over everyone else, hands slapping the wall and trying to make their voices heard.

'I like that.'

'Who cares about us? Why would anyone want to see us on a map?'

'I care.'

'Me too.'

'If we're on a wall, will we be proper famous then?' the little one who's always on at me to fix the bike asks, then looks at me to see if I think it's a good idea too.

Flea nods. 'Yeah, Silas. That's right. Like the maps in my shack that tell all those stories. No one forgets those stories because they're on a map. We can put *our* stories on the map. Like, *The coppers took our money here*, and, *He who killed music lives here*, so everyone knows and can boo that man and throw eggs at his shop and never buy their shoes from him again. Then no matter what happens, hundreds of years from now, people will look at this wall and say, "This used to be a City of Beasts. They existed and were true."'

Flea's eyes are burning with excitement now, imagining that map blooming on the wall, spreading and stretching across the city. Imagining the whole world seeing it and taking note. Flea has the best imagination in the world.

'A map is stupid,' Squizzy says. 'I reckon we should paint a giant fish.'

And everyone is yelling over everyone else again.

'Who would want to look at a fish?'

'Fish are stupid.'

'What about a raven? They're like guardians, aren't they, Flea?'

'No, the map is what we're here for—' Flea tries to shout over the rest of us.

'Crows are better than ravens,' Squizzy says.

'They're the same thing, aren't they?'

'Ravens and crows are both dumb,' Preacher says. 'I reckon a skeleton.' And she uncaps the spray can and without waiting for us to say that a skeleton is a good idea or not, she starts on the outline. The scrawny black bird picking through the rubbish looks at the wall and squawks angrily.

Squizzy whines that skeletons are more stupid than a map even, but it's actually a pretty good skeleton. It has a top hat and walking stick and a briefcase and looks like it's about to dance right off that wall. I didn't know Preacher could paint.

'Where are we going to paint the map now? How will Twig's dad know he's waiting? And how are we supposed to get revenge on that shoe shop fella?' Flea kicks at the rubbish. 'That was the whole point of the map and now you've gone and ruined it with a dumb skeleton. It's not even Halloween or Day of the Dead or nothing.'

'How about a bag of roaches?' Preacher says and shakes up the can again. 'We could wait until that man gets in his fancy car and then steal his keys and empty them in through the window, so he's covered all over and we could lock the door and trap him in there until he dies from roach bites.'

'Roaches are stupid.' Squizzy tries to light a cigarette butt and burns his fingers instead. He always says Preacher's ideas are stupid. He thinks he's so smart, but he never has any good ideas either. This time though, he's right. Roaches *are* stupid.

'And roach bites don't kill you.'

'Sometimes they do. If you can't get them clean in time.'

'And you can't lock someone *in* their car, only out.'

'In jail they train the roaches to carry stuff between the cells. I seen it.' But no one cares.

'Don't you worry, Twig. We'll work out a good and proper revenge. No one goes around breaking our stuff and getting away with it,' Flea says, but they know as good as me we won't, because the fella was a proper fella with a suit and a car and a house probably, and those sorts can do whatever they want.

'Rats,' one of the little ones says. 'Rats are better than roaches. We'll catch 'em, and set 'em loose in his house and they'll charge, all biting and scratching at him and they'll probably have rabies or something too.'

'How are we supposed to catch rats without getting bitten and turned to rabies ourselves?' Preacher shakes her head. 'And don't touch that paint. You're only here to help carry, got it?'

'You don't turn to rabies, stupid, you turn to

135

zombies. You catch rabies from the rats.'

'Rats don't turn you to zombies, vampires do.'

'Nah way. Zombies turn you to zombies, and vampires turn you to vampires. You lot know nothing about nothing. You all dumb as stone.'

'Cat pee is worse than rats. I had a cat pee on my jacket once and had to throw it away 'cause that smell won't never get out.'

We all fall about laughing then, thinking of Squizzy being peed on by a cat and because he reckons it would be easier to get a bucket of cat pee than a bag full of rats. And now everyone's yelling and arguing and throwing rubbish and Preacher stops painting to shove the kid who called her dumb and Squizzy grabs the can and starts spraying everyone's feet pink and we're all so caught up squealing and yelling we don't even notice when a metal door down the back of the lane opens wide.

Later we'll say there was always a door there. But there wasn't, cross my heart, hope to die, stick a needle in my eye. That was a dead-end lane as sure as a dog barks. But we don't notice the door appear and we don't notice it open. We don't even notice when two men in their black jackets walk out with baseball bats, thumping their big fat fists and their big red faces full up with shock. I guess they weren't expecting a skeleton and a pack of dirty kids to appear in this particular lane.

The bat smashes hard against the bins, and those

Black Jacket Men are yelling and pointing at the wall and throwing us down on the rubbish like we're rags. 'What are we going to do with them?' the man with a scar the size of a river running down his face says to the really big man who's shaking his head slow and scary. I think of the cage fights set up in the black markets, and how sometimes they use cocks for the fighting, and sometimes they use dogs, and sometimes, they use kids.

BigMan leans right in close so we can smell the smoke on his breath. 'Do you know,' he says slowly and the way he says it makes me think of a snake waiting to strike, 'whose lane this is?'

None of us is dumb enough to answer. The bat swings hard and slams the bin again, right next to my head, so my ear rings with the clang of it. We shake our heads fast. The man stands up. 'You mean to tell me, you live in this city and you don't know whose city this is?' I know Flea will be thinking *this is the City of Beasts* and I hope more than anything they're clever enough not to say it.

And then. And then the door opens again. And my heart stops beating in my chest. And my blood freezes in my veins. And all the air in my lungs turns to stone.

Because there she is. Standing right there in that lane. The Hoblin.

Chapter 25

Little Mouse

I stop breathing, staring up at the Hoblin. All this time I'd told myself that she wasn't how I'd remembered. That I'd just been little, and scared was all, and that she was just some regular old thief stealing Da's black market goods and I just got in the way. But there she is, right in front of me. Bigger and more powerful than she was before, and I swear she doesn't even move her feet, just glides over like she isn't made of skin and blood and bone and I wonder who howled her here without us even hearing. I don't look at those snake eyes.

She looks around at the lane and a long finger twirls in the air as if she is smoking up all the paint and rubbish into a cloud. She turns to us and stares.

'You want us to deal with them, boss?' BigMan points his bat and the Hoblin stops time and glides closer.

'Do you know who I am?' she asks in her pretend human voice. You can tell straight off it isn't a real voice because there's no deepness to it. Not one of us looks at her. Not one of us even breathes, just in case she can suck our souls straight from our mouths and into her own.

'Do you know' – and she bends down and her claws scratch under Flea's chin and lifts it so Flea is stuck looking her in the eye and my little finger links tight with Flea's – 'what I do? I keep this city safe. Respectable.' She stands up; her hand flies at the scattered rubbish and sprayed paint. 'Does this look safe? Does this look respectable? I do not tolerate thugs and hoodlums and thieves on my streets.'

When we don't say a word, the Hoblin turns to ScarFace. 'This is the work of thugs and hoodlums.' And her head flicks back to us so fast her face blurs and I swear I see all the souls she has eaten for breakfast flash across her face, their mouths open and screaming to be saved. 'Are you thieves as well? Are you the ones who my shopkeepers are complaining about? Are you the ones the police tell me are snatching bags and wallets from our tourists? The Mayor was telling me only yesterday that our city has a problem with . . .' She looks at us with disgust, her nostrils flaring. '. . . with beggars and thieves. The Mayor asked *me* to fix it.' She turns to ScarFace. 'Tell them what happens to people in my streets who create trouble for our mayor. Who make our streets dirty. Who turn away the tourists and worry the businesses.'

ScarFace smiles and squats down so he's looking right at us all piled and tumbled on each other. 'The first time,' he says, and his voice is the voice of the dogs growling over scraps down the tips, 'is a warning. We're good like that, aren't we, boss?'

The Hoblin doesn't answer. Just looks at us with her snake eyes flashing.

'The first time' – ScarFace grabs Squizzy's arm and pulls it forward, holding tight to his fingers and I hear him squeak – 'we just break a couple of your little thieving—'

'You.' The Hoblin points at me. ScarFace drops Squizzy and he grabs me instead and now he has me standing up against the wet paint of the skeleton, his bat pinning me to the wall and when he smiles I can count all the teeth that are missing. Out on the street, a copper strolls past, spinning his stick and whistling. I think it's Doughnuts, but it's hard to tell. They all look the same. He looks at us with the spray cans at our feet, and the Hoblin and her men, and he nods and his smile grows bigger. He keeps walking.

'I don't . . .' I tell the Hoblin but my voice is shaking so the words come out more of a whisper. 'I don't actually thieve. Ask anyone. I never . . .'

It's true. I'm never the one to *actually* steal. I just get in the way and distract a little, and that's not technically thieving. I've never technically thieved. Not proper things anyway. Only things that don't count like fruit from the markets or the money from the gospel church down the road. But that's not stealing, because when they collect the money, they say 'for the poor' and we are the poor, so all we're doing is cutting out the middle man and doing everyone a favour. And anyway, if we don't take that money then it's just the vicar who does. We saw him pocket it and go buy himself a great big burger down the shops, so if anyone's fingers should be given a warning it should be his.

All the others nod their heads.

'It's true. He's rubbish at thieving,' Squizzy says and I think he's trying to help, but all it gets him is a kick from BigMan and Squizzy yelps and shuts his mouth.

The Hoblin looks at me, moving her head to see me from different angles like her snake eyes can't quite focus right. 'Little Mouse,' she hisses and it isn't her pretend voice now but the real voice of a Hoblin for sure. Cold and dead. 'How you've grown.'

My brain starts fuzzing and the black starts creeping in from the edges and the air is suddenly too thick to breathe.

'Does your father know you are here?' Da? She's talking about Da? He's alive? He's here? 'He was so very upset when you ran away from him like that, so angry.' And I don't know if she means I was so angry or Da was so angry with me. 'Such a small child in such a big city. He wondered where you would go. I don't think he ever thought you would join a crew though. Surely he taught you better than that . . .' She looks at the Beasts and shakes her head and frowns. 'What a pity. Come. We are late, Micahel.'

She turns to BigMan and glides from the lane, pulling on long white gloves that go all the way up to her elbows so no one notices her sharp Hoblin claws and I want to ask her about Da, to make her tell me everything, but my voice sticks and she keeps walking.

ScarFace points his finger hard at my face. 'We'll be back in two hours. This lane will be safe and respectable when we get back.' He spits on the ground, which isn't very safe or respectable, but no one says so, not even Squizzy.

We don't talk much. Not for the whole two hours. Only Flea did once, and that was a whisper in my ear. 'She isn't a Hoblin, don't you know? There's no such thing. It's just a stupid story.' I pretend I knew that already even though we all agreed it was the work of a Hoblin just the other month when that whole bunch of sniffer kids were found dead outside the stations.

'You can tell because their lips are blue and frothed where their souls were sucked out,' Squizzy had said in his show-offy-know-everything way, but Preacher said, 'Their lips are blue and frothed from the glue and paint they sniff, stupid.' And even though that was more true, we all still believed Squizzy.

The whole time, all I can do is think how the Hoblin was talking about Da. How the Hoblin knows Da. And maybe, the Hoblin can bring me to Da.

'Flea? Do you think she really knows where my da is?'

'Of course not. She just said that to trick you into

142

giving up your soul. You think if your da was here, he wouldn't find you? You stay away from her, squirt – are you listening?'

And when we have given up scrubbing the paint because it won't come off, we get the black cans and spray the whole wall black instead. I feel a bit sad for Preacher's skeleton vanishing under the paint, but the wall looks better black than it did before we came. Proper fancy like all the hipster cafes down Old Fitzroy Road.

We clean up the rubbish and take the spray cans with us in case anyone sees the store tags still on them and decides to give us a warning after all.

'It's been two hours,' Preacher says, and we run flat out away from that lane and the Hoblin and her Black Jacket Men, through Potters Field and past the old miners' cottages in Canning Street. And when we find a watermelon sitting unguarded in the car park on Dodds Road, we take turns carrying it down the park and Preacher draws eyes on it and we all get sticks and beat the watermelon to death. We watch its brains explode all over the grass and cheer and yell at it that this is what happens to thugs and hooligans and thieves in our city and then we eat the pieces and pretend we are Hoblins eating its soul for breakfast. And we laugh great big pretend laughs that empty out our fear and make it easier to pretend that the lady is just a lady and not a Hoblin at all, and the trees and bushes start laughing with us and the buildings are all holding their big building bellies and laughing so much the whole world shakes and the leaves shake down harder and faster on top of us and we go deeper deeper deeper under the green.

Krruk was calling to him. Twig knew it was Krruk. Knew the words Krruk was saying, but his mind was still flitting, back and forth. He let himself drift back, allowed himself to follow the shadows again, through the wind, across the skies. He saw it in the way one sees a dream. Felt it happening. It wasn't that day, or even a time he knew. But he felt the fingers reaching, the knowings whispering across time and place, and he released the Bone of Lost Wonders into the hand that looked for it.

This hand was old and wrinkled, her fingers tickling at the roots of a seedling being patted into a patch of flowers on top of a hill. Twig felt his way down into the roots of the flowers, became the dirt beneath her fingers, pressed himself under her nail, edged at her papery skin, and when she dug the white bone from the ground, Twig twirled on the wind and roared with the evening sun.

Twig was only vaguely aware of the shadows around him, swirling and disappearing, a handful of meeples swirling and disappearing with them higher and higher into the sky, going, going, almost gone, and Twig didn't mind the feeling of being pulled with them . . . didn't mind staying in the calm, quiet of his memories . . . he let himself go.

Chapter 26

Fading

There was a sharp pain on his hand and Twig pulled back, toppling off the bench and on to the dirt. He looked at his skin, at the beak mark, red and bleeding. 'You pecked me!'

'You went too far into that Crossin' and almost didn't come back! You almost *unbecame*! What else was I to do? The meeples tried bitin' you, but it was no good. You were too far gone.'

Twig looked at the bright red marks dotting his arms and legs. His mind was still flitting between now and his memories. It had felt so easy to just let go . . . And even thinking it, Twig suddenly saw again the silver. The hand aiming. And a voice. Voices. He could hear them now, clear as day—

'You want us to deal with them, boss?'

and—

'Twig! Twiggy!'

The voices became muffled, running on top of each other. And there was a song, a tune being rung on bells,

and he knew the words to the tune, sang along with the
bells in his head—

'Oranges and lemons sing the bells of . . .'

And then the sound got fainter and he couldn't tell any
more if he was really hearing it or if it was only a dream
echoing. He shook his head and rubbed his eyes. There
was something wrong. When he looked at his hands
they seemed all wobbly, like he couldn't quite focus
properly. And they tingled, as though he had pins and
needles in the very tips of his fingers.

Krruk gasped. 'Oh, my bones! Look at your hands!
They've faded they has! I said it was too hard for you,
that you wasn't strong enough in the mental department.
I said you was in there too long! Listen, boyo. Once you
start fadin', the weaker you are and the easier it is to
unbecome! I can't just peck you every time neither. Pain
works at first, but there's the risk that it will send you
further into your memories to escape the pain.' Krruk
hopped from foot to foot.

'Faded? Can I stop it? Can I unfade?'

'Oh, sure. If you stop messin' about with Crossin's
and memories and the like and concentrate on all the
wonders this realm has to offer . . .'

Twig looked up at the deep orange, almost red, of the
sky and could see where the sky seemed thicker now, as
if it had been sprayed into being by a ginormous paint
can. The mountainside seemed to have shrunk back to
its normal size, and as Twig looked out across the land,

he was overcome with its beauty. He sighed softly, and turned back to the atlas, circling the key symbol on the Map of Fish Mountain with shaking hands. What choice did he have? The Gatherer had said that there was no time to wait for anyone else. He was their last chance. He couldn't just stop.

Krruk huffed then pecked Twig's finger gently. 'I know. How abouts we make a safe word, like. So, if in your memories you hear someone say "bones" you'll think of me, and that means yous are in a bit of strife, and fairly close to unbecomin', and to get back here quick sharp.'

'Will that work?'

'I don't rightly know, but it's worth a try, isn't it? Better tried and failed than failed and whatsit.'

Twig nodded.

'Righteo and Bob's your uncle Markus. Where to's it then?'

Twig flicked through the atlas, searching for more keys. Four to go. He looked again at his hands. Would he last that long?

'Here. The next closest key is on the Map of Running River Lake. There, in the Falls of Despair.' Twig was hit with an image of deep, dark water, churning, eating at him, pulling him down. 'Are they really falls of *despair*?'

'Oh, we-ell. Despair is a strong word. You could say they were falls of misery, desolation, hopelessness, anguish, gloom even. The *Falls of Gloom*, now that has a certain ring to it, don't you think?'

Twig didn't know if he could do it. He was so, so tired. The Gatherer hadn't said how draining it was, releasing the bones into the world. She didn't say how easy it was to just let go. 'We might just sit for a while, I think. Just a little while . . .' Twig leaned against the bench and watched the passing fish and the meeples secreting odd rocks and pieces of shell into his shorts' pockets.

He glanced quickly at his tingling hands, then away. 'Look at that bird,' Twig said to Krruk, trying hard to concentrate on all the wonders the realm had to offer.

'Oh, yap. Always the colourful ones that get the attention.' Krruk looked rather offended.

'Crows are lovely too though,' Twig added, then stopped. Krruk was glaring again.

'Crows are nothin' but trash! You do remember I'm a raven, not a crow, don't you?'

'Oh, I . . .'

'And crow's feathers are nothing but a dull *meh* colour and not a bit lucky, but have you seen the way a raven's feather is not only full of luck, but holds every colour of the rainbow and then some, in the one deep shade of black? Of course not. No one bothers to see the beauty in somethin' so simple. And anyway, you can admire that there birdy, but I'll tell you now that you wouldn't be admirin' it so much once it got close. That beak is wicked sharp, believe you me.' Krruk fluttered on to Twig's shoulder. 'Have I told you the story . . .' he began . . .

Down the mountain, across the valley and at the very edge of the Wilderforest, two Officials sat atop a giant furred spider, looking at the **MISSING: LOST SOUL** notice nailed to the tree. 'This is where the trail left by the wind ends,' one of them mused.

'The boy was here, not long ago.' The taller Official rubbed his moustache and jumped from the spider's back. He picked up a piece of yellow paper fluttering on the ground. 'It's a map of some sort.' He handed it to his partner and together they examined the jagged edge where the map had come loose from the atlas. *Map of Lost Words*, they read. And then, scrawled in the corner of the map, *FIGHT THE FORGETTING!*

'The boy has an atlas.' The Official sighed deeply. 'This is more serious than we thought. He isn't just lost. He's fighting.'

The word MISSING shivered, then detached itself from the notice and fluttered into the sky. A thick line of red ink rose up from the dirt and slithered on to the paper to take its place. The Official glanced back at the notice and nodded.

WANTED: LOST SOUL

'Time to call in the cavalry,' the smaller Official said.

The spider reached out a long, furred leg, and raised a bugle to its lips.

Chapter 27

Falls of Despair

Twig traced his finger along the map, following a swirling river that snaked across the page, over the *Great Sands of Fire*, around the *Lakes of Fear*, and to the *Falls of Despair*. This was definitely it. He'd almost hoped they had followed the map the wrong way and that they wouldn't really have to venture any closer to the churning black waterfall raging before them.

'I see what they mean by despair,' Twig said. All around the waterfall, the land lay ruined and destroyed. Trees were toppled, leaves blustered in small swirling clouds of dirt, and rainbow bees lay twitching on the ground. Twig turned back to the notes scribbled across the atlas.

Focus on the good times.

Roots entwine beneath our feet and tell secrets
we can not know.

They share, they warn, they nurture. While above
the ground they grow.

Take it step by step, moment by moment . . .

And then the voices were back, writhing and worming in Twig's mind and he dropped the atlas and covered his ears with his hands.

'Agh, scrimpkins! Not those pesky Gods again!' Krruk plucked two dead bugs from the ground and shoved them in his ear holes.

'GOOD DAY, YE . . . YE OF LITTLE . . . GODLINESS. BEHOLD. THIS IS YOUR GODS SPEAKING.' There was a pause and some muttering and whispered argument. 'THE TIME HAS COME, MY LITTLE FRIEND, TO TALK OF MANY THINGS. OF SHOES AND SHIPS AND CEILING WAX. OF CABBAGES AND—' There was a muted thump and then a slightly different tone of voices leaked into Twig's brain.

'AHEM. THAT MESSAGE WAS NOT INTENDED FOR EARS SUCH AS YOURS. *SOMEONE* – NOT NAMING NAMES – BUT THE GOD OF SOMETHING STARTING WITH "W" AND ENDING WITH "ONDER" WAS SWITCHED ON TO DREAM STALKING . . . AND IT IS SEALING WAX. NOT

CEILING WAX. I DON'T BELIEVE CEILINGS NEED
WAX. NOT LIKE THOSE SEALS. YOU WOULDN'T
WANT TO SEE AN UNWAXED SEAL. DREADFUL.
WAX IS WHAT MAKES THEIR FUR SO SHINY.
AND WHY THEY MAKE THAT SORT OF
SQUEAKING NOISE WHEN YOU RUB THEM—'
There was the shuffle of more arguing, 'START AGAIN,'
and moving and, 'RIGHT. STARTING AGAIN.' And
now both sets of voices were speaking into Twig at
once and his eyes watered with the unbearable tingling,
scratching itch of it, like his brain was crawling
with spiders.

'HEAR YE. HEAR YE. YOU HAVE DISREGARDED
OUR WARNING. YOU HAVE FAILED TO OBEY
OUR DECREE! YOU WILL BE FOUND. YOU WILL
BE DEALT WITH UNPLEASANTLY. IF YOU HAND
YOURSELF IN NOW, WE WILL TAKE THIS INTO
CONSIDERATION BEFORE WE OBLITERATE YOU.
I MEAN, YOUR RECORD! HA! NOT YOU. IF YOU
HAND YOURSELF IN, YOUR *RECORD* WILL BE
OBLITERATED AND ALL WILL BE FORGIVEN. IF
YOU CONTINUE ON YOUR WAY, HOWEVER,
YOU WILL BE *CONDEMNED* WITH OUR GODLY
JUDGEMENT. AND KNOW THIS. WE DO NOT
LOSE. WE ARE GODS. WE *NEVER* LOSE.'

There was silence and Twig gasped for breath.

'WELL, THERE WAS THAT ONE TIME—'
followed by another thump and crackle and then the

voices faded and were gone.

Krruk crossed his wings and tapped his foot and glared at Twig. 'Happy now, are we? Did you hear what they said? Obliterate! Obliterate! You could be happily retired now, chuggin' off in the train, doin' yogawhatsits. But would you listen? No. Of course not.'

'Should I hand myself in then?' Twig thought of never being with Da. Of never seeing him, never knowing him again and he was filled with an agonising ache.

'What? Are you for real, like? There is no forgiveness! It's a trick, isn't it? The Gods are verr-rry tricksy and not to be trusted, like. Them Gods is the worst tricksters in all the realms they is, the lot of them. I bet you think they are great big wonderous spirits floatin' along in clouds or some such nonsense, don't you? That's because that's what they drip into people's dream wells. But let me tell you they is nothin' but skeleton people no taller than a squirrel, and with great big butterfly wings and little antennae that bob about and get in the way.' Krruk nodded. '*And* they aren't even real Gods. God*lings* more like, been given free rein to play with a realm. Little pests they are. Their day will come, mark my words. It always does. And who will be left to pick up the pieces? Well, not me because I'll be obliterated, thanks to you.'

Twig tried to imagine the Gods as Krruk had described them. 'So why are we running from them then? If they're so small? Why doesn't the Gatherer just go and demand that they release the memories?' Twig couldn't imagine anyone arguing with the Gatherer.

'Oh ho! You think size has anythin' to do with anythin'? The smallest bug can take down the biggest beast if they knows how. But those in power protect themselves. And anywhatsits, the Gods may be pesky little blighters, but they have the Officials on their side, don't they? And those Officials are not to be messed with. They is just plain mean, they is. They enjoy the hunt and the power. How else could they take on such a job? I'm afraid the only thing for it is to enjoy the last days of existence before the agonisin' pain of obliteration. The best we can do is try to cover our tracks as we go. They don't know where we are – all-seein', all-knowin', my beak – if they did, the Officials would have us surrounded, wouldn't they? Move on quickly, that's all we's can do. Here. Have a feather. They're good luck, you know. We'll need it. In fact, take two. No, three, even better.' Krruk produced three feathers from the air between his ribcage and handed them to Twig. 'Righteo. In we go. Watch the ground beneath your toe.'

They followed a track etched in purple pen on the map, guiding them to a small ledge that led to an alcove eating into the rock behind the waterfall. 'I have to walk along that?' Twig's voice shook, looking at the thin ridge. He was shaking so ferociously by now that meeples were jumping from his body and scrambling up the wet rocks themselves. *To know yourself you must be*

156

strong. He took a deep breath and gripped his fingers to the cliff face—

> *'All you're doing is standing against a wall.*
> *What does the drop matter?'*

Yes. Twig held on to the memory. *Standing against a wall* . . . The water raged before him and he struggled to find a grip on the slimed rock ledge. He could do this.

He couldn't do this.

'Come on, boyo, tick tock. What's the hold-up?' Krruk nudged at his leg.

'Meep?' The littlest meeple was running back and forth along the ledge, skipping and jumping joyously in the puddles that had formed from the spray. 'Meeeeeep!'

Take it step by step. Slowly, carefully, Twig edged his way along the ledge and finally made it into the alcove. The noise from the waterfall was deafening. Twig dropped to the ground and wrapped his arms around himself, trying to still the shivering in his body and the meeples rubbed their heads against him and meeped soothingly. Krruk, meanwhile, was fixing the pictures drawn throughout the alcove. Rubbing out those he didn't like with his wing bone and adding crooked raven pictures in their place.

As Twig watched the water raging in front of him, a face seemed to appear from within, forming in the droplets of spray. At first, it was an old man's face, kind and smiling, and then, as Twig watched, it twisted and spun, revealing the face of a fox, then a chicken, then a deer, an otter, and then finally settling into the form of a giant beetle. With a human face. And glasses. Twig thought it looked quite friendly really . . .

'Agh, scrimpkins!' Krruk hissed. 'Twisters. They is the worst of the lot they is. Terrible sports, always tryin' to trick you into sayin' somethin' you don't mean. You have to play this one well smart now, boyo. She won't give you a second chance, like. Do not say a word, unless that word is the answer. You hear me? Not one word.' Krruk drew a single claw across his beak.

Twig opened his mouth to say 'got it' but was struck with a wing bone on his head before he had the chance.

'Smart I said! Not one word!'

Twig nodded. The beetle peered at him over the rim of her glasses. She smiled and began to rub her forelegs together. A thrum of music arose, blooming into words as it reached Twig's ears. It was the most beautiful sound Twig had ever heard. He thought he really must tell her how lovely it is . . . A meeple gave him a warning bite, and he clenched his mouth shut tight and concentrated on the words of the song instead.

> *'I have cones but not for eating,*
> *I have needles that will not sew.*
> *I can shout a storm is coming,*
> *but my voice you'll never know.*
> *I am home for some,*
> *and food for more,*

158

my family travels far.
While underland I spread my love,
above I reach for stars.'

Twig breathed in deeply. He felt he was getting better at this whole riddle thing. There was a way of thinking about the riddles. You had to twist your mind a little bit. All it took was a small twist . . . and suddenly Twig could see it. It was something Flea had said, all that time ago. About pine cones warning that a storm was on its way. Twig went through the riddle in his head, making sure he had it right. *Cones – pine cones. Needles – pine needles. A pine tree could be a home for animals. Animals could eat pine cones, and people eat pine nuts. Pine trees are spread across the world.* And now the clue in the atlas about the roots entwining while growing above ground made sense. *While underland I spread my love. Above I reach for stars.*

Twig nodded. 'Pine tree,' he whispered.

The beetle smiled again, then spun faster and faster, twisting into myriad different animals and beings. Perhaps he had got the riddle wrong after all. Perhaps this was the end. For a moment, Twig felt an incredible pull to be part of that churning water, to become one of the Twister's creatures, but then, as quickly as it had come, the beetle was gone, and the waterfall was just a waterfall again.

Twig smiled and tried to catch his breath. The

159

meeples cheered and Krruk rubbed his head against Twig's cheek. 'Well done, my boy. Well done. Hurry and cross now before she comes back. But please remember not to dwell too long in your memories! Please be careful.' The raven pecked Twig's nose gently.

'I'll try. I'll really try.' Twig reached into the bundle and took out the largest of the stone-white bones. He closed his eyes, and howled, just the faintest howl this time – it was all he could muster. And when the shadows tumbled towards him, churning harder and faster than the waterfall, he hesitated for just a moment, wondering if he had the strength to face his own memories again. He thought of his da. Of being wrapped in those arms. Being lost in those eyes, and suddenly it wasn't Da's eyes but Flea's and they're pleading for help, calling his name, and he's hearing the Hoblin laughing and—

> *'Oh, my. Didn't he tell you? My, my, Little Mouse. Keeping secrets. Tut tut.'*

And the hurt on Flea's face and the way they turned from him—

> *'Blood Family for ever, remember?'*
> *'Go on. Do it then. I dare you.'*

And Twig was wrenched back into the deep, dark shadows.

Chapter 28

Blood Raven

We're all down the river, trying to get clean even though it's close to freezing, because the mammas reckoned it was us bringing the sicknesses into the Boneyard. They tried to blame us for the baby that died last week but everyone was coughing as much as us and everyone knows that babies' coughs are a sure sign of dying and that it was scrawny as a chicken since the day it was born and its eyes never looked right anyway.

When it's hot, I don't mind getting clean in the river. I sit in the sun and let the warm mud squeeze between my toes and watch the others race. No one ever beats Flea, because they're the best swimmer of all. Even underwater they can hold their breath for so long the rest of us get bored. But there's no racing or sitting on the bank when it's cold like this. Days like this all you can do is get in and scrub as fast as you can while your body starts aching, then jump out and try to rub some warm back into your bones. Even the people living in their boats all lined up along the river bank don't swim in this weather.

I'm already wrapping the newspaper back around my body and helping the little ones get wrapped so we can stay extra warm, and Squizzy and Preacher are over with the others, poking through the mud looking for treasures worth selling.

'Twig,' Flea says, and grabs at my arm, pointing out to the river. 'I thought I saw . . .'

But there's nothing there but our reflections, wavy and shimmery and not quite right. 'Do you think that's what ghosts look like?' I say. 'Maybe when you die you turn to reflection and move through water and mirrors and windows.' And when I say it, for just a second my reflection changes and it's like I'm looking at a different me. An older, sort of sadder, raggedier me.

'When you die,' Flea says, eyes wide staring at that water, and just like that, a body pops up to the surface. A real-life dead body, right there in front of us, right where we'd been swimming and washing, like it had been called up by Flea's words.

A big black bird flies on to the branch above the river and starts calling out to that body, and I remember what Flea said about ravens being messengers of the Gods and I don't even know if it's a raven or a crow and I don't even believe in omens, but if this isn't an omen, then what is?

Everyone has joined us now, all of us bunched up together and watching the body bobbing on the water like a boat. I've never seen a dead body before.

'Do you reckon he still has a face?' Squizzy asks.

'The fish probably ate his face already,' Preacher says.

'Why do you reckon it's not floating off down the river?' A little one tugs on my sleeve.

I shrug. 'Probably snagged on something.'

Some of the little kids start the game of throwing rocks to try and hit the body loose, but it's too cold even for that and in the end we get bored.

'What if he's wearing a chain or something? Or a watch? He won't need it now. His time's up.' But nobody laughs at Preacher's joke because it's bad luck to laugh at the dead. Preacher says sorry to the body and spits in the dirt.

'Someone should check.'

But nobody is going back in that river. It's just about evening now and everyone knows that as soon as the sun starts setting, those water spirits work their way up from the mud and just wait for someone to come swimming. Then they grab at your toes and your legs and your arms and your hair and they pull you under no matter how hard you struggle. That's what happened to that girl a few months back. She was down there for days. Then the coppers came with their yellow tape and their boats and their frogman swimmers and they pulled her body out of the river and it was all blue and blown up like a dead fish. They only bothered with all that because she was some rich kid run away to the city for fun. There were no police tapes when the baby died in the camp. I wonder if they'll send the coppers for this fella or if he's not important enough to bother with.

'Go on, Flea,' Squizzy says. 'You're the best swimmer.'

Flea laughs. 'Go yourself.'

But Squizzy won't let up. 'Are you scared? Do it, I dare you.'

'Don't.' I grab at Flea's arm, and the bird caws out again from the tree and sends shivers up my back, but Flea's eyes are already set. Flea never, ever backs down on a dare, and they get undressed slow and sure, and walk into that river like it's a bright summer day and not freezing and nearly dark at all.

'Why did you dare them?' Preacher shakes her head and pushes Squizzy.

Squizzy shrugs.

'If Flea gets pulled down, you know their spirit will come for you.'

'And the spirit of the dead guy. They'll team up. That's how they do,' I tell him.

Squizzy hadn't thought of that. 'All right! Flea! Come back. Forget it!'

But Flea won't stop. They swim right up to that dead man and poke and prod.

'Now Flea's got the touch of death on them for sure.' Preacher shakes her head.

But then Flea throws their arm in the air and we can see the watch glinting and we forget about spirits, and whistle and stomp and cheer Flea all the way back to shore.

'Is it a good one? How much will we get for it?'

'Was his face still there? Was it eaten by fish already?'

'Who was it, do we know them? Was it Big Tall Fred? He's been missing for ages. Where's he been at if not dead?'

'What did it feel like? Did it feel like jelly? When I found that dead dog in the bins out the back of the bakery it felt like jelly and his stomach was moving with all the maggots eating through from the inside and I heard those maggots buzzing inside him.' But we've all already heard Preacher's dead dog story a hundred times before and no one is interested in hearing it now.

'Beasts!' Squizzy crows then. He takes out his knife and it's my hand he grabs first. 'Blood brothers! For ever!' Squizzy slices the knife slow along my hand. He's enjoying it, I can tell. I don't let on that it hurts. Just wait until it is my turn to slice his hand and I'll get him back.

'Why not blood sisters?' Preacher takes the knife and does her own hand before Squizzy can.

'Because that's not what it's called.'

'Come on. My hand is bleeding.' I pull Flea into the circle before they start in on the argument as well and we pass around the knife and pile our hands so our bloods mix and drip into the dirt and all our blood sparkles in the setting sun like stardust.

We watch it splatter and send tiny dirt clouds into the air. 'Look at that,' Flea says. 'It looks like a raven rising up out of the dirt.' And we twist our heads to try and see what Flea is on about. It just looks like blood splatter to me. I look back at the tree but the actual raven has gone.

'Now spit,' Flea says. 'Then we're all tied by blood and spit and that's stronger than anything ever in the whole universe and nothing can break a blood-and-spit tie, not nothing. Blood *Family* for ever.'

And we spit on our hands and we scream to the sky, all our voices as loud and long as each other's. 'Blood Family for ever!'

And then we hear the sirens coming and we run fast back to the Boneyard before those coppers reckon it was us that did that man and threw him into the river. I guess he was important after all.

The next day, we light a candle for him in the church to say thanks for the watch, and then we take turns blowing out all the other candles and pretending it's our birthdays until the vicar throws us out, and we walk away booing and throwing rocks and calling that vicar a thug and a hoodlum and a hooligan and a thief and telling him if he doesn't watch out we'll tell the Hoblin about him and her Black Jacket Men will come give him a warning and then she'll suck out his soul and his lips will be blue and frothed because of it.

'Don't make me call the police!' he threatens,

but that just makes us boo even louder.

And I guess it's because of the watch that Flea doesn't think much on the body being an omen. I guess it's because of the watch that none of us even think twice about what that bird was trying to foretell. I guess we just didn't know to listen.

Chapter 29
A Million Swarming Bees

We sit under the fountain in Federation Place and make a list of things we're going to buy with the money from the watch. Squizzy writes it down, but he doesn't say it back right the way we told it, so either his reading or his writing aren't as good as he thinks they are. Flea says I should be the one writing, but then Squizzy glares and whispers, 'Tower Boy thinks he's smarter than us?'

But I've been a Beast for over a year and a half now, so Squizzy can shut it. I wrap Da's coat around me tighter and don't listen to the scratchy voice in my head hissing that I'm a fraud, that if I'm really a Beast, why do I keep sneaking back to Hidden Skeleton Lane to wait for the Hoblin? It's been five months already and she hasn't shown once, but my feet keep taking me there, hoping.

It's the not knowing that keeps me going back. I just want to know where Da is. I want to know if he's dead like Flea reckons. Or if he's missing like Charlie. And that Hoblin lady *knows*.

'We could buy a house,' Preacher says then. 'Write down "Proper House".' And everyone boos and laughs because she thinks a watch can be worth more money than a house. Squizzy writes it down anyway.

'What makes a proper house then?' a little one wants to know.

'I don't like them fancy ones,' someone else says. 'There's too many rooms, you'd get lost. In one of my foster homes the floor was all cold and dead and too smooth so my feet couldn't feel a thing.'

And then everyone is scrabbling and tapping at Squizzy to try and get heard.

'It needs one of those great big wooden doors like on a palace, with a head of a dragon you use to knock so not just anyone can come in, and spikes on the top, and so heavy you need two people just to open it.'

'A palace door!'

'And a window so when it rains you can still see out.'

'And a bed made all of feathers.'

'Or water. So you sleep like you're floating on the sea.'

'Who would want to sleep on the sea?'

'I lived in a proper house once,' Squizzy says. 'It had lots of rooms and I didn't get lost once.' And we look at him hard and shake our heads because this is the first time he's ever said about living in a proper house before.

'Yeah, sure you did. Where is this house then?'

Squizzy shrugs. 'Down the way. It's yellow with a

white roof and red windows and a vine that grows all the way to the chimney. And it has a red gate but the hinge is always broken so it never swings right.' He looks at us with his chest pushed out and daring us to say he's lying even though it's obvious he is.

We all stop talking about the house then because Squizzy isn't writing any of it down anyway, and the little ones scatter back to playing tag around the fountain.

'Come on then.' Squizzy folds the paper carefully. 'We can't do anything until Flea sells the dumb watch anyway.'

'I'm waiting until the coppers stop asking their questions. What? You want to get me arrested for killing and taken to their jails and beaten to death?'

'They don't arrest for killing.' Preacher spits on the ground. 'They arrest for murdering. And anyway, there's no law about taking watches off dead people in the river. You're allowed to. Anyone is.'

'Are you a fancy lawyer now?' Flea pushes Preacher, then marches off down the street and doesn't stop until they reach the Grand Hotel, the rest of us following behind. We climb the fence and practise hanging from the bars while we wait for one of the fancy cars to drive up.

'You see that car over there?' I point to a car parked across the road. Everyone looks.

'That old thing? What about it?'

'You don't know what that is, Squizzy? I thought

you knew everything there is to know about cars.' Squizzy thinks he's so good, just because he reckons he knows how to fiddle car wires together and make a car start, even the ones that don't have keys. He reckons he can drive too, but we've never seen him do any of it so none of us believe a word he says.

'I know proper cars, stupid. That there is nothing but scrap metal.' Squizzy spits on the ground to prove it.

'That car is worth more than anything.' I try to remember what Da told me. 'It's a . . . DeLorean, that's it. It was in the most famous movie ever and those doors open up into wings so it can fly and everything.'

Preacher starts laughing at me then and throws the stick she was chewing at my head. 'No way.'

'It's true. Ask anyone. They didn't make many, that's why it's worth so much.'

Squizzy shakes his head at me, but I see him looking back at the car, and those doors, and wondering.

'Here comes a proper car,' he says and smiles at the man pulling up next to the hotel.

Flea jumps up to the car window first. 'Hey, sir, good afternoon, sir, want us to watch your car for you, sir?' It's a big silver car and even the tyres are shiny.

'It's still morning,' Preacher hisses, but Flea doesn't take any notice, just keeps smiling their angel face at the man in the car. He isn't smiling back. His face is turning red looking us up and down and understanding what's happening here. We all nod and smile back. He knows if

171

he says no to us watching his car, then his car won't be the same when he comes back. But he's also one of those coin pinchers who never wants to give a cent away.

'No, I do not.' He spits the words at Flea.

'Are you sure, sir?' Squizzy says and opens the man's door like he's one of those drivers who's paid to open doors. He even puts one hand behind his back and stands up tall and straight. 'There are some thieves and hooligans and thugs around here, sir. A nice car like yours . . .' And then the man has Squizzy by his shirt and is throwing him on the ground and pinning him down with his foot.

'Nothing will happen to my car. Because if it does, I will hold *you* responsible. Just you. Understood?' The man takes his phone out and takes a photo of Squizzy so he remembers just what he looks like when he comes to hunt him down.

Squizzy nods and the rest of us run back to the shadows so that man can't hold us responsible too. The man steps over Squizzy and walks through the hotel doors, not listening to Jack the doorman apologising and saying how 'it won't happen again and these kids you know, trying to make money, so many of them nowadays, who would have thought ten years ago, hey? Things sure do change. But don't worry, your car is perfectly safe, not to worry, sir, sorry again, sir.'

Jack is nice. He never chases us away except for show, and he tells the chefs to leave the leftover food out the back for us, and one time he got them to bring out a table with candles and a whole meal and it was the best night ever, until the coppers came and we had to run even before dessert. But now Squizzy is stuck looking after a dumb car all day and not even getting coin for it.

'We'll bring you a hot dog,' I tell him, but he doesn't look up, just kicks at the wall of the Grand Hotel until Jack tells him to quit it or there'll be trouble for real.

'What now?' Preacher asks. 'Just sell the watch, Flea. You only want it to pretend you're important like the dead man but you're not.'

Preacher's right, but still I shove her on to the road. 'Next time, *you* push through all the river monsters to get the watch off the dead man.'

'I will then,' Preacher says, but she knows dead men are hard to find, and she stomps off to wait with Squizzy.

I look at Flea. 'It's a stupid watch. It doesn't even work. There's no ticking. Give it here and I'll try to fix it.'

'It's not a ticking one, don't you know anything?' Flea shakes the watch and taps it a couple of times then holds it tight to their ear to listen. 'Fine then. I'll sell it. But if the coppers kill me for this, may a million swarming bees make their hive in your brain.'

Later I'll remember Flea said that. Later, I'll think I hear those bees coming for me. But by then, it will be too late to change a thing.

Chapter 30
Tasting Souls

Flea stomps off, harder than Preacher did, splashing through the puddles and still trying to find the tick in the broken watch.

If I had my accordion I could make serious coin. But instead I'm left dodging cars and trying to find gold in the rubbish bins because that's what happened to a group of kids who used to sleep behind the casino. One day they were there and the next they were gone. Word is, they found a whole bag of gold thrown out in the rubbish and took off to live a life of luxury. Squizzy tried to tell us they were thieving from people who won big and the casino found out and had the Hoblin suck their souls and throw their bodies into a great big body pit and that he's seen the pit and everything. We all laughed and threw rocks at Squizzy and he didn't even try to pretend he was for real.

I don't find any gold though. And after a bit I give up and walk down to Miner's Park where we painted our wings all that time ago. That's where we always meet, me and Flea.

Flea is already there, smiling bigger than ever, and I think of all the money that they must have made from selling that watch to make a smile that big. 'How much did you get? Was it hundreds? Thousands? Millions?'

'Close your eyes,' Flea says, and I hold out my arms and get ready for the weight of a million dollars. 'For you, squirt.' But it's not money. It's not a case. It's even better than that and my tongue juices, knowing right off the waxy feel of the Fruit of the Gods in my hand. 'For always.'

I don't even ask how much money Flea made from the watch then. I don't even care. We just sit with our backs against the warm of those bricks, and our handprint wings still bright white, rising up above us, and I'm not even scared of the cliff now, not really. We chew on the seeds from that fruit so that the red spurts from our lips and runs down our chins and we talk about how we're going to make a kite strong enough to beat Squizzy's kite in a battle, with bits of broken glass on it so that it tears at Squizzy's kite when it gets too close. And everything is so perfect, and the sun is so warm and the fruit so good and our kite is so certain to win that we don't even notice the coppers driving up all quiet in their car. We don't even see them until their boots are chomping up the dirt and their hands are slapping away our fruit.

'Hey! That's ours! Do you know how much that cost?'

'On your feet, both of you.' They have us by our

shirts and are smushing our faces into our wall and twisting our arms so we can't struggle and not even looking at the cliff, and what if they trip and fall and pull us over with them?

'This them?' One of the coppers looks at a photo on his phone and nods. 'Right. Come on then, and don't be silly about it.'

'Flea!'

But I'm still being held, and Flea is being pulled into the car, yelling and barking and spitting in the coppers' eyes. 'You're the scum of snail rot, you've got nothing! You can't take me. May a thousand spiders lay eggs in your eyes! I know my rights. It isn't legal. I need an adult present.' And the coppers only laugh when I try to bite them and kick them and then one of them kicks me back and threatens to throw me off the cliff and holds me right on the very edge and the laughing stops.

'Wait. I took the watch,' I say. 'Not Flea.'

'What watch is that then, sonny?'

'Shut it, squirt, you're not helping.'

'No. Take me.' But the coppers drop me on the ground right on the edge of the cliff and laugh and shake their heads and get in the car.

I chase after them and bang on their car and try to open the doors to get Flea out, but then the window comes down. One of the coppers is waving his gun. 'If there is a single scratch on this car, then you are dead where you stand. Do you hear me, kid?' There are lots of scratches on his car already. I wonder if the people who made them are dead where they stood or if he's just full of it.

When they drive away, all I can think about is Flea being beaten to death and that it's all my fault.

An old scabby dog comes sliding up to me on his belly and I can see all the scars on his skin where the fur won't grow back. He licks at the Fruit of the Gods stomped and sticky in the dirt, and then at my face and even though you have to be careful of dogs because just one bite can kill you, I reach over and pull this dog on to my lap and he doesn't mind when my tears fall on his head and wet his fur. 'You want to come home with me, fella?' I say. 'Flea will love you. When they get back, I'll give you as a present, OK?' And I just keep thinking of that moment because if I don't think hard on it, maybe it won't happen at all.

The dog starts howling then, and I join in because it seems to be the only way to let go of the ache. I should have known not to. I should have remembered. And the voice in my head hisses I knew exactly what I was doing and how could I ever forget a thing like that and why hadn't I thought of it sooner? The voice in my head whispers that this is how I can fix *everything*.

Later, when I'm telling the others about what happened next, I'll say it was just the dog that howled and not me, and I'll swear that the whole world turned ice-cold for at least a minute, and that my ears filled with the sound of fifty-eight snakes hissing. And because I'm telling it, my brain starts thinking it too, until that is the truth, the whole truth and nothing but the truth, so strike me down dead if it isn't.

I think probably the world didn't turn to ice, but I did hear the hissing, because that's what you hear when a Hoblin sneaks up on you. That little dog saw her, and he trembled so hard in my lap I thought he would break into a thousand tiny dog pieces, and then he turned and sped out of there because dogs know Hoblins when they see them.

'Oh, Little Mouse,' Hoblin Lady hushes. BigMan is standing behind her in the shadows. 'Why, what has you so upset?' The Hoblin is using her pretend lady voice and I can see the hunting in her snake eyes and when her tongue pokes from her lips a little I can just tell she is tasting my soul. I shake my head because it's never any good saying more words to a Hoblin than you have to, but suddenly my tongue is talking without me even trying and the whole story falls out. All about the coppers taking Flea for selling the watch, but then I remember what she said about thugs and hooligans and thieves. 'But it wasn't thieving. He was already dead,' I tell her. 'So you're allowed to take stuff from the dead if they're floating in the river already.'

When she doesn't say anything, my tongue starts back up again. 'All Flea did was take his watch. It's not even a very good watch. It was broken. But Flea sold it and then the coppers came and . . . and . . .' My tongue runs out of words and I snap my teeth tight to stop it telling any more.

The Hoblin smiles her fake lady-smile and pats my shoulder with her gloved hand hiding her Hoblin fingers. 'Now, now, Little Mouse. Don't worry. I'm sure it is just a mistake. How about I talk to those police for you, hmmm? I can make them see sense. There is no need to worry.' And she brushes my face with her finger, and I watch to make sure she doesn't try and take even a single hair. 'I look out for the people in my city. Like family.' She smiles again and a whisper in my brain says that maybe we were wrong. Maybe she isn't a Hoblin at all, just a lady with snakey eyes. That can happen to someone, especially if their mother steps on a snake when they're a babe in the stomach still.

'Would you?' I say. 'Now? Because they can beat you to death right quick in jail.' Then I remember to be polite because I think that being polite might be important to people with snake eyes who own cities, and definitely important if those people happen to be a Hoblin. 'Please.'

'Of course,' she says. 'I am very good at fixing people's problems. I will go right away and sort out this whole mess. That's what family do.' She gives my shoulder a squeeze.

I guess it's the way she said 'family' that makes those next words come, so soft I could hardly hear them myself. 'Do you know where my da is? Have you seen him? I thought he was taken on the bus. I thought he might have been sent off somewhere or . . . Because some of the other kids say . . . And it's been so long . . .'

Hoblin Lady smiles. 'Little Mouse, I have known your father since before you were born. He wasn't anywhere near those buses. Come see me Friday morning. At the Highett. We can have tea and cake and talk all you like.'

I guess it's the way her hand on my shoulder reminds me of Da and the way he used to put his arm around my shoulder to tell the whole world I was his and he was mine, that makes my head nod and my mouth smile and my voice say, 'Thank you.'

The Hoblin lady looks at the sky. 'What a beautiful day it is. Aren't we lucky?' I follow her eyes and look up at the dark clouds gathering and there is definitely a storm sneaking in and I don't know what she is talking about, because there is nothing especially beautiful about today at all.

When I look back, the Hoblin is gone.

Chapter 31
StreetKing

'You did what?' Flea's eyes are wide and their lips are thin and why am I getting the angry look when I should be getting the thank you look instead? 'You're as stupid as your feet. Why would you do that? Why did you tell her?' And Flea leaps up on to the gargoyle's tomb, cocks a marble into their shooter and fires, pinging the marble off a stop sign all the way over the fence and across the road. It's what Flea does when they're angry. Target practice. And it's just a little scary. That slingshot could kill a person the way Flea fires it.

'I didn't. Well, I mean, my mouth did, but that wasn't me. And anyway, you're alive now and not beaten to death, which is a good thing, right? That Hoblin lady, she just popped up out of nowhere. BOOM! and there was smoke coming up all around her in a cloud.' I threw that last bit in to try and make it not so much my fault for telling.

Flea's eyes get small and thin to match their lips and they fire another marble, this one across the Boneyard.

It hits an angel statue and the nose flies off the angel and we all stare. That can't be good luck, shooting a nose off an angel. So that's when I tell about the whole day icing over and the fifty-eight hissing snakes.

'It's because she's a Hoblin,' Squizzy says.

'Yeah, that's how they do. Appear in smoke, for real,' a littlie says, nodding big, solemn nods.

'And the cold and the hissing,' I add.

'Why fifty-eight snakes? You can't even hear numbers in hissing,' Preacher says but I roll my eyes and tell her because that's how many there were, stupid, and does she want to hear about it or not?

'Man, you dumb as a thumb.' Preacher throws a clump of mud at my head. 'She's no Hoblin. She's a StreetKing is all. Keeping her city in order so the coppers don't have to, and the tourists keep coming and the city keeps looking good in all them photos and TV shows. And in return, the coppers turn their eyes blind and their ears deaf to everything the StreetKing does, and she's left free to run her business just the way she wants. It works for everyone who's anyone and not for a single person who's not. That's the way of the world. And now she owns you, don't she? She did you some big favour there and now you owe the woman.'

'Nah, that's not right. She's definitely a Hoblin.' Squizzy shakes his head and chews on his lip, thinking over what that means for us all.

'Ask the Magic 8 ball then,' Preacher says and

spits in the dirt.

'Yeah, see what it says.'

And we gather round and whisper, 'Is the lady a Hoblin for real?' and wait to see the answer. *Concentrate And Ask Again.*

Flea glares at me like I was the one not concentrating and turns the ball again. This time it says, *Better Not Tell You Now.*

We all just stare at it then, because why wouldn't it tell us? What does that mean?

'If she's not a Hoblin, how do you explain the smoke and ice and hissing then?' Squizzy says.

'StreetKings are worse than any Hoblin. Don't you remember when the Olympics came to the city? Didn't you see how every street sleeper and sniffer and beggar suddenly disappeared and the city looked all nice and clean? What do you reckon happened to all them people? They weren't given a holiday. Not even bussed out. Not one of those people came back to the city. Why do you reckon that was, hey? Damn, Twiggy. We're the killables. You don't pay her back on time, she's goin' to kill you dead and probably take out all of us with you and not one person will even bother to think on it. We're nothin'.' Preacher sucks spit through her teeth and nods likes she knows anything and we all start booing and throwing mud back.

I look at Flea. 'What do you think?'

Flea tsks, but the slingshot goes back in their belt. I

try not to smile. 'Whatever, she didn't do you no favour anyway. They knew I didn't kill that man. How could I kill a man that big? They just wanted me to tell them everything I knew, about where the body was, what it looked like, if I'd seen anything, if I was *with* anyone . . .'

'You didn't tell about us, did you?'

Squizzy is such a baby.

'Of course not. They didn't believe it though, so I told them to go cook their own stomachs. Those coppers couldn't prove a thing. And that was it. They took our watch money and threw me out of the car and I had to jump on the back of a bus to get back. But that dead man, he was real important. They had a whole big room full of people working to find who did it and his picture is in the paper and everything.'

'How do you know it was his picture? He was face down and probably didn't even have a face any more. You full of it.'

But Flea just waves Squizzy away. 'I know 'cause they slapped that paper down in front of me and their fat fingers poked at it and they said, "See right there? That watch? That's the watch you sold". And I told you all that watch was real special.'

Then the little kids run through, pulling on Preacher's arm and begging her to show them how to make those rubber-band necklaces she fiddles together. 'We found rubber bands,' 'A whole heap of them,' 'Look at all the colours,' and Preacher picks up the bag of rubber bands, still with the store tag stuck to the front.

'Your mammas are goin' kill you dead if they find you've been thieving,' she says and the little ones shut up except for the sniffing of their noses and the scratching of their scabby heads and the slapping of mosquitos.

'And there's a Hoblin who runs the city,' Squizzy says and glares at Preacher to say different. 'She finds out, she'll suck your soul.' And all their eyes turn big as the moon.

'Twig.' Flea grabs me and pulls me away from the others.

'Don't worry, Flea. I don't owe no one. And if she's a Hoblin I'll stick one of those wood picks through her heart, easy.'

'Pft. That's not how you kill a Hoblin. Those wooden pick things are for werewolves.'

I know that. Hoblins can't be killed anyway. I was going to tell Flea then, about saying how I'd meet the Hoblin and how she said she was going to tell me about Da. I was going to ask Flea to come with me because that's not the kind of meeting I want to have on my own.

But then Flea reaches into a pocket and pulls out a piece of leather, all knotted and tied with extra bits and pieces hanging from string. 'I've been making this for you,' Flea says. 'It's a memory bracelet. See? Each one of these is a memory.' Flea flicks a wheel from a toy car.

'This was one of the treasures you left in the church, years back, remember?'

Flea kept that? This whole time?

'And this.' Flea tugs at a rock with a hole in the middle. 'This is my old seeing stone – even though you could never make it work, you will, one day. And this is from my bandana.' Flea flicks at a piece of red material knotted around the leather. 'And all these knots are charm knots, tied with wishes. I tied the first one the day we painted our wings. They'll protect you.' Flea stops. 'You have to keep adding to it though. All our memories, OK? For ever. You can't forget. And this. This is my favourite. It's from the museum shop. I didn't even thieve it.' Flea pulls out a dark black knotted rock, with a small brass ring to connect it to the bracelet. 'It's a piece of a star. For real.' Flea smiles. 'Remember? We are all connected,' Flea whispers. 'To each other. To this world . . .'

'To everything that ever was, and everything that ever will be,' I say back.

'So whoever you are,'

'and wherever you are,'

'you are never alone.'

'Because we are all made of stardust,' we say together.

Flea ties the memory bracelet around my wrist. 'There. So you'll never be lost.' And I wonder how Flea knew that's exactly how I've been feeling. Ever since the Hoblin said about Da still being in the city,

I've had this hollow, empty spot in my stomach that I can't fill. And that's what the feeling is. Lost.

Chapter 32

Presence Requested

I'm not going to meet the Hoblin. Flea's right. That lady is just messing with me. If Da's been here this whole time, he would have found me. Which means he isn't here. Which means he's either locked up, or dead, or on his way, and whatever it is, that lady's lying. So I'm not going. Nothing can make me.

We're down at Queen Vic Park, sitting on the dried-out fountain, watching the circus tent go up and wondering if we could sneak in under the flap and watch the show. 'Watch the show? We could *be* the show. Make our own circus,' Preacher says and tries to juggle rocks, but she's hopeless and all the little ones fall about laughing.

'You should be the clown,' Flea calls and Preacher throws the rocks at Flea instead.

Squizzy's looking at the cars passing by all packed up for the holidays and not moving anywhere in the traffic.

'This is when you need the DeLorean,' I say.

'Your stupid flying car? That rubbish?'

'It's not rubbish, cars can fly!' one of the little ones says. It's the kid who loves motorbikes. He's always backing me up, this kid. I smile and give him a wink.

'We should go on a holiday,' Flea says then.

'Yeah, Squiz. You should steal us a car so we can go on holiday.'

'Holiday? Yeah. If I got one of those big ones with the mud-chewing wheels and the snorkel we could go on a proper adventure.'

'We could go anywhere! We could go to Disneyland!' Flea looks all excited, like they think Squizzy could actually steal a car.

'Disneyland is for babies. Who wants to go hug a giant mouse? We have enough rats here,' Preacher says.

'I want to go to Disneyland!' a little one says and they all start up nagging us and I'm not going to be the one to tell them that they aren't invited. That this is for the big kids only and anyway, they wouldn't all fit.

Squizzy pulls out the same piece of paper he had been writing our plans for the watch money on, and I didn't know he'd bothered to keep it. It wasn't even a proper plan, or proper writing even. 'Then after the holiday, we could sell the car and buy our proper house.'

'And necklaces so we can put them on and go down the city so everyone sees how much money we have and we'd walk along up on our tiptoes and speak all, "Oooh, this? This is nothing really. Come let me see your face, aren't you just a darling?"' Preacher is doing her workaday people act. '"What would you like to say to the cameras? Would you tell them you are happy? Really? Living here in this big old city . . . but you have no necklaces . . ."' And her voice is so much like the ladies that come down with the vicar in their bus to the Boneyard and get to work putting up a schoolroom and take photos of all of us smiling kids and read to us and bring us teddy bears and dolls because what do they think – there aren't enough real babies around here that need looking after that we need pretend ones now too? And as soon as they get back on the bus, that school doesn't become a school for us any more because what's a school with no books and pens and paper and no teachers to teach? And those teddy bears get taken and sold or ripped apart by the dogs and that schoolroom becomes a nice new storeroom to keep stuff away from the foxes and everyone is happy. Preacher has the voice so perfect that we are all rolling around laughing so hard our guts almost rip and the kids in their holiday cars watch us with mouths open wide and smiling like they're joining in on our joke.

That's when the car rolls up, driving along the emergency lane, all super black and shiny with windows like mirrors. It stops right next to us. And when the mirror windows slide open it's not our own dirty faces we're looking at, but the ugly face of BigMan. My stomach twists around so tight I'll never eat a thing again. 'Flea,' I say.

'Little Mouse,' BigMan says and everyone jumps off the fountain and steps away from me. Everyone except Flea. 'Your presence is requested.' Flea stands up with me. 'Just you,' BigMan adds, and there is no space to argue in his voice. Flea catches their finger in my bracelet, and I know what it means. It will protect me. I won't get lost.

From behind the fountain Preacher whispers, 'I told you, man. You owned now.'

'Just do what they say, Twig.'

'Don't get her mad.'

'You get a Hoblin mad, she'll suck your—' There's a thump and I know without looking it was Flea getting Squizzy to shut up.

'Go on, Twiggyman. Go before he takes us too.' Squizzy leans forward and gives me a push towards the car.

My legs walk me all jelly to the car, and when the door shuts on the street and the Beasts and the little ones watching with eyes wide, I hear Squizzy – 'Damn. He's been taken by a Hoblin. He ain't never coming back, for real.'

Even Preacher nods.

Chapter 33
High Tea

I watch the Beasts as we drive away. ScarFace hands me a T-shirt that's clean and not even a bit ripped and watches as I put it on. Then he throws me a pack of baby wipes. 'Clean up. You're not going for High Tea like that.' And my stomach twists even more and the voice in my head laughs and claps.

'I don't really . . .' I start to say, but then BigMan looks at me and those words die right there in my mouth.

I try to pretend that I'm a movie star, being driven in my fancy limo to High Tea with the Queen, but all I can think of is Hoblins eating souls for breakfast and is tea technically breakfast?

By the time we get to the Highett I'm so scared my hands are shaking and I wonder if I can make a run for it because I'm not as fast as Squizzy, but I'm still fast, and I don't reckon any of them could catch me once I got moving. ScarFace opens the door, then leans in close and hisses in my ear, 'Don't even think about it, boy. We found you once, we'll find you again. And we don't take kindly to boys who mess our boss around.' He squeezes tight with his fingers on the back of my neck. 'Now smile. This here is a respectable place for respectable people.' And he walks me, holding my neck the whole way, through the doors with the doorman who looks at me with suspicious eyes, and through the restaurant, and all the way to a table at the back with a window looking out over the lake. The Hoblin is waiting.

She doesn't look up when I sit down, just keeps writing in a book with a pen made only of gold. I think maybe even the ink is gold, or blood maybe because a Hoblin would probably write in blood, but when I try to look, BigMan grunts and stares at me like he is promising all the pain in the world if I don't stop what I'm doing *right now*.

A man comes up then, twisting his hat in his hands and shuffling his feet. 'Excuse me, ma'am?' he says, and Hoblin Lady stops writing and smiles at him. 'I'm sorry to interrupt. I just wanted to say thank you. My wife—' He stops and glances at me and then back at Hoblin Lady. 'Those last months of her life, in your care home, she was so happy. Surrounded by gardens and listening to the children in the kindergarten. I can't ever thank you enough.' And Hoblin Lady takes his hand in hers and stands up.

'I am so happy I could help in some small way,' she says and he kisses her on both cheeks, and when he walks away, her cheeks are wet with tears and I don't know if they are hers or the old man's.

'So, Little Mouse.' Hoblin Lady sits and smiles at me and BigMan pours us tea from a proper teapot. 'I hear you are quite a gifted musician.' How does she know that? I choke on the tea and it spits back into the cup and ScarFace glares and clenches his teeth. But the Hoblin lady just laughs quietly. 'It's hot. Be careful.' And she gives me a cake and a sandwich with cucumber in it. I've never had a sandwich with cucumber in it before.

'I play the accordion,' I say.

'But not for a while, I hear. Whyever not?'

'It broke.'

'That is a shame,' she says, but the way she says it makes me think she knew this already. 'What happened?'

So I tell her, about the shoe-shop fella and the coppers and the truck.

'He give you trouble? This fella?' BigMan asks.

'I guess. We don't go there any more.' I shrug and take another cake. I wonder if they'll let me take some back for the Beasts.

'So.' And even though I wasn't going to, I figure now I'm here, I might as well ask. 'Do you know where my da is?' I want to say, *Is he alive? Is he locked up where he can't see the stars?* but the words stick in my throat.

'Ah yes. Your father.' And she frowns, just a bit. 'I'm afraid I haven't seen him for quite some time now. Last I heard he was leaving the city. He said it didn't suit him. After you ran away from him, I suppose he figured there wasn't much for him here.'

The words bounce around my head and I can't understand what they mean, because I wasn't running from *him*, and he wouldn't leave without me. Would he?

'Perhaps he realised you'd chosen . . .' She pauses and her nose turns up like she is back in the lane again. '. . . other people to be with now.'

'It wasn't like that . . . I tried to find him but the bus came . . . and I looked for him, and I waited and . . . I left messages with Charlie . . .' And now they're all looking at me and wondering just what I *did* do to find my da, and I think maybe I messed it up. Maybe it wasn't Charlie I was supposed to leave messages with but someone else. And everything I'm saying makes me see that I didn't do enough. Not enough at all. The cake turns hard in my gut.

Hoblin Lady takes my hand in hers and her fingers are cold even though she's had them wrapped around her tea this whole time. 'He didn't get on the bus. He wasn't even there that day. He was helping me with some business. But how about I ask around for you, hmm? See if I can find out just where it is he has got to. Would you like that?'

I nod yes, thank you, lady. I would like that. Very much. And she smiles again and gives me another sandwich, and when it's time to go she gets the restaurant to pack a box full of cakes to take with me.

BigMan takes me back to the park where the Beasts are all waiting, but before I can get out of the car, ScarFace puts his hand on my shoulder. 'People come to her with their problems. She looks after people. Gives money to the church and the schools. That care home didn't exist before she came along. She makes sure the streets are clean and that no sniffers hassle the little kiddies on their way to school and no thieves rob their parents. There's no gang violence in this city any more. Do you know how many lives she's saved by cleaning up the streets and getting rid of those gangs? No one else cared. This city is her family. Don't you *ever* forget that.' And the look he gives starts me up shaking again because maybe, that Hoblin lady, maybe she does own me now after all.

Chapter 34

Truths

'So what did she do to you?'

'She gave you cake? What sort of job is it to eat cake? Is it poison cake? Are you a poison tester? Like what the kings and stuff used to have?'

'Are you going to die, then?'

'Do you owe her still?' Squizzy says. 'She should have got me to come pay back the favour. I could have done a better job. I know where the hooligans are. I could show her so she could clear out all those streets as well.' Squizzy turns his cap round because he thinks it makes him look tough, but it just makes him look stupid.

Then all the kids are crowding and yap yapping at me and I can't get my thoughts straight, or a single word out even.

'Did she have you kill someone for her?'

'Yeah! No one would think of a kid! I bet kids get away with murder all the time! Is that what you did then, Twiggy?'

'Is that why you're shaking?'

'Is that why she gave you cake?'

'Don't be stupid. Twig can't kill a fly.'

'You don't pay a person for killing in cake.'

'Were you guarding for her, Twig?'

'What were you guarding?'

'Money. It's always money. Or gold. Were you guarding gold?'

'Did they give you a gun? Where's your gun?'

'Can I have a turn shooting it?'

'Of course he doesn't have a gun.'

'How can you guard without a gun?'

'Flea could with their shooter.'

'But Twiggy can't hit a thing.'

'He's *not* guarding, is he?'

'Guard dogs would be better than a gun. Do you have a guard dog?'

'Do you see a guard dog? You dumb as a rock.'

'And guns can kill dogs, but dogs can't kill no gun. So the gun wins.'

'The shooter wins.' Flea whips out their slingshot and pings a marble off a truck parked across the road. We can see the dent from here.

'How is he supposed to guard without a weapon? He's scrawny as a cat. Did they give you a taser even?'

And now because they're still crowding and tugging at me, my mouth starts spurting out all sorts of rubbish. About hidden weapons and treasure to guard and how she is a Hoblin for sure. Saying it out loud though just makes it seem even more ridiculous and soon everyone is laughing and shoving and Squizzy puts his cap back round the right way and tells me how next time I should run for it.

'The trick is to pretend you're The Flash. Believe it and you'll be it, for real. That's what I do. Only takes a single second of them looking away and boom! I'm outta there.' We've all seen Squizzy get away from the coppers like that before. I don't say that BigMan and ScarFace are scarier than any cop though and that no one can outrun a gun.

'Come on, let's get hot dogs.'

'No mustard.'

'Give me one of them cakes.'

'Are these sandwiches with cucumber? Who eats sandwiches with cucumber?'

Flea waits until the others have walked ahead before leaning in. 'You got to be careful, squirt. That Hoblin, she has eyes and ears and toes in every pie. You know the people pay her, right? The shopkeepers and council people and coppers and everything. They all pay her to keep the streets clean of sniffers and pickpockets and street rats so everyone can keep pretending we don't exist. And anyone who tries to fight back, or asks questions, or make a fuss, gets disappeared right along with them. She thinks she owns everything. She probably thinks she owns you now too. But she doesn't. A cat can't grow into a bird, right.'

I have no idea what that even means. 'Don't worry, Flea. She doesn't own me. I won't get lost.' I smile and touch the rock hanging from the bracelet, and when I tell Flea that we just had tea and cake because I wanted to know about Da, and that I wasn't a guard at all, Flea just says, 'Of course you weren't a guard. What, you think I don't know anything? I knew you would go running and ask that dumb lady about your dad. You never listen to sense. What did she tell you?'

'That he's left.' Saying the words out loud makes my heart ache even harder. 'That he didn't get on the bus. But he left anyway.'

'Nah way. He's not left. He wouldn't leave unless he had to. And he would have come back if he could. You know what the Magic 8 ball said. He's dead as a donkey's doornail, Twig, no doubt about it.'

And for some reason hearing that makes me feel better. Hearing that he isn't alive and hurting and locked up and worrying. Then I feel worse for feeling better.

'Here, while you were off having tea and cake, I got these for us.' Flea hands me a walkie-talkie.

'Where did you get them?' I turn it on and the static turns to high-pitched squealing.

'They were just left in someone's garden, waiting to be saved. You carry yours, and I'll carry mine, and if ever I'm not there and you need help, you can use it.'

'What if *you* need help?'

'Don't be stupid. I'm too clever to ever need help.'

200

I don't argue.

'But you can only talk in code,' Flea adds, 'because these radio waves can be picked up by truck drivers and coppers and everything, so be smart, right?'

'Right,' I say. 'Flea, if she was a Hoblin for real, she couldn't eat cake, could she? I'm sure I've heard that, right? That they don't eat real things because they're too full up of souls? So she must be just a lady then, right?'

'Of course, that's what I was saying. She isn't ever a bird, just a dumb cat.' But Flea won't look me in the eye when they say it.

Chapter 35
Selling Out

The next time I see BigMan, it's just me and Flea. We're walking down the canal, and how is it that BigMan knows where to find me, every time?

'I told you. Toes in every pie. There's nowhere you can go that your Hoblin lady won't know,' Flea whispers, and I whisper back that she's not *my* Hoblin lady, and then I hear myself telling Flea what ScarFace told me, about how she looks after her people and solves their problems and makes the city safe for the little ones and gives money and stuff and maybe she isn't *so* bad after all.

Flea stops and looks at me. 'She brainwashed you that quick, Twiggy? Sure. She solves people's problems. But haven't you worked it out yet? We *are* the problem. Whatever. Go run on up to your saviour lady because who knows, maybe she can tell you something worth selling out for.' I've never seen Flea mad like this before. Not with me.

'Flea . . .' But then BigMan winds the window down

and I walk all jittery legs up to the car. BigMan looks at me a bit, like he's trying to figure me out.

'You know the vicar?' he growls. 'Give him this.' And he's still staring at me while he hands me a big yellow envelope, full to the brim with money. I can tell it's money by the feel of it and my brain flies to Squizzy's plan and I think of all the things we could do with this much money. I nod at BigMan. 'Sure.' And I act like people trust me with envelopes of money every day.

ScarFace leans across BigMan then. 'Oh, and kid. That shoe-shop man . . .' He's smiling when he says it, and my blood turns cold. 'He won't be hassling you no more.' ScarFace smiles his devil smile and winks and BigMan stares at me even harder and the window goes up and the car pulls away nice and slow.

Flea stares at me with eyes bug wide. 'What does he mean? What did you do, Twig?'

'I don't know. I didn't do anything . . . she asked what happened to my accordion . . . but I didn't sell him out . . . I didn't . . .'

Flea looks back at the car. 'I know. Come on. They're watching.' Flea doesn't say anything after that, just chews on their lip the whole way to the church and we take the envelope to the vicar, who smiles and sniffs the envelope like he can already smell what he's going to buy.

'It's good to see you're turning into respectable young people,' he says then, and gives us a fiver for our trouble and Flea glares at him and steals a whole bunch of candles and a little metal saint on the way out.

It's not until we get back that we hear the news. How the shoe-shop fella was hit by a car that broke all his bones.

'Serves him right,' Squizzy says. 'See? We didn't need to draw that map after all. Karma, isn't it.'

'Is he dead then?' Preacher asks.

'Nah, not yet. But the shop has a "For Sale" sign on, so maybe soon.'

Flea looks at me. We don't say a word.

Chapter 36
Lake of the Dead

Preacher, Flea and me are on our way to the markets when the car comes past. The DeLorean. It slows right down, just crawling that road, and we're all watching and seeing if it's going to start flying. Now I can see it up close I think maybe I mixed that bit up because it doesn't look like this car could fly even a bit. It looks like it can hardly drive.

Preacher starts whistling and hooting and Flea thumps her to shut her up. 'What're you doing? You want people to think we're hooligans now?' But when the car stops Flea is the one hooting louder than any of us because it's not just anyone driving that famous movie car. It's Squizzy. I guess he wasn't so full of it after all.

'Come on! Get in already, would you?' he says and his smile is so big and wide we all cheer and watch the doors open like wings rising, and we clamber in quick so we don't get left behind. Squizzy takes off so fast my head smashes the seat in front and Preacher screams, then starts laughing so hard she can't stop.

Squizzy wasn't technically lying about being able to drive. It's just he can't drive very well is all. He goes through about a hundred stop signs, speeding faster than a train. After a while we get bored though, and Preacher says to take us home before the coppers catch us. 'This isn't a holidaying kind of car. Go for the one with the snorkel next time.'

'I want to show you something,' Squizzy says and stops the car at a road so long and thin, he'll have to drive straight and proper if he's not going to crash. There are houses on one side and fenced-in trees and bushes all twisted together along the other.

'Why have they put a fence around an old dead forest?' Preacher shakes her head and watches the birds all cawing at us from the fence.

'It's an old quarry,' Squizzy says. 'But if you climb the fence, there's this track, and if you follow the track, all the way to the middle, you get to the Lake of the Dead. It's so quiet down there, it's like every single sound in the world has been sucked into the water. Even when you talk it sounds empty. And the branches on the trees all creak and move, even when there's no wind. The water is darker than anything. Not dark like mud, but dark like *death*. And anyone that has ever gone swimming in there hasn't returned to tell about it. It's the cold that gets you. It cramps at your muscles so you can't swim.' And we're all dead quiet and itching at every word that creeps from his lips. He isn't looking at us. He's looking out the window and it's like he isn't really even seeing the world in front of him. Like his mind has whisked him down to the quarry, and he's looking at that water and feeling the cold tugging at his toes.

'There's a pull in the water that sucks you down and in and under the rock and that's why no one finds the bodies.'

'Why do people keep swimming there then?' Preacher asks.

'They don't any more. But that don't mean there aren't bodies.' He looks at us as if this is supposed to mean something. 'That quarry, that's where the Hoblin takes them. Out to the lake like I told you.'

'You said it was a pit, not a lake.'

'What's a lake if not a big pit? The Hoblin marches them there in the dead of night. Then she sucks their souls clean out of their skin and their bodies fall, BAM! That's how they do.' And he slaps his hands together so we can hear what a body falling into a quarry lake would sound like. 'Right into the lake. I've seen it. It's where those casino kids ended up, just like I told you. They dump you there and wait for the fish to eat your skin until you're nothing but *bones*. I can show you.'

Something pulled at my thinking then. Like there was something I was supposed to remember but couldn't. Something . . .

'You're full of it, Squizzy.' Preacher shakes her head. 'There's no Hoblin. If there even is a lake, I bet you anything that every one of them bodies has been done for, StreetKing style. That's the BAM! No soul sucking about it. You all dumb.'

Squizzy shrugs and starts the car rumbling down that road again, jumping it a bit so Preacher's head hits the window. He drives slow, looking out into that quarry, then stops at the very end of the street and points at a house just the other side of a white wooden fence. 'I told you it was real,' he says softly. And it's just like Squizzy told. Yellow with a white roof and red windows and a vine growing all the way to the chimney. Even the red gate is hanging off a broken hinge.

'Is that your house? For real?'

Squizzy nods. We sit and look at that house, imagining. 'Are we going in then?' Flea asks. Inside, the curtain twitches, and a man in a tie and suit looks out of the window at us. Squizzy's face turns hard. He jams his foot on the pedal. The car jumps and the tyres screech and we're speeding down that long thin no-room-for-mistakes road.

'Squizzy! Slow down!'

But his face has twisted so he doesn't even look like Squizzy any more.

'Squizzyman! Stop!'

I knew he wasn't a good driver, but now he's going so fast . . .

and that road is so thin . . .
and he spins around the corner and we're still spinning
and the whole world is spinning
and I hear
Preacher scream and I'm
holding tight to the door handle
to hold myself still and then
we are
flying.

For a moment I think I was right about the car, that it really can fly . . .

But no cars can fly, not even the DeLorean.

This time, the pull was stronger, fiercer. Twig wasn't flitting and curious, but wrenching, gut-hauling into clouds of thunder, screech of tyres, cold black water, churning, falling, and everything was so, so cold . . . and then he was the splat of a fly, the lick on a cat's whisker – he saw the eyes waiting, the open-wide brown eyes of a young man shivering under the bridge, sifting in the piles of dumped rubbish, and Twig was the aching teeth of a rat, wanting to bite . . . he released the Bone of Lost Wonders. The man picked at it and went to toss it, hesitated, then felt it, weighed it in his palm, listened to it, and placed it carefully in his pocket.

From somewhere far away, Twig could feel the pull

of the other bones. He *was* the other bones. He was being carried in the child's pocket, kept close and sure; he was sun-warmed and glowing on a wooden altar watching over the old woman as she slept. He drifted further, skimming on the sun-dropped dust, and he felt so right, and so safe here, that Twig almost let himself seep further still, to where his shadows flowed into the trees and the rain, drifted and spun on the waves, whispered through every grain of sand—

> *To know yourself you must be strong. Fight*
> *the forgetting . . .*

A memory whispered.

'*Bones! Bones! Ah, scrimpkins. BONES, for cryin' out loud!*' It was Krruk's voice. Twig knew it was Krruk's voice. He tried to concentrate on it, but it seemed so distant . . .

Twig fought the promise of peace. He followed the soft echo of Krruk's voice, the roar of the waterfall. Concentrated on the burning cold of ice water against his skin . . . everything was so, so cold . . .

Twig opened his eyes and felt his lids heavy with frost. Even the waterfall had frozen solid.

'I don't believe it! It worked, it did! Did you hear me in your memories, like? Was it my voice bringin' you home? I never thought it would *actually* work, like. I only said it to make you feel better. Who would have thought? Righteo. No time to be wasted not and wanted not. Let's to it. I didn't see that weather descending quite so quickly, like. No wonder they call it the Falls of Despair. It's mis-err-able weather, this.'

The meeples surrounded Twig, rubbing at him with their little hands, warming him up, rub by rub. They were like tiny points of fire, heating his blood in nips that weren't particularly pleasant.

'Come on, boyo, no time to waste recoverin', like. You heard them Gods. They is after you, they is. And you sit here too long, you'll freeze! Suspended animation is no way to spend eternity. It is verr-ry borin'. I knew a Guardian once who was suspended mid crouch. His knees were never the same after. We've to get to the next Crossin' quick smart. City of Lost Wonders, so says the atlas. You see? While you were there rememberin' all la-de-da, like, I was here doin' the hard work of figurin' where we're to. What you'd do without me I don't know.'

Twig couldn't answer through his chattering jaws. He tried not to look at where his arms were tingling and had now become wobbly and out of focus, as though the rot of fading had spread up from his hands. *Only three more Crossings to go.* He forced himself on to his feet and followed Krruk back down the path, and away, leaving a long trail of footprints in the freshly fallen snow.

Chapter 37

The City of Lost Wonders

Twig stared at the map. The atlas had led them to the City of Lost Wonders, but now they were here, it was impossible to tell just *where* in the city they were. Most of the map had faded, leaving roads and streets unmarked, and the uncircled key symbol sat off to the edge. Even with the added advice scribbled into the margin, Twig couldn't work it out. Someone had stuck a tea bag in an envelope, with the words *EMERGENCY USE ONLY*, and there was an old business card wedged into a pocket, but there were no words on the card. Just a picture of a triangle with a single white eye and what appeared to be wings.

The city itself was full of old crumbling buildings and signposts leading to places like *Atlantis; City Library; Babylonian Hanging Gardens; Pristine Untouched Wilderness; Dragon Nesting Site; The Swan's Head Pub; Unicorn Sanctuary; Great Auk Isle;* and *Phoenix Rebirthing Facility*. This last one seemed to be nothing but the remnants of a burnt-out building.

'Like lookin' for an egg in a stack of needles,' Krruk huffed. He flew on to Twig's shoulder and peered at the card in Twig's hand. 'Well, why didn't you show me that before, like? Is that where we're to? We've been wanderin' around these old ruins for hours, tryin' to make sense of that old map, and all along you've had that? Un-be-liev-able that is.'

Twig looked at the raven, then back at the atlas.

'You know what this is?'

'Well, of course I do. That's a symbol of a fellow raven such as myself.'

Twig looked at the triangle. '*That's* a raven?'

'Well, of course it is! The eye is all white! And I thought you was clever. Now, think carefully. Where would one go to be like a raven?'

'Um. A tree? The tip?'

Krruk muttered something under his breath. 'You do know that ravens, such as myself, are symbols of powerful wisdom, vast knowledge, great mental clarity and the active pursuit of knowledge, don't you? So? We go to the . . . ?'

Twig shrugged.

'Oh, for the love of fish. The library. That's obviously where the Crossin' will be. At the library. For goodness' sakes . . . And look at them clues in the margin for the riddle! *I is only 1; Ignore the wives and sacks and cats.* Oh, even I knows that riddle.'

'What riddle?'

'You *know* the one! *As I was goin' to St Ives, I met a man with seven wives. The seven wives had seven girls, the seven girls had seven sacks, the seven sacks had seven cats. Cats, sacks, girls and wives, how many were goin' to St Ives?*'

Twig started adding numbers in his head.

'Noooo! No maths! The only thing worse than riddles is maths. Look here. *I is only 1*. The "I" of the riddle was going to St Ives! The rest he just met on the way. You see? The answer is one.'

'Oh.' Twig smiled. It felt good knowing the answer before the Crossing. Like a weight had been lifted.

A long line of meeples who had been busily scavenging suddenly exploded into a flailing throng. 'Meeep! Meeeeeeeeep!' they squealed, abandoning their treasure and floundering in circles.

'What is with them then? Little pests.' Krruk shook his head, then froze, his head cocked to the side. 'Ohhhhh, scrimpkins. Scrimpity scrumpity scrimpkins. Nonono. Can you hear that?'

Twig listened. There was a soft whooshing rising up from the valley. 'What is that? A wind storm?'

'That sound, my boy, is the unmistakable scuttle of one hundred and seven musically challenged and oversized spiders with bugles heading this way . . .'

'Spiders? With bugles?'

'Musically challenged spiders with bugles! The

Officials! They is on to us. Theys is comin'! Run, my boy. RUN!'

Chapter 38

The Library of Wonderers and Wanderers

The library was closed. Twig tried the door again. 'You're sure about that clue?'

'I'm sure I'm sure.' Krruk pointed to the rusty sign leaning up against the wall and half buried in broken bricks – LIBRARY OF WONDERERS AND WANDERERS – and the picture of the raven engraved in black under the letters. 'Now hurry up and open that door!'

Twig rattled the handle and wished Flea was here with their pins. 'It's no good. Without the key we're stuck . . .'

'Don't panic!'

There was the call of a single bugle, and the responding cacophony of a whole army of bugles.

'OK. Now panic.' The raven started spinning circles. 'Ooooh nooooo. It's the snuffin's for us. Ooooh nooooonononono. The obliterations! We're done for.

Donnnne for . . .' Krruk cawed mournfully.

'It's locked!' Even Twig could hear the distant scuttling of the spiders' feet now, and the sound shivered at his spine. There was a sharp 'meep!' from Twig's shoulder, and the littlest meeple emerged from under Twig's shirt, tugging with all his stick-arm might at the Gatherer's key around his neck.

'That's it! THE key! Of course! It's a skeleton key. It opens *any* lock.'

'Oh, you brilliant little blighter! Why didn't we think of that?' Krruk flipped the meeple up into the air with his beak. 'And to think I almost ate you!' The meeple landed on Krruk's back with a cheer and the rest of the meeples clambered on. Twig stuck the skeleton key into the lock and the door swung open with a creak of hinges and a cloud of dust.

'Quickly now! Close the door behind you! Lock it! Barricade!' Krruk's voice was muffled under the horde of meeples dangling from his beak. Twig locked the door and heaved a small bookshelf in front of it. Then some chairs. Then a table. He wondered how strong musically challenged over-sized bugling spiders could be. Perhaps he should use the books too.

Dust hung thick in the air and across every surface. The shelves were full of books that looked as though they hadn't been opened for thousands of years, and more were piled high on tables and lending trolleys. A cup of tea that was so old the tea bag had disintegrated sat next to a box of blank index cards, a pen abandoned on the floor. It was decidedly eerie. It didn't feel like a Crossing. It felt . . . like somewhere that had been interrupted, frozen in time. Like the place itself was waiting.

'Should we hide?' Twig whispered.

'Hide? Are you for real? Those spiders are trained trackers! They would sniff you out in under a minute. It's quite impressive to watch actually. No, there must be a back way out . . .'

'Through there . . .' Twig pointed to a dark hallway, closed off by a pair of automatic gates that lazily blinked yellow. A sign hung from the arch above the gates.

RESTRICTED AREA –
EMPLOYEE ACCESS ONLY

It was the only way out. Twig lifted a leg over the gate and the yellow light turned red and went from slow flashes to a mad frenzy of flashing. An alarm spun to life overhead and in an instant the entire library erupted into a buzzing, shrieking cacophony of sirens.

'Scrimpkins!'

Twig pulled his leg back and the noise stopped instantly.

'It's too late! Give yourself up, boyo. Save them the bother of the chase and they might be kind to you . . .'

218

From behind the shelves, seven great big silver heads ballooned up like bubbles and spun in the air around them.

'I don't believe it,' Krruk sighed. 'What are they still doin' here? No one has come to the library for at least three thousand years.'

'Are they the Sentries?' Twig watched the heads spin faster and faster, their eyes rolling back into their skulls, their mouths stretching wide in grimaced smiles.

'No. They is the bloomin' librarians. Talk like a pepper mill, they do. They take their job verr-rry seriously, like. There will be no getting through that gate with them lot here. We is most definitely trapped.'

'Welcome,' the first head said, and spun a circle in front of Twig.

'They are new visitors to the Library,' said another and did a loop the loop.

'A new visitor is a cause for Morning Tea.'

'Yes. Tea.'

'Who has the tea?'

'Biscuits? Where are the biscuits?'

'Look.' Krruk turned to the closest head. 'We really don't have time for this . . . can you just let us through that there gateamajig and we'll be on our way and not bother you again . . .'

'Can you read?'

'Did you see the sign?'

'It says *employees only* . . .'

'Are you an *employee*?'

'He's got an atlas!'

'An atlas!'

'Did he borrow it?'

'Has he got a library card?'

'Is it overdue?'

'Maps, atlases and other cartographic documents can be found in the MAP ROOM on the sixth floor. The older and less consulted documents are kept in the depositories . . .' a rather squished-looking head added helpfully.

'When someone tells me to stop acting like a flamingo,' an ancient-looking head floating near the floor said, 'that's when I put my foot down. BAAAAAAH HAAAAAAAAAH HAAAAAA!!!!' Then it drifted away, still giggling.

Krruk leaned close to Twig. 'They've been holed up in here on their own for too long. Follow me, my boy, there must be another way.'

From outside, a scraping could be heard. As if a giant, hairy leg was pawing at the door . . .

'Don't go,' a head said from behind Twig. 'You've only just arrived.'

And they were suddenly surrounded, the floating heads spinning faster and faster around them.

All the heads opened their mouths. Moths began to crawl out from inside the gaping jaws. More and more of them, flying, fleeing, filling the room, joining the heads in a swirling mass, circling closer and closer to Twig and Krruk.

'Ha.'

'Ha.'

'Ha.'

Chapter 39

Hopeless

The moths swarmed, flapping at Twig's hair and crawling across his face. 'Wait!' Twig said, as the heads squeezed closer. 'I've come to open the Crossing . . .'

'What did you go and tell them that for? They are *librarians*! They don't break rules for nothin'! Most law-abidin' of anyone! Worse than teachers they are! Worse even than parkin' inspectors!' Krruk snapped up a moth and swallowed.

The heads stopped spinning. They stared at Twig.

'A Crossing?' asked a greyish head.

'A Boundary. A Veil. A Space Between,' the squished head added. 'The Crossing is located with other transitional places of waiting in the LIMINAL SPACES room, located in the Restricted Area in the basement tunnel.'

The heads thought about this for a while.

'Is he an employee then?'

The heads all turned and blinked at Twig. 'Well, no. But the Officials are after me . . . they've got spiders . . .

and bugles . . . and the Gatherer told me to—'

'The Gatherer?'

'She gathers that which is at risk of being forgotten,' a small head whispered.

'*We* gather that which is at risk of being forgotten . . .' the greyish head mused.

'Those spiders will break through the doors any moment now.' A large head smiled. 'It's hopeless.'

'The bartender says *We don't serve time travellers in here*. A time traveller walks into a bar. HEEEE HEEE HEEEEE HOOOOO HOOOOO HAAAAAA HAAAAA!'

'I'm sorry, boyo. This is it, I'm afraid.' Krruk nudged Twig gently with his beak.

'I'm sorry, Krruk. For getting you into this—'

There was a loud bang on the door and every head started laughing. 'Knock knock, who's there?' a spinning head gasped through giggles.

Krruk squeezed Twig's shoulder with his claw. 'You did well, presh. Your da would be proud.'

Twig nodded and looked at the meeples, their shoulders sagging, swaying softly with their arms wrapped around each other and standing between Twig and the door in a miniature stick-figure barricade.

'Give the Gatherer back her key, can you? And the atlas? Just in case someone else . . .' Twig took hold of the skeleton key and began to lift it from around his neck. He wondered if it would be painful, being

223

obliterated. A single tear ran down Krruk's skull and dropped off the end of his beak.

'Wait a minute!' The ancient-looking head butted up against Twig's stomach. 'You can't just give up! Aren't you even going to try?'

'You just said it's hopeless.'

'I never said *hopeless*.'

'He never said hopeless.'

'I'm pretty sure he said hopeless,' Krruk mumbled.

'If the boy works for the Gatherer . . .'

'Then maybe . . .'

'We've done it before . . .'

'For the nice little lass with the funny dog. Do you remember?'

'Maybe what?' Twig tried not to shout. The barricade was shaking. A single hairy leg snaked through the crack and then pulled back as a meeple bit flesh.

'Maybe we could all sit down and have a lovely Morning Tea to work it all out . . .'

'I was thinking we could make him a provisional employee . . .'

'Just for today . . .'

'Would he make the tea?'

'The pay won't be very good though, you understand . . .'

Twig remembered. He flicked through the atlas and grabbed the emergency tea bag from the envelope.

'Here! For the tea! Please hurry . . .'

'Oh, you can't hurry bureaucracy . . .' The small head shook from side to side but took the tea bag in its mouth.

'Perhaps we could let him through the gates, just for a tour.'

All the heads stopped and thought about this for a moment, and then as one, they turned and gestured towards the gate. The gate whooshed open.

'Welcome! We'll be your tour guides.' Two identical floating heads with large purple eyes bubbled up in front of them and set off through the gates.

They hadn't even reached the basement stairs when they heard the crash of the library door being thrown open.

'There's no time . . . we're done for!' Krruk flapped madly at Twig.

'Oh, don't worry,' one of the heads murmured quietly.

'When that door opens our mouth moths will swarm towards the light of day. The spiders won't get through them for a while . . .'

'We are Librarians, remember.'

'We take our job very seriously.'

From down the hallway came a voice, squealing, 'I haven't done the Hokey Pokey in such a long time. I guess I forgot what it was all about . . . HEEE HEEE HEE HOOO HAAA!'

'And time works very differently in a library.' One of the heads smiled.

'It can be stretched.'

'Lost . . .'

'Wasted and killed . . .'

'It passes.'

'You have it on your hands . . .'

'But it can slip through your fingers.'

'It is a great healer.'

'Except' – Krruk nipped at Twig's heels – 'for us it is runnin' out, so get a move on, would you!'

'Moving on, now,' said the head. 'Here we are.' It butted itself up against the handle of a small black door. The door opened silently.

A library message board scattered with advertisements and messages scrawled on bits of yellow paper hung lopsidedly from a hook.

Dr Desmond Cay – Spirit Guide to the Stars
This card entitles you to one free session.
Guidance guaranteed.

Missing Cat
Goes by the name of Bastet
Last seen October 4, 2004BC
Reward Offered

To: Caroline
From: Pearl
Message: Last Word

Keys Cut and Souls Mended
Best Price
Est. 47AD

From: Maha
Message: To Get to the Other Side

Twig took this last message from the board. It was torn in half and he wondered who it was meant for. He looked at the crooked writing. It seemed as though a child had written it, and he tried to imagine what other child had made it this far, and what had happened to them.

'What are the messages for?'

'People used to come here to send messages through to their loved ones,' a head explained.

'How do you get a message through?' Twig thought of Flea. Of everything he wanted to say to them. *I never meant . . .*

'Psychics mostly,' the head replied.

'And bored teenagers with Ouija boards.'

'And tarot card readers.'

'And very occasionally, an old granny who likes drinking tea. Although it is harder to get a message through in tea leaves . . . they are quite often misunderstood.'

'We really don't have time . . .' Krruk pushed Twig forward with his head.

'Through those doors you will find the Crossing,' the heads said in unison. 'We won't let anyone approach while you are crossing over.'

'The Sentry has been waiting for you . . .'

From behind the doors came a loud crash, followed by a squeal of despair. Twig's eyes grew wide.

'Good luck.' The two heads smiled, and Twig thought it was a rather sad sort of smile. Like they knew what was coming and were sorry for it.

Twig took a deep breath and opened the door.

Chapter 40

Impossible

The Liminal Spaces room was covered in flour. Pots and pans and baking trays littered the floor. Melted cheese dripped from the ceiling and tomatoes stuck, splatted to the walls. It was like a kitchen that had exploded, and, as Twig watched, a small grey mouse erupted from the oven in a blaze of flames. It rolled once on the floor, then jumped into the overflowing sink with a sizzle.

'Oh my bones, it's like pigs' feet in here,' Krruk whispered, and eyed the steaming mouse suspiciously.

She eyed them back. 'Ohh. Oh ho! Oh ho ho ho ho ho ho!' she squeaked. 'I've been waiting for you, I have. I had a meal prepared, I did. But it got cold, it did. Years of waiting makes food go cold, it does. You are very late, you are.'

'Sorry,' Twig mumbled.

'Hmph.' The mouse hopped, dripping, from the sink and scurried closer to Twig, leaving a trail of footprints in the flour. She peered at him. 'Ah. You want to cross, you do.'

Twig nodded.

'Hmm. You are after a riddle, you are.'

Twig nodded again.

The mouse rolled her eyes. 'Fine then. Answer me this, you might. *As I was going to St Ives, I met a man with seven wives . . .*' And then she stopped. She looked at Twig again, and started pacing up and down, muttering to herself, 'No. No, it won't do. Everyone knows that riddle, they do. I'm bored of the same old riddle, I am. All I really want are my biscuits, I do. But how can I when they keep exploding, I ask?' She paused and turned to Twig. 'Not that riddle, no,' she told him, and Twig's heart sank.

'Help me bake my biscuits, and you may use the Crossing, you may.'

Twig looked at Krruk. The bird shrugged. 'Just do as she says, like. These mice Sentries are the worst . . . you don't want to get her angry . . .'

Twig tried to smile at the mouse.

The mouse scurried over to a cupboard and started pulling out mixing bowls and measuring scoops and large wooden spoons. 'We are going to make Blueberry-Boysenberry-Bushelberry-Blast-Biscuits, we are. With white chocolate chips.' She gave Twig two measuring scoops. 'The problem is, I have misplaced the one measuring scoop I need, I have. So you must figure how to measure the *exact* right amount, you must.'

Twig nodded. This was much better than a riddle.

'*Exact*, I say, I say. Because, if it is not *exact*, the biscuits will blast. And then I will not be making Blueberry-Boysenberry-Bushelberry-Blast-Biscuits, I won't, but I will be making Blueberry-Boysenberry-Bushelberry-Boy-Biscuits, I will.'

Krruk leaned close to Twig's ear. 'I think she means that you will be in those biscuits, like . . .' he whispered.

'Yes. Thanks. I got that.' Twig looked at the measuring scoops. One scoop had *3 blobs* written on it, and the other was labelled *5 blobs*.

'The recipe calls for exactly four blobs of Blueberry-Boysenberry-Bushelberry puree, it does,' the mouse said, and heaved a large vat of swirling blue, red and purple gloop towards Twig. 'Get blobbing. The oven is almost at the right temperature, it is . . .'

Twig looked again at the measuring scoops. How could he possibly measure four blobs when he only had scoops for three and five blobs?

The mouse began throwing ingredients into a mixing bowl and stirring them together, squeaking a song as she stirred. It reminded Twig of a witch stirring up a cauldron. The mouse looked at him and smiled. Twig tried to ignore the sharp teeth glistening with drool.

'Come on, boyo!' Krruk hissed.

Twig filled up the five-blob scoop with puree. What now? This was hopeless. He couldn't guess because she said it had to be exact. But there was no way to make it exact!

'And now the other scoop.' Krruk pecked Twig to hurry.

'But then we would have eight blobs, not four! Hang on . . . wait. Four is half of eight. Maybe we could . . . no, that wouldn't work.' He looked at the scoops. Maybe there *was* no way. Maybe it was impossible . . .

The meeples meeped sorrowfully from his pocket. Even they had given up. The littlest meeple ran down Twig's arm and stared into the scoop of gloop. He paced up and down along Twig's hand for a moment, and then began to jump up and down with excitement. He pointed to the three-blob scoop.

'But we need four blobs . . .' The meeple shook his head. He mimed pouring from one scoop to the other.

'Oh yes! Yes! He is on to somethin', he is! Clever little thing!' Krruk hopped excitedly from foot to foot.

'Of course!' Twig carefully poured from the five-blob scoop, into the three-blob scoop until it reached the top. He was careful not to drip even a single drop. 'Now we have three blobs in here, and two blobs in here!' Twig poured the two blobs into a mixing bowl.

'Now do it again, and you'll have four blobs and Bob's your blobbin' uncle!'

Twig smiled as he emptied the next two blobs' worth into the bowl and handed it to the mouse.

'It is exact, is it?' The mouse sniffed at the puree.

'I think so . . .'

'Think and is are different, they are. We shall see, we

shall.' The mouse put safety goggles on and pulled a giant pair of earmuffs over her ears. Krruk and the meeples took a step backwards. Using a pair of silver tongs, the mouse carefully poured the puree into her mixture.

It began to bubble. And fizz. Smoke rose up from the middle of the bowl. The whole bowl began to shake . . . and then – nothing.

The mouse turned to Twig. 'Well, well, well.'

Twig gulped.

'Do you know how long I have been waiting for blast biscuits, do you?'

Twig shook his head.

'One hundred and eighty-seven years, four months and twenty-nine days. And you come along and tell me you can help . . . and you did! This is the best batch of blast biscuits I have ever seen, this is! They will be perfect, they will! Thank you! Thank you! Please' – she nodded to a corner of the room – 'cross over! Enjoy! Enjoy!' She shuffled him away with her paws and started dolloping the batter on to a tray.

'Oh, my bones. I am gettin' too old for this. If I had a heart, I reckon it would have stopped with the fear of it. Right. Quickly now . . .' Krruk pushed at Twig with his head.

Twig sat down in the corner of the room, breathing deeply and trying to slow the mad pounding of his heart. He took a large bone from the bundle and held it tightly to his chest. The mouse's song turned to an almost lullaby, and Twig felt himself being carried away on the tune of it, felt himself calm and relax, as though a sea of quiet had washed over him.

Twig tipped back his head and howled for his memories. Slowly, surely, the wild shadows came.

Chapter 41

Oranges and Lemons

Stupid Squizzy. I knew he couldn't drive. I wrap my shirt tight around the cut in my arm to stop the bleeding.

'It wasn't my fault,' Squizzy keeps saying. 'It was the fox. Ran right across in front of me. You saw it, didn't you?'

None of us saw it.

Squizzy has taken off his shirt and is wiping the car clean so no one can find our fingerprints. I'm under the seat, looking for my shoe that came off in the crash. Preacher is just sitting in the gutter, her head in her hands, blood seeping between her fingers.

'We'll get you some mangoes, OK?' Squizzy says, which I guess is his way of saying sorry. It's lucky for him that fence stopped us crashing into the trees and we're not all lying dead in the ditch.

Squizzy climbs out of the car and smiles. 'Can you hear that? All them bells ringing out that song?'

We listen. There's a tune playing. I know it. It's an old nursery rhyme that Da used to sing. There was a game that went with it but I can't remember how it went. I smile, listening to those bells. Remembering the words.

'"Oranges and Lemons", that is,' Squizzy tells us. 'There's a proper person ringing them bells. He took me up the tower one time and showed me how to make them ring the song. There are numbers on the bells and music to follow and everything. He rings them every day, no matter what. Bang on twelve o'clock, and if it's a Saturday, he rings them again at seven. My sister and me would sing along to the song. *Oranges and lemons, say the bells of St Clement's. You owe me five farthings, say the bells of St Martin's. When will you pay me? say the bells of Old Bailey. When I grow rich, say the bells of Shoreditch . . .*' Squizzy sings in time to the ringing bells and Preacher starts laughing.

'Enough with your stupid apples and bananas. What do we do with all this stuff?' Flea points to where a folder full of papers and photos have exploded from the open boot and are blowing along the road. I look at the photo near my foot and think it's a photo of a copper. He isn't in a uniform, but he has that copper look about him and he looks kind of familiar with his little moustache and sneering mouth. I hope to every God in Heaven that this car doesn't belong to the police.

'There's a phone here too. And a camera. A proper one with a big lens and everything. Like those ones the newspaper people have. We could sell this for loads.'

Flea holds up the camera. 'These are like spy photos! I bet whoever took them wants them back. They'd pay us, wouldn't they? To get them back?' Flea's getting excited now.

'No way! You want to get done for this now, too?' Squizzy says, acting all big-man leader again.

Flea shrugs.

'We're not taking a single thing. Put that stuff back in the car. We don't want no one coming after us.'

'Maybe you should have thought about that before stealing the car, stupid.' Preacher spits blood on to the ground. At least she's talking now.

'You all thought I'd made it up, about the house. I just wanted you to see . . .' And he says it so sad that none of us have the heart to keep nipping. 'And anyway, Twig said the car could fly.'

I'm picking up the papers and trying not to get blood on anything because coppers can read blood like fingerprints, can't they, and that's when I see the map. It's peeking out from under some papers. It's a map of *Queen's City and Surrounds* and there are circles and arrows and Xs drawn on in red, and a phone number scribbled down the bottom. I wonder what the Xs are for. Flea would say they're for treasure – X *marks the spot*. A real-life treasure map. But there's too many crosses for it to be that. I find the Boneyard – *Old Queens Cemetery* – and smile. Flea's right. There's something amazing about seeing where we live, printed out all official on a proper map. I get why Flea wanted to paint the map on the wall now. There's something about seeing yourself there, for real. Makes you *feel* more alive somehow.

I look back at the others but they're all busy cleaning up the car so none of them see when I take the map and put it in my pocket. I don't care what Squizzy says. He's not the boss of me, and Flea will love this. They've not ever had a map like this one before, a map of us. We can draw an X over the Boneyard to show that this is our place, and we can mark down all the places that are special to us and stick it in the shack and add to it each day. Here lies the death of music. Here a car flew. Here the river gave back the dead . . . And just thinking it makes me feel like part of something bigger.

Preacher stands up and kicks the wheel of the car with her foot. 'We're not ever getting this clean. There's blood and stuff everywhere.'

'Maybe we should burn it?' And everyone looks at me. 'That's the way you do it, right? Then the coppers can't find nothing.' I shrug. I'm even a little impressed with my own thinking.

Flea smiles. 'It's actually not a bad idea.' I can't help noticing that Flea seems surprised.

'How are we supposed to burn the car then?' Squizzy shakes his head at me like it's the stupidest idea in the world but stealing the car in the first place was stupider, so I win.

'Put a match in the petrol tank, or something?' I shrug again.

We all think about that for a minute, remembering the time Squizzy filled a jack-o'-lantern with petrol, and how when we threw a match into it, it exploded pumpkin everywhere. I imagine the car exploding DeLorean bits everywhere and am a little sorry I thought of it.

'Has anyone got any matches?'

We look at each other and shrug. It looks like the DeLorean is saved after all.

'Teach us that song, will you, Squiz?' Preacher asks, and she isn't joking. She's really wanting to learn some stupid old nursery rhyme.

Squizzy smiles, and starts up singing again. I join in, and Squizzy even smiles at me then. '*When will that be, say the bells of Stepney. I do not know, says the great bell at Bow. Here comes a candle, to light you to bed . . .*'

And when we hear a siren, we run, and leave the car sitting all nested in the fence, still laughing and singing, '*and here comes a chopper to chop off your head! Chip chop chip chop the last man is dead . . .*' and thinking that everything will be OK.

Chapter 42
Soft Eyes

The doorman at the hotel doesn't look at me all suspicious any more. He even nods and smiles when I walk in, like he knows I'm due. I've been here six times over the last few months, and each time the cakes and sandwiches taste better and better. And each time they give me a big box to take back to the Beasts, and we sit in the Boneyard and have our own High Tea and talk all fancy like the people at the hotel do. And each time I wait for Hoblin Lady to tell me something about Da. She hasn't though. Not yet. Each time she says to be patient, that these things take time. Come back in a few weeks and we'll see.

Last time, she showed me plans for a new school, set up only a block from the Boneyard. She said it was going to be for the local kids and it took me a minute to understand that she meant us. A real, proper school for *us*. All the Boneyard kids. The Beasts. I haven't even thought about school for two years now, not since Da, and I think, *I'd really like to go back to school again.*

This time, BigMan and ScarFace are sitting right up next to me, and Hoblin Lady is tapping her finger on the table and looking like something is itching at her. It makes me nervous, that tapping. There's another man there too. He has a crooked nose and a scar splitting his eyebrow in two. He doesn't look at me. There's something about him though. He doesn't look nervous, but there's something that makes me think he is. Maybe it's his eyes. He looks all tough and hard, with tattoos all over his neck like BigMan, but this guy has soft eyes and lots of lines on his face. Lots of lines means you listen and look and feel things for proper. His eyes remind me of Da's eyes.

'Your friend.' Hoblin Lady doesn't pour me tea or offer me cakes, just stares hard at me. 'The one with the red bandana thing.' And my heart stops and I think I might drop down dead right here at the table and wonder if that would count as unrespectable behaviour. 'We need to speak to your friend.'

'Why?' I say and BigMan's hand whips out and thumps me hard on the back of my head. The man with nice eyes looks at me then, like he's figuring me out.

Hoblin Lady takes a sip of her tea. 'Why?' she says and somehow she makes that word full of darkness.

'I mean,' I say, and BigMan eyes me, 'just that, I'm with Flea all the time. We tell each other everything. So if anything's happened, it won't be Flea, 'cause I'd know about it. Flea would never . . .'

'Ah. I see.' Hoblin Lady smiles now. 'So would this . . . Flea . . . never steal a car, for example? A very particular car, belonging to this gentleman here, who happens to work for *me*?' A lump in my throat grows so big I think I might choke. 'You see, we've heard that your Flea has a certain . . . *knack* with locks. What was it they said? I believe lock whisperer was the term used.'

'But not cars. Flea doesn't do cars. And not house locks or anything neither, just gates or . . . or . . . old post offices or . . . maybe a . . .' And I'm talking too fast and I'm trying to work out how to get Flea out of trouble because it's not like they go into big old fancy mansions to steal jewels even though they could if they wanted to. Although there was that one time, but that was to steal food and a warm jumper just left on the ground, and those people whose house it was were on holiday, so the food was just going to waste and the jumper moulding from the cold and the damp . . . I stop talking.

'So you know nothing about our friend's car that was stolen.' The Hoblin looks right through my eyes and into my soul and I know she knows I know.

'What car?' I whisper. I clear my throat and ask again.

'DeLorean. Like in the movie,' the man says, his voice gravel-hard and rough and I think how it doesn't match his eyes at all.

'It wasn't Flea,' I say, and ScarFace smiles and

BigMan leans forward and the man with nice eyes and the dog-growl voice raises just one eyebrow and for a second he looks almost sad – and they all know now. I think of the pit full of dead bodies Squizzy told about and suddenly it doesn't seem so ridiculous. 'We just went for a drive.' But even as I'm trying to explain it, I don't know how to fix this one. 'Squizzy, he wanted to show us his house but it was too far to walk. We didn't know it was your car, honest. We didn't know you worked for—'

'A drive?' Hoblin Lady says. Her finger has stopped tapping.

'I can show you where the car is. Down that thin road near the old quarry. It's just that, well, Squizzy, he isn't a very good driver. He said there was a fox, there probably was, but he kind of, just, crashed the car. Just a little.'

The man leans forward then and suddenly his eyes don't look as nice as they did before. 'You crashed my car?'

'So this – Squizzy – stole it then?'

And I try not to think how much I hate the way Squizzy never listens when the little kids tell him *no* and to *stop* and he keeps on teasing until they cry, or the way he's always picking on Preacher and gets her so riled that sometimes she runs off and doesn't come back for days. I try not to think of the way he pins me down and calls me Tower Boy and lets his spit drop slow on to my face, and the way Flea always stands up for him just because he's Blood Family. I try not to think of any of that because that wasn't why I do what I do. It's just, what else can I say?

I nod.

Chapter 43
A Single Voice

In the hotel tearoom, everyone is talking and laughing and eating and drinking and not knowing that the whole world is about to erupt. ScarFace looks at me and smiles. It isn't a nice smile.

'We're really sorry,' I say. 'I can show you where the car is . . . I think it's fixable. I can fix anything. I've never tried a car, but . . . and it's just a little bit crushed, at the front . . .'

'A little bit . . .' The Dog Growl man's eyes go thin. 'Crushed?'

'We didn't take anything, honest, and we put all your papers and photos and everything back in the boot, and we didn't take your phone or camera or anything. They're still there, honest.' And the Dog Growl man's face twitches just a bit and I see his teeth clench tight together.

Hoblin Lady stops drinking her tea and turns her head slow to look at the man like she'd just worked something out. She doesn't move. Just stares. 'Papers?

Photos? A phone and a camera? Javier, you never said you were missing more than your car. Isn't that your phone there?' Her voice is the pretend proper-lady voice and that is the scariest voice of all. I don't know what's happening. I don't know what I've said, but that man looks at me. He doesn't look at the Hoblin lady. Just at me. And his eyes are nice again, and they look so very, very sad.

'I don't know what the boy's talking about,' he says and doesn't take his eyes off me. 'Maybe it wasn't my car they stole after all. It doesn't matter. The truth will be heard, eventually. All it takes is a single voice. A single voice can change the world.' He keeps looking at me, as if those words are just for me. I think then of what Flea had said. About the camera being like the kind of ones the newspaper people use and how the photos were like spy photos. I look at the man again. Maybe he doesn't really work for the Hoblin. Maybe he just wanted her to think he did. Maybe he was here to tell the truth. I get now why his voice is mean but his eyes are nice. He was trying to *beat* the Hoblin. But he should know, a Hoblin can never be beaten. And I'm so sorry. I never meant— But I never do mean. It doesn't stop things from happening though.

Hoblin Lady smiles her snake smile. 'Oh, it sounds like your car, Javier. There can't be that many DeLoreans driving around the city now, can there? I think it's very important that we get your things back for you. A phone and a camera and photos, they sound important. We wouldn't want them to get lost. And I do like looking at photos. I know, why don't we go take a look at your car together, shall we?' Hoblin Lady smiles even bigger and pats his hand with her claw fingers and Dog Growl Man laughs a soft, small laugh. Like he knows what is about to come and has accepted it. 'After all, that's what families are for now, aren't they? To be there for each other. To help each other. Isn't that right, Twiggy?' Hoblin Lady doesn't look at me when she says it. 'You can always trust your family. Without trust, what is there?'

A lump grows hard in my throat, and I hear the Beasts shouting, *Blood Family for ever!* and try to ignore the scratchy voice laughing in my head.

'Oh, I almost forgot.' Hoblin Lady turns to me then. 'Speaking of families . . .' And she hands me a black-and-white photo of a man walking into a building. 'Your father, we believe.'

'Da?' And I can't tell if it looks like him or not. The photo is too fuzzy to see right. He's all stooped over though. Da did that when he was tired. I touch the photo and try to stop my eyes from burning up. 'The address is on the back,' Hoblin Lady says and puts her gloves on.

I look at the photo in my hand. And I wonder what it is I have done.

Chapter 44
Be The Flash

'Where's our cake?' Preacher says, her head all blue and swollen and her eye black from the crash.

'You went and had cake and didn't bring any back?' Squizzy spits on the ground and shakes his head. 'That's low.' And the little kids spit on the ground and shake their heads at me too.

'Twig? What happened?' Flea pulls on my sleeve. 'You look like you've been bitten by a ghost.'

'There's no cake,' I say and everyone stares, hearing the way my voice shakes. 'Squizzyman' – and the words tumble thick and fast from my mouth – 'that car. It belongs to a fella that works for the Hoblin. Or at least he wants her to think he does. Maybe he really works for some newspaper, or maybe he's another kind of police or something. Maybe he was here to get proof, so he can tell the world what happens in this city. But she knows now. About him and his camera and photos and . . . and about us taking the car.'

'How does she know?' Squizzy's eyes are fear-wide

and popping.

'That Hoblin has eyes and ears everywhere. She knows everything.' I look away so the Beasts can't see what really happened written right there on my face.

'It's true. She does,' Flea says slowly and squeezes my shoulder.

'I told them it was an accident, and where to find the car and I think they just want it back, you know?' I look at the ground and think of what happened to the shoe-shop man. Flea squeezes my shoulder again.

'Good thing we didn't sell it all then, hey?' Preacher says.

'It'll be OK,' I say.

'Except it won't, stupid, because the car's not there any more.'

I look at Squizzy and the whole world turns dark and cold as ice. 'What do you mean?'

'I burned it, didn't I? Like you said. A match in the petrol tank.'

'What did you do that for?'

'For us! So no one could do us for it. Our fingerprints were everywhere.' Squizzy is jitter-walking up and down and up and down and his hands are flapping and we're all looking at each other and wondering what we do now.

'We could run,' Preacher says, and maybe that's what we'd have done, except then BigMan's shiny car comes slow around the corner. It stops right in front of us. I hear Squizzy whimper. ScarFace gets out from the back and we can see Hoblin Lady in the front and Dog Growl Man in the back. His hands are tied together. I think of what Flea said. *Anyone who tries to fight back, or asks questions, or makes a fuss, gets disappeared right along with them.*

ScarFace points at Squizzy. 'You,' he says. 'Get in.'

Squizzy looks at us. I think he's about to cry. 'Don't tell them you torched it,' Flea whispers. 'They'll think it was someone else.' But we all know. There is no fooling a Hoblin.

'Squizzy. You have to run for it, man. First chance you get. You're the fastest. You can vanish. You have to.' Preacher is tugging at Squizzy's sleeve and hissing into his ear. 'Please run.'

'Be The Flash, Squiz,' I say, but even as I say it, the voice in my head hisses, *'and their bodies fall, BAM! That's how they do . . .'*

Squizzy gets in the car.

I don't tell the others where I'm going. Just say I need some space. Flea grabs my arm and looks at me. 'Twig?' But I shake away their hand.

'I won't be long.' I turn and start walking so I don't have to look in their eyes.

When I'm far enough away, I take my da's photo from my pocket and run my finger over the address on the back. It's not even that far. All this time, there he was, just the other side of a walk. That makes me even sadder. Knowing everything we've missed. Knowing if only I'd looked harder, I'd have found him sooner.

My walkie-talkie stutters to life and Flea is saying, 'Twig? Twiggy? Are you there?' I look at it and imagine Flea tapping their foot and crossing their arms and getting angry at me being gone too long. I don't answer. Just turn it all the way off so I can say I didn't hear it. So I don't have to think about Squizzy. So I don't have to think about what I've done. So I can do just this one thing for me.

I run the whole way and try to quiet the voice in my head saying, *Why would he want to see you, after all this time? What will he think*, the voice hisses, *when he sees what you've become?* I run so I can't change my mind. And when I get there, I don't even stop to think. Just run straight up those steps and ring the bell and hammer on the wood with my fist bang bang banging. And the door opens, like he's been waiting for me all this time . . .

'Da—'

And suddenly, Twig was spinning and twisting, faster and further. He whisked through time, across place, floated in the dark black of nothingness and for a moment, he was nothing but absence itself, hard and heavy in the heart of a young woman. He flowed down and into the water lapping at her toes, whispered to her from the banks of the river, called her back from the edge, and when she knelt her body to the ground, Twig flew himself into the sands and pushed the Bone of Lost Wonders towards her fingers, and she held tight to the ancient gnarled bone and everything she had lost, and in that moment, she knew somehow, she would be all right.

Twig let himself drift away from the woman, and all around him was noise, bang bang banging, louder, harder, faster, alarms and sirens wailing and suddenly he was pulled wide awake.

The banging, wailing sirens continued.

'Agh, scrimpkins!'

The two heads with purple eyes came crashing through the door and into the Liminal Spaces room.

'Have you come for biscuits?' the mouse asked.

'Did we come for biscuits?' one head said to the other.

'I don't think so. No . . . We came because of the alarm. Can you hear that?'

'I can hear that,' the other head agreed.

'We can all hear that!' Krruk screeched. 'They've broken through! I don't believe it. What kind of librarians have you got running this joint, that just lets any old Official through and into the Restricted Section? Un-be-lievable that is! I bet they isn't employees!' Krruk swept the meeples up and on to his shoulders and the rest clambered on to Twig, desperately trying to drag a heavy pot and an old cookbook up with them.

'It's OK,' the first head said peacefully, 'we know a secret way out . . .'

'Would you like some tea first, perhaps?' said the mouse. 'Tea goes very nicely with biscuits . . .'

'No tea! No biscuits! Get us out of here!' Krruk flapped madly at the heads.

'Goodbye, then.' The mouse waved. 'Perhaps the Officials would like some biscuits . . .'

The heads led them to a trapdoor in the corner of the kitchen, covered in a thick layer of dust.

'Goodbye,' one head whispered.

'Good luck.' The other smiled.

And then, at the same time, the heads sang, 'Use the Map of Paths Less Taken – page 109 if we're not mistaken – they won't follow so easily then.'

'Thank you,' Twig said. He handed the first head a small scrap of message paper. 'Just in case someone comes along who knows how to give a message, could you . . .' He shrugged.

'Of course.' The head nodded. 'But maybe you'll find a way to pass it on yourself. Never give up believing. Just listen to the whisper of your soul . . .'

Twig opened the trapdoor.

Chapter 45

Predicting the Tides

The desert stretched out in front of Twig, twisting and rolling like waves. Every so often, a creature leaped from the sand and twirled in the air before vanishing again, deep down into the Underland. They had been walking for what felt like days while they followed the Map of Paths Less Taken, crawling through great burrows, climbing towering mountains and traversing tattered rope bridges that swayed hundreds of feet above the ground. From time to time, they heard a bugle call, but they kept on following the map down long-forgotten paths, and for the moment at least, all was quiet. And now, here they were, staring down into the Valley of Olds where the next uncircled key waited. Twig looked into the bundle. There were only two bones left. And despite the fading that had now started to tingle at his toes and was eating its way up his foot, for the first time, Twig truly, honestly believed he could do this.

The rain started to fall from the sky then, in great long drips of colour that puddled into swirling seas of blues and reds and purples and greens and when Twig looked closely, he could see whole worlds bloom to life in those puddles. A beast waddled slowly past on two fat, round, rhinoceros legs and trumpeted music from its long snout. The notes floated and fell from the beast and trailed through the air as though they were seeds caught on the wind, and Twig wondered at how he could see the music, and without hearing a single note, could feel it deep inside him.

Twig and Krruk stood together, watching, listening, the drips of rain running down their faces and colouring the tears that came suddenly to Twig's eyes. He understood then, that he was only a very, very small part of everything that was. But he was part of it, all the same.

Krruk squeezed his shoulder. 'It's lush, isn't it, presh?' The raven nudged Twig's forehead with his own, and they stood, heads together, as the rivers of colour grew higher around them and the meeples meeped softly in what sounded like a sort of stick-person song.

'Well,' Krruk said eventually. 'That's the Valley of the Olds. Where to's that Crossin' then?'

Twig looked at the map. 'I don't understand. Are we not reading it right? It says we are standing in front of the valley, but this doesn't look anything like the valley on the map. There are meant to be trees and hillocks, and right down in the very middle of the valley is supposed to be a ring of standing stones. That's where the Crossing is. And none of the advice even mentions sand.'

Krruk peered at the atlas and the scribbles scattered over the map with one eye, then flew upside down to peer with the other eye. '*The hillock is a hill of locks. Walk around,*' Krruk read. 'I mean, that is good advice, I suppose . . . *Answer with certainty* . . . alrighty then. *The rules of the game will save you.* Hmm. Not sure about that one. *Sandwiches appear when the Crossing is neared.* Oooh. I love a good sandwich, me. I wonder what sort? I must say I have been hungerin' after a really good BLT. Or even one of them three cheese toasties with red pepper relish, with a bit of salad on the side . . .'

Twig looked in the pocket on the map. There was nothing there except a string of bells and a strange circular paper wheel. 'Krruk, do you know what this is?'

'Oh, yup. That I do. They don't call me Bird Extraordinaire for nothin', you know. That there, my boy, is what is known in the parlance as a *volvelle*. They're used for lots of things. Tellin' fortunes, the phases of the moon, and so on and so forth. This one I believe' – he spun the uppermost circle with his beak – 'is a tide predictor. It is tellin' us that right now in a minute, the tide will go out. Which would make more sense if we was by the sea, really. Why on earth would they put a tide predictor in here, like?'

And then it started. Sand slunk from beneath Twig's

feet, sliding out from under him, pushing him down the hill in a golden wave of moving, rushing sand. Twig tried to keep his feet, struggled against the tide of sand, but it was too strong – and then the sand began to rise up around them. Single grains zipping into the sky, like rain falling backwards, higher and higher, until they found themselves at the bottom of the valley, right on the very edge of a standing stone circle, the ground covered in brilliant blue-green moss, and not a speck of sand in sight.

Twig stepped inside the circle and felt the energy surge deep inside him, so forcefully it took his breath away.

'Here comes the Sentry, then,' Krruk said, and pointed up.

A small wooden boat was floating gently down towards them, a simple fishing rod of a stick and string hanging over the side of the boat. The Sentry himself was a very large skull atop a small thin body and wore a waistcoat and grey top hat. He reminded Twig of the old men who would sit at the park playing chess and never minded about the Beasts sitting around to watch. The boat landed at Twig's feet.

'For those who wish to cross,' the Sentry began, and his voice was ancient and cracked, 'an answer they must give.' He waited.

Twig nodded. He wasn't frightened of this Sentry. He wondered if he should be. The Sentry smiled and started to reel in his fishing line. Dangling on the end of it was a large bird cage. Inside the cage were two mole-like creatures, with small eyes, long snouts and three forked tongues. They didn't seem to be able to see Twig, but they could clearly smell him, their noses twitching excitedly as they clawed at the bottom of the cage. One of the creatures was covered with bright blue fur, and the other had beautiful silver feathers all over its body.

'You have but one sentence . . .' the Sentry began. 'If you lie, the Furred will devour you. If you tell the truth, the Feathered will consume you. What say you?'

Twig's eyes darted between the Sentry and the cage. That was it? This wasn't a riddle. How was this a riddle? *The rules of the game will save you*, Twig remembered, but he wasn't convinced anything could save him this time. Behind him he heard Krruk moan, 'Agh, scrimpkins.' Twig looked at the meeples. They stared back at him and shrugged.

Twig tried very hard not to panic. He had a vague memory of his da giving him a puzzle like this one time. There had been something about a fork in the road and two guards. One always told the truth and the other always lied. The trick of it was to ask one guard what the other guard would say. Twig had liked that puzzle. It had taken him days to work it out though, and it didn't help here anyway. Twig looked at the atlas open in his hands, reading through the clues again. *Answer with certainty*. He thought for a moment more. Perhaps, there *was* something in the riddle his da had given him . . . he thought some more, *rules of the game* . . . and tried to ignore the creatures now panting and drooling in anticipation of their meal. What if . . . he paused, thinking through his answer carefully. Then he smiled.

'It is certain,' Twig started slowly, 'that the' – he paused again, to make sure he got this next bit right – 'Furred will eat me.'

Behind him, Krruk began to wail. The Furred and the Feathered joined in, screaming and gnashing their teeth. The Sentry smiled, bowed his head and slowly began to paddle away, back into the sky.

Krruk stopped wailing. 'What in the name of fish heads just happened there, like? How are you not devoured or consumed? They aren't coming back, are they?'

'No. I worked it out. I said, *It is certain the Furred will eat me*. But he can only eat me if I lie. So if he eats me that means I was telling the truth. So then the Feathered should eat me. But if the Feathered eats me, that means I lied. So then the Furred should eat me. You see, by the rules of the game, it's impossible for either to eat me.'

'Are you ser-i-ous? That's it? I told you I hated riddles, me. Righteo, my boy, you go ahead and do your Crossin' thingy, and I'll sit here and wait for the sandwiches, like. I'll try to save you one, but I'm not makin' any promises.'

Twig took a large, smooth bone from the bundle, and the howl that came from within him this time was so sure and true that the surrounding countryside erupted with howled replies of their own. Twig closed his eyes to wait. And he was so overcome with awe at the place, at the spirit and strength that surged through him, that he didn't think about the *volvelle* again. Didn't wonder about when the tide would be coming *in*. And by the time the first grains of sand began to flutter softly down again on the breeze, Twig had already followed the memories, falling, deep down into the tumbling shadows of his knowings.

Chapter 46
Forgetting

'Hello? Can I help you?' the man says. He hasn't taken his hand off the door.

'Da?' But I already know. I already heard. A person might change their look after a time, but not their voice. And this is not the voice of stories and whispers and laughing. These are not the lips that kissed my hand and brushed against my head when I woke from a nightmare. These are not the hands that caught me and spun me around and around so that the whole world was mine. This is not the one who could make everything better again. This is not my da. Just someone who maybe could look enough like my da to fool me into believing everything would be OK, just for a moment.

I don't say a word then. Just step back down the stairs and on to the street and the city breathes in all my pain and turns darker and colder and greyer than ever.

I walk slowly, my legs all heavy and shaking. I just want to be curled up in Flea's shack, looking at those maps and imagining I'm someone else and somewhere else and I wish that I could just stop *being*. I wish that I could unbecome.

It takes a long time to walk back to the Boneyard. I wish it took longer. I wish it took days and days and weeks and months and years even, because walking back, I don't know what's happened. Walking back, I still think everything will be the same and no one will think I had sold them out to find my da because I didn't find him, did I? So no one will ever know a thing.

I still think that Squizzy's face will be red from crying like a baby because the Hoblin's men will have beaten on him a bit for taking what wasn't his, but not too bad because he's in my crew and somehow I think I'm kind of in the Hoblin's crew, and so Squizzy will get a kind of protection from that, won't he? I still think that Squizzy will be proper angry and ready to beat on me to get even for it, but that we will all roll our eyes and agree he had it coming because you can't go around stealing cars and crashing them and burning them and get away with it. Especially super-expensive rare cars from old movies that might fly if you know how to make them. And we'll all climb right to the very top of the big stone gargoyle that sits on the top of the tomb room, and we'll crow our cry to the skies, and everything will go back to normal.

But nothing is normal. Nothing will ever be normal again. I can tell even before I step across Kingswood Road. Clouds of smoke and dust are blooming from behind the old stone fence, choking up the air and curling the inside of my nose with the smell of burning car tyres. I can taste that burn right at the back of my throat and my head starts aching like a watermelon split straight down the middle.

'You.' One of the mothers grabs me at the gate and stabs her hand against my chest. 'What did you do?' Her voice spits out cold and hard, and the little ones holding back in the shadows pull at their hair and the scabs on their lips the way they do when they're scared.

I look at the Boneyard. Everything is gone. Everything has been crushed to the ground and all our homes are just bits of broken wood and plastic flapping in the dirt. Even the graves are nothing but crushed rock on the ground. The only thing still standing is the gargoyle's tomb, and the gargoyle looks at me and sees into my soul and turns from me in disgust.

Where is everyone? Where are the rest of the kids? Where's Preacher? Where's Squizzy? I can't get enough air in. Where's Flea?

'Where are we supposed to go now?' Mamma Out'é hisses. 'Where will our babies sleep? In the cold? At the station with all the sniffers? May the world fall down around your ears for what you have done.' She turns bigger than the sky and angrier than thunder and spits on the dirt to sink her promise deep into the earth and make it come true.

'What happened?' My voice is just a whisper on the wind.

'You know what happened. Those men came. They were looking for papers and photos and phones and cameras. Your Preacher told them you didn't take a single thing. They didn't believe her.'

I think of the map still in my pocket and how I was waiting for the perfect night to give it to Flea. If I had been here, if I had given it to the Hoblin, would that have been enough? Is that what the Hoblin wanted? If I had been here, Hoblin Lady would have listened to me. She would have believed me. If I had been here . . .

'That lady burned everything. She brought her crooked police to come and crush our homes. Do you know how many times we have been moved on and moved out so people do not have to look at us? So people can forget we exist? It is so easy for people to forget. Finally, we found somewhere to call home, because even the police know a churchyard is a sacred place. But they do not care for anything. Not even the Gods themselves could rise up against those bulldozers and that fire and those sticks.'

'Where . . . where did the others go? Flea and—' I pick up two silver pins from the ground, all bent and twisted out of shape. Flea's lock-whispering pins. The ones their sister gave them. The ones they never go anywhere without.

'Where's Flea?'

Mamma Out'é turns away.

Chapter 47

Not Ever

I need to know where Flea is. Nothing else matters. 'Please!' I call after Mamma Out'é.

She turns and there is only disgust on her face. 'Flea has gone. They have all gone. There is nothing left for any of us here.'

'Gone? Gone where?' A burnt piece of Flea's story map drifts past on the wind, Ferryman's Cove, and I grab for it, but it turns to ash in my fingers.

Mamma Out'é starts laughing then. 'You think they want to see you? They know what you did. That lady said to say thank you, to *you*, for telling her it was Squizzy who stole the car. She said he won't be stealing anything again. Not ever. She said that there is no place for thieves in *her* city. And she said' – Mamma Out'é shakes her head – 'she hopes you found your father with the address she gave you.'

Her words fall – BAM! – in my ears and I try to say it wasn't like that – but I don't know what it *was* like. I stop.

'You are not one of them. Do you even understand what family means?' And I wish it was me lying broken under all those bricks.

One of the kids is standing looking at me, not bothering to push away the flies from the corners of his eyes and sucking the pus from his belly. It's the kid who loves motorbikes, and I think I never did help him fix up that bike. He holds out his hand and gives me Flea's maps, muddied and ripped and burned and saved. 'Silas,' I say, but he shrugs and turns away.

The little ones watch me leave.

I go to the square but the Beasts aren't there. I go to the markets. I go to the rail where we jump the trains. I go to the Grand Hotel but Jack hasn't seen any of them. He asks if I'm OK. I go all over the city, running even though the air in my lungs is burning and my throat is on fire. I yell into the walkie-talkie, over and over and over again, and listen as nothing but static yells back.

I think how Flea tried to call me.

I think how I turned the walkie-talkie off.

And when there is nowhere else to go, I go to Miner's Park. I wrap Flea's maps in a plastic bag and hide them in the dirt under the slide so Flea will know I have been here, waiting, because only Flea knows that hiding place. And then I sit under our wings. I wait for Flea.

I hold tight to my memory bracelet and whisper over and over that with this bracelet, with the knots, with my small piece of star, I can't be lost. I will be found. I tie

Flea's bent and broken lock-whispering pins to my bracelet and I don't care when the tips scrape at my skin and make me bleed. I tell myself over and over that it wasn't my fault. That Squizzy will be OK, he'll have run like The Flash, and that the others do want to see me, to be with me, because we're Blood Family, aren't we? For ever. Aren't we?

I wrap Da's coat to hold me tight and wait for Flea. I don't move. Not to get food or water or to get out of the rain, even when it turns so cold the drips from my nose turn to ice.

But Flea doesn't come. And when my body starts shivering and shaking so hard that my back slams the wall, I think the bricks are falling and I think the paint is swirling me in its colours and that wall is crashing, falling, crushing and I am falling, over that cliff and deep down into the dark water beneath and I am happy then, because under the water, it is too dark, and too heavy for my ache, and I can forget that I ever really existed. I can forget that Flea ever really left me.

I can just forget.

Chapter 48

Burning Souls

It's Hoblin Lady who finds me. BigMan picks me up like a rag and I try to hold on to the bricks of the wall, to tell him to leave me alone. I tell him I am waiting. His face turns to the face of a dream and becomes a silver head, floating in front of me. '*Just listen to the whisper of your . . .*' And his voice gets further and further away, echoing in and out, and his eyes are hypnotising, spinning, twirling and he whispers, '*burning up*' in the hiss of the voice inside my head, and he is talking about my soul. Not even a Hoblin would suck a soul so hot.

I am on fire. I am on ice. I am dying in a bed so soft it is like lying on feathers and Death is a giant skeleton crow that looks down at me and says, 'Ravens are messengers of the Gods, don't you know?' and his eyes are the colour of the setting sun only more brilliant, and I am glad that I am dying.

When I wake up, still in that bed of feathers, Hoblin Lady is sitting on a chair next to me, smiling her pretend lady smile and trying to spoon warm soup into my mouth. 'There you are. Come now, Twiggy, have some soup.' I don't want any, but my mouth opens and the soup on my tongue is warm and full of memories of being small and cared for and part of me wants more.

'I know how you are feeling,' she says, her voice soft and gentle. 'I know all about growing up with the streets the only parent you know. When I was six,' she says, 'I watched as a man, high on drugs, killed my father for the change in his pocket. When I was seven, my mother died from the grief of it.' She puts the soup down. 'There was no justice in the law. No justice for my father. No justice for my mother. When I was seven, that is what I learned. But we can make our own justice. We can make this world the world we want to live in. And I promised that one day, I would make the city what it should be. I would stop the people who fed poison to the children so they grow up to be killers who stab a man for change.' She stops and looks at me. 'Tell me. What would you do if you saw a poisoned dog dying a long and painful death? Would you watch it die? Or would you put it out of its pain? Would you stop it attacking others in its agony, or do nothing and watch as it did? What would you do, if you could stop the man who poisoned it from poisoning other dogs? Would you clear him out of the city? Or would you stand by and do nothing?'

I don't answer. But she nods anyway. 'You see, I do

269

know how you are feeling, because' – she smiles – 'you are just the same as me.'

And I turn to the wall and close my eyes and wish that I were dead. Sometimes, the best way to fix things is to take them apart. It doesn't work with people though. If I could take myself apart and put me back together again I would. But I think maybe people can't be fixed. Or maybe I'm just too broken. I wish that the Hoblin lady would see that I am poisoned too. I wish that she would put me out of my misery.

I wake again to the Hoblin singing. I know that song. It wakes something in me, pulling me from the safety of dark and dreaming and my chest aches to hear the rest of those words. The Hoblin lady brushes the hair from my head with her hand, singing those words that I know deep inside my bones.

I turn over and look at her. 'What is that song?' I ask, and my voice cracks with the newness of being used again. I wonder how long I have been here for, and if Flea knows where I am. I wonder if Flea even cares.

'Ah, that is the song I used to sing to my daughter, when she was just a baby.'

'Oh.' I look around at the room I am in. At the sun shining bright through the window. At red sneakers, brand new beside the bed. 'How long have I been here? Where is my coat?'

'You've been in and out of fever for almost three

weeks now. And don't worry about that old coat.' She flicks her fingers and twists her mouth. 'It was probably full of disease. No wonder you were so ill. There's a new one hanging in the cupboard for you. Micahel chose it. Said it is the best and warmest that money can buy.' She starts singing again, and when she stops she says, 'And this song is the song your mother sang to you, when you were growing inside her. She sang that song, every single day.' The Hoblin lady looks at me and smiles, and it isn't her pretend lady smile. It isn't a Hoblin smile. It is a real smile. Soft and sad.

'You knew my mum?'

'Of course. Didn't you see the way your father fell at my feet? It was shame that dragged him down. Shame because I knew what he had done to your mother. How he had left her when she needed him the most. How she had been all alone when she died. How if he hadn't taken her away and made her go with him, she would have been looked after in a proper hospital with proper doctors, instead of bleeding out in some dingy, dirty flat.' And the Hoblin's words are crashing through my ears and I'm trying to make sense of them, but it's like the whole world is a puzzle that's been put together wrong.

'It is no surprise that he has done the same to you. Run away and left you when you needed him the most. It's what he does. He is selfish. It is shame that has stopped him coming back for you. Shame that now you

271

see him for the coward that he is. But you don't need him, Twiggy. I am here now.'

But I still don't understand.

She laughs then and takes my hand in her own. 'Don't you see, Twiggy? Don't you know? I am your grandmother.'

Chapter 49
Every Day

It has been five months, two weeks and three days since I last saw Flea.

Five months, two weeks and three days since I stopped being a Beast of the City Wilds.

Five months, two weeks and three days since a whole family were suddenly mine, with a house and a bed and more food than we could ever eat.

Five months, two weeks and three days since my soul shrivelled and died and I stopped knowing who I am.

And now, every day is the same. I wake in a bed softer than silk with blankets piled high and pillows made from the feathers of the fluffiest geese and it takes me time to remember everything.

Every day I hold the star on my memory bracelet and whisper the words to the wind, hoping they somehow find Flea's ears, wherever they are. 'We are all connected. To each other. To this world. To everything that ever was, and everything that ever will be. So whoever you are, and wherever you are, you are never alone. Because we are all made of stardust.'

Every day I listen for Flea over the walkie-talkie, but there is only ever static. Once, I thought I heard breathing. 'Flea? Is that you?' But then the breathing stopped, and the static came back on. It was probably just one of the truckies. Flea probably doesn't even have the walkie-talkie any more. But still, every day I send a message out into the radio waves and hope it falls in their ears.

Every day, I look for Flea and the Beasts. For a message. For anything. I go to the Boneyard and kick through the ruins and try to remember how it was before. I try to imagine the clothes strung in rainbows between the trees and the sounds of chatting and arguing and laughing. I try to imagine the little ones playing in the dirt and throwing dice and building towers with bones and stones and sticks. I try to imagine all of us, back here again, together. I can't. And the raven watching me from the top of the gargoyle tomb caws, and it sounds like he is crying with me.

I leave messages. I draw wings on everything I find. I leave knots tied in a trail across the city, and hope Flea knows it means I am lost. Come find me. I'm sorry.

Every day I go back to Miner's Park to wait. Every day BigMan picks me up. Every day he tells me again that I am better off without them. That the Beasts are better off without me. 'It's the way of the world, kid. You're made of different stuff.' I don't tell him that we are all made of stardust, doesn't he know?

'Leave him be,' the Hoblin says to BigMan. 'He just needs time. It is hard to let go. But soon you will forget about them, Twiggy. I am your family. Blood is thicker than water, darling.' And I hear the echo of *Blood Family for ever!* ringing in my ears.

She tells me to call her Grandmother. She pulls me to her and asks would I like to help her design a new park for the children of the city. 'One with a great big tower and slides and swings so you can imagine you are flying. I was thinking, darling, we need to make up for lost time. I'm going to take you on a trip to the coast to meet the rest of the family. All your aunts and uncles and cousins, down by the sea. They are just desperate to meet you. Would you like that?' She smiles and squeezes my shoulder just like Da used to, and I'm filled again with a confused anger that chews at me because Da said we had no family. That it was just us. Da didn't say a word about aunts and uncles and cousins and a grandmother and the sea. Da didn't say how Mum was alone when she died. I think of being part of a great big family and I nod. 'Yes.'

Every day Hoblin Lady takes me places with her. 'This is *our* city, Twiggy.' And sometimes I deliver packages or messages to people in my new red shoes and warm-as-money-can-buy coat that smells nothing like the smell of rock skin and night wind and tunnels that weave through stars, and that cannot ever warm the cold inside my bones. And now everyone in the city knows that I am the Hoblin's, and they all bow their heads to me and listen, and say to tell the lady thanks for looking after us, thank you, thank you.

And some days the lady is happy and gives me things, and other days she goes quiet and cold like ice and I wonder what it is I have done wrong. One of the things she gave me was an accordion. Just like my old money maker, except brand new and beautiful. 'Play something for me?' she said, and I closed my eyes and started to play. But the sound that came out was like a cat being strangled and nothing like music at all. I guess my spirit has forgotten how to sing.

And one of those every days I was in the car with BigMan and I saw the Beasts. They were stomping in the water of a broken-down fire hydrant and the water was rushing out faster than a waterfall and those days when you find the hydrants first are the best, because then all the other kids have to wait until you are done playing before they can come take their turn. And the Beasts were squealing and laughing and Flea was flicking the water from the ground on to Preacher, and they were spinning around and around, arms in the air and their faces turned to the sun. I banged on the window and waved and yelled and hooted and laughed with them and they turned and saw me.

And they stopped their squealing.

And they stopped their stomping.

And they stopped their laughing.

And they stopped their smiling.

And they watched me in the big black car as we drove away, all of them turned still as statues. And when I opened the window and stretched my body all the way out to look back, they were already walking away.

BigMan patted me on the back. 'Don't worry about those street rats. They're nothing. You have your real family now.'

And I sat back in the car and watched the city blur past.

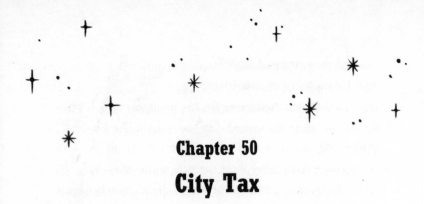

Chapter 50

City Tax

I'm out with one of the older boys, Mupp. The older boys are the ones who go up and down Hoblin Lady's streets, making sure there are no hooligans and thieves and thugs and sniffers hanging about, and the ones who collect the money from the shopkeepers to keep the streets so nice and clean.

They don't even need to say a word, just stand in the shop until someone comes and gives them an envelope.

I am only out with Mupp because there is a new shop down the High Street. It's a woman who bought it, and she is like the older boys, thinking she is bigger and tougher and more clever than she is. Hoblin Lady wanted me there so this shopwoman knows who to answer to.

The shopwoman has skin so white and shiny and clean it must blind her even, because she always has her sunglasses on and her hair pulled back so tight it flattens all the lines from her face and makes it look like she is wearing a mask. She makes me think of the workaday ladies and the TV people with their cameras and I wonder if they notice I am not there any more with the others. I wonder if they ask about where I am now and what happened to me. I wonder what the others say.

But this woman is dumber than stone. She sells all shiny things that are no good to anyone and for so much money it makes me laugh out loud. She doesn't understand the ways of the world, not one bit. She doesn't even see that she needs to pay tax for her shop full of nothing.

'Now listen here, young man . . .' And Mupp starts laughing at who she thinks she is.

'I bought this shop and pay my council tax and I am not giving you a single coin. So you can stop this right now or I will call the police.'

Mupp looks at me, to show the woman in the shop that I am the one to be spoken to.

I pull my shoulders back and stand tall like BigMan. 'The police?' I ask and I can feel my eyes turn to ice like Hoblin Lady's, and I can feel the shopwoman stumble and stop at my stare. Mupp picks up a little glass dog that costs more money than a motorbike even, and he gives it a shake and looks at the woman.

'Now put that down!' And she flaps her hands at Mupp.

Mupp smiles. 'Sure.' He drops it on the ground so it smashes into thousands of tiny sparkling glass pieces.

'You don't understand. This isn't council tax,' I tell her, and my voice is soft but it stops her screaming and yelling and waving her arms. 'This is city tax. You pay, so the city can be kept nice, and neat, and respectable, and tidy.' And on the words 'nice' and 'neat' and 'respectable' and 'tidy', Mupp drops four more things that shatter on the floor. 'It is to keep thugs and hooligans and thieves off the streets. To keep the sniffers away, so the tourists come and buy your beautiful things. Do you understand?'

Two coppers walk past the window. The shopwoman turns from me and starts yelling at them to come and see what is happening and pointing to us and pushing and pulling and ordering them like she owns them the same way she thinks she owns the shop. They walk into the shop and the big one looks at me and nods and even bows just a little.

'How stupid is she?' Mupp starts laughing again.

'Ma'am,' the big copper says very slowly. 'It's not hard to understand for someone of your intelligence. You live in this city, don't you? You work in this city? You make money from this city?' And suddenly the shopwoman is beginning to see. She stops yelling. She stops stamping her foot like a baby. She looks at the police in their uniforms with their sticks and their guns. She looks at us. The coppers smile and step over the thousand and one pieces of shining glass and walk out on to the street without another word.

Mupp smiles. 'Taxes?' he says loudly. And the shopwoman looks like she has been shattered on the floor along with her shiny things. But she goes to her machine and takes out the money and offers it to me. I nod at Mupp, so she knows it is him who will take the money.

'You need to put it in an envelope,' he tells her. She blinks at him, one, two, three times, then shakes herself awake and puts the money in the envelope.

'Thanking you very much.' Mupp tips his cap and he's laughing as we walk outside.

Mupp has just put the envelope in the backpack with all the other envelopes from all the other shops when Preacher steps out from the crowd. She isn't looking like Preacher. She's wearing a hat pulled down tight on her head and walking all slouched over. She won't look at me, and when my mouth opens to talk to her, she shakes her head just the tiniest shake. She walks past and I see her liberate Mupp's phone up her sleeve, smoother than silk. And even though Mupp must've liberated at least a million phones himself, he doesn't feel a thing.

But then Preacher stops. She takes the phone from her sleeve and holds it high in the air. 'Hey, fish guts,' she yells, and Mupp turns. 'Thanks for the phone!' And Preacher darts off down a lane.

Mupp looks at me, eyes wide, then starts after her. Preacher is fast, but Mupp's legs are longer and his anger is stronger, pushing him closer and closer and I'm trying to run after them and my brain is fuzzing and all I can think about is the shopwoman blinking three times and the sad in her eyes with understanding.

Preacher gets to the end of the lane and turns the corner. Mupp is right on her. There's a thump and a cry. I turn the corner and see just a flash of black before a bat cracks my back and sends me flying on to the ground next to Mupp.

And there they all are. Hoods pulled down and shirts pulled up and black scarves wrapped tight around their faces and I can make out just the tiniest scrap of red poking from Flea's hood and even though my back is screaming from where Preacher cracked me with her stick, my heart feels close to bursting with strong pride at my Beasts and how easy they took us down. Little ones drop from the roofs and the windows and swarm all over us, their thin little fingers reaching into our socks, our pockets, poking and slapping at our skin, pulling at our hair, laughing like it is the most fun they have ever had and more than anything I want to be laughing with them.

Preacher has me on my stomach now, that stick ready to fly at my head if I try anything and Flea has Mupp on his stomach and is standing with their foot on his face and pressing it into the stones. Mupp is calling Flea every name on earth but doing just what they say because Flea is aiming their shiny silver slingshot right at his head without even a tremble, and there is no doubting the damage that thing could do.

One of the little ones takes the backpack from Mupp and spits on him. There must be thousands in that backpack. I wonder what they'll do with all that money. I wonder if they'll buy a house. Or a car. Or go on holiday. Without me.

Flea takes a big black marker out of their pocket and the little ones hold Mupp still. Flea looks at me, then draws a pair of black wings on Mupp's face. *Come with me. I can show you how to fly* . . . And the tears fall hard and fast from my eyes.

'Tell your boss lady it is time for *her* to pay city tax,' Flea says to Mupp. 'Tell your boss lady that this city does not belong to her. It is the people that belong to the city. And the people are taking the city back. You got that?'

Flea only looks at me for a second, then bends down and I think I hear them whisper, 'Run, squirt! Run!' But then they are gone and I think maybe I just imagined those words. I think maybe Flea didn't say anything to me at all.

But after that, every time one of the older boys gets taken down, and every time they come back with no envelopes, just shaky voices repeating the same message and big black wings drawn on their faces in marker that doesn't come off for days no matter how hard they scrub, I can't help but smile. And every time, Hoblin Lady's face turns harder and her eyes turn thinner and she looks again like a Hoblin for real. And every time, I feel the memory of standing up against that wall, those wings beating hard against my back and my soul sings. Every time.

Chapter 51

Hood

'Somebody must know something,' Hoblin Lady says and her hand thumps hard on the table and spills the tea. 'This has gone on too long. Nine months! Nine months and you know nothing? I can't send a single runner out without wondering if he will get taken. Even in groups it is happening. Who are these people?' But all BigMan can do is look away.

The stories of who is stealing the money get bigger and better with each telling, so now it's gangs of grown men with guns stealing the money instead of a crew of little kids with bats and slingshots, some of them not even five years old. No one tells that they are being robbed by kids, all swarming over them just like how we used to liberate the purses from people in the square. No one tells because of the shame. That shame is what keeps the Beasts safe.

'I want the truth,' Hoblin Lady hisses, and the Dog Growl man's words echo loud in my memory – *The truth will be heard, eventually. All it takes is a single voice. A single voice can change the world.* He had looked right at me when he said that, like he needed me to do something. To *choose* to do something. But I didn't do a thing. And suddenly, I understand that there is always something you can do. It's just a matter of choosing whether or not to do it. *Not* doing is just as big a choice as doing.

Flea chose. Flea is doing something. Following the plan from all those years back when we talked of robbing banks and leaving money in piles for everyone who needed it.

I think of the Beasts, of what they will be doing right now, and my whole body aches knowing what it is missing out on. At all it has already missed. I know the Beasts will be playing football in the square and making plans for their kites, because it is getting close to kite season now. Flea will be climbing the old city wall near the market, higher and higher, to see all there is to see of the world. Preacher will be playing with her little toy soldiers that she thinks we don't know she plays with, and Squizzy will be bouncing his ball on his knee and making out like it's the ball's fault every time it— Then I remember that Squizzy won't be doing anything at all. And I choose. Hoblin Lady said blood was thicker than water. I guess she doesn't know we are Blood Family. And we are for ever.

'I know the truth,' I tell her then, and my voice is super loud and super strong and everyone in the restaurant goes quiet and BigMan and ScarFace might be scared but I'm not, because if you can't fight your own fear, how can you ever stand up for what you believe in? I'm tired of being scared. I'm tired of trying to do right and only doing wrong. I'm tired of not doing anything at all. 'Those ones taking the money, they aren't keeping it. Don't you know? They are giving it away. Like Robin Hood.' I never did tell Flea about Robin Hood.

'Giving it away?' Hoblin Lady looks like she can't understand the words. I speak more slowly.

'All of it. Every bit goes back to the people who need it most. The people who everyone wants to vanish, to forget that they even exist.' The words *fight the forgetting!* storm through my brain and I wonder where I heard that. 'They take the money and leave it in envelopes in the tent city and down the stations and in the drain town and under the bridges. Everywhere the forgotten and lost people of this city are.' My voice doesn't shake, even when I call it 'this city' and not 'your city' like she expects me to.

'No one sees them doing it, so no one can say who it is. No eyes and ears. And those people, they buy blankets for the cold and food for the babies and . . .' And as I am talking I can see my Beasts. I know how they will be sneaking, trying not to laugh out loud, keeping to the shadows like we did when we played Capture the Flag and Hunters through the Boneyard. They'll make sure everyone gets some, tiptoeing from tent to tent, from bench to shack, across every sleeping bag, every cardboard box, every newspaper blanket. I smile and pull my shoulders back proud, thinking of my Beasts, my family doing all that.

Hoblin Lady leans across the table and her hand slaps the rest of the words from my mouth and all I am imagining from my head. But still I am not scared. I am not scared because I can see that she is. It is her words I am remembering too. *We can make this world the world we want to live in* . . . It's just that the world I want isn't the same as the world she wants. I don't think she will ever understand that.

'Remember who you are,' she says. 'We share the same blood, the same marrow runs in our *bones*.' And her finger pointing at me has the smallest shake to it. I see it though. She sees it too. I smile.

'I remember,' I say. And I do. I remember who I am. I am a Beast of the City Wilds.

'You tell all those *people* that this is *my* city. I will find out who is doing this to us. I will hunt them down, and anyone who is not loyal to me, and to this city. I will show them who this city belongs to.'

I nod my head and I smile the great big smile us Beasts smiled for those TV people, showing all our teeth and shouting CHEEEEEESE like they told us to, and I pretend I am the boy she thinks I am. *The trick is in letting them think they have the game worked out.*

Letting them think they have already won. Just like Squizzy fooling those people with his cards. I say, 'Of course, Grandmother. I'll find out for you. I'll find out who is stealing from you. I'll bring them to you. Trust me. I can get anyone to tell me anything. No problem.' I stand up from that table, my head high and shoulders up and strutting my walk better than Squizzy even, knowing for real now, that it's for the very last time.

I am not yet at the door when I hear Hoblin Lady telling BigMan to set the traps. 'Make sure every envelope has a watcher on it. Not a single package gets stolen without us being there to take them down. And when we do, make sure everyone knows what happens to those who steal from me. I will not abide rats in my city.'

And all the strut thuds hard from my bones and the sun outside turns black and the world shivers and the grass becomes ice and snaps under my feet and the roads buckle and bend and every voice in the whole world screams.

I need to warn Flea. I need to find them. Before the Hoblin does.

And Twig was hovering again, shivering, shaking, ice on glass, cracking mirrors and he's swirling in the dark water of the sewers, screaming through broken roads.

He is the squeal of tyres and the bending of metal. He *is* pain. He twists and writhes, aches and burns. He is the shock of a breaking bone, the sinking of hope and the pull of fear. And when a tug jerks at him, when he feels the call of the one who waits, whose ears wonder, he charges hard and fast and furious, sweeping them, swirling them, faster and faster – and he can hear the cry of the tiny child, panicked with Twig's spinning madness, with eyes so soft and true they make Twig slow and stop. These are not the knowings Twig wants this baby to feel. He stills and becomes. He edges on the wind, dances in the tree, whispers every true thing there is in this world and the next. He breathes wonder, and curiosity and hope and love and happiness into those eyes. *May you always have the courage to dream*, he whispers, and edges the Bone of Lost Wonders towards the child's reaching fist. And when the child laughs with delight at their new find, Twig becomes the laughter and the joy that the babe grasps tight to. He follows the breath of the child, and slips away, quietly, tripping back through the shadows, and into the Valley of the Olds.

Chapter 52

SandWitches

'*Bonnnnnesss!*' Krruk screeched in Twig's ear.

Twig opened his eyes. The Valley was not covered in brilliant moss any more but was refilling with sand that fell like snow from the sky. The sand was already waist-deep around Twig.

'Quickly now!' Krruk pecked, frantically trying to claw him free, the meeples all digging with their hands and feet in the sand surrounding him. 'The tide is coming back in!'

'There's something in the sand!' Twig gasped. He could feel claws pulling at him from under the sand, tugging at his clothes, his skin. Pinpricks of pain burned at his legs. 'Something's biting me!'

'Oh yes, we-ell. About that,' Krruk said. 'You know how I read that cluesywhatsit about sandwiches coming when you enter the Crossin'?'

'Yes?' The sand was almost up to his armpits now, the weight of it squashing his chest.

'Well, I may have read it a little wrongly, like. Because

it wasn't sandwiches so much as Sand*Witches*. They is a bit like mosquitos. Except that they is the size of large rats and wear pointy black hats, and they zoom through the sand on little broomstickys so they can suck your blood for their potions, and are unfortunately quite hard to squash.'

Another pinprick of pain burned at his stomach, and this time Twig heard a gleeful cackle rise up from the sand. He dug harder.

'Can't we get rid of them somehow?'

A haggle of SandWitches flew out of the sand and started circling his head, darting towards him as Krruk tried to flap them away.

'Agh, scrimpkins! It's no good! The only thing gets rid of the pests are bells. They can't stand the smell of a ringin' bell. Gets up their noses, it does.'

'There's a string of bells in the atlas!' And suddenly Twig was reminded of Squizzy, singing 'Oranges and Lemons' and the words of the song echoed through his head in tune with the tolling of the bells.

Krruk grabbed at the atlas, tipping it upside down and shaking it until the string of bells fell free from their pocket. 'Ah ha!' he crowed, and rang the bells as hard as he could.

There was a cacophony of agonised screeching, and the SandWitches grabbed hold of their noses, sneezing and sniffing, and swarmed upwards, hundreds of them diving out from the sand. As the sand caved in around the fleeing witches, Twig was finally able to pull himself free.

'Let's to it! Quick shakes, boyo!' Krruk coughed up a great pile of sand and a soggy-looking meeple. 'Now, before it sweeps us away!'

On shaking legs, Twig ran.

From his look-out on the hill, the High Official sipped at his coffee and watched through a telescope at the boy and his guardian running across the dunes. He hadn't expected them to make it out from under all that sand. He was sure the tide would have taken them as it had taken so many that came before. He had underestimated the boy. It wouldn't happen again.

'Ahem, Your Mightinessss,' a thin voice slithered. 'I have done assss you asked.'

The High Official eyed the creature swaying before him. 'You have it?'

'Yesss. I dooo. It isss here.' The creature opened its clawed paw to reveal the ancient white treasure within.

'And this, this was taken from the boy?'

'Of coursssse, Your Mightinessss. Asss you asssked. He didn't even know I wassss there, not with all the SsssandWitchesss about.'

'Very well. Thank you, Boris.' The High Official took the treasure and untethered his eight-legged steed. He smiled. The boy would not last another day. Of that, he was certain.

Chapter 53

Keepers

Twig was more exhausted than he had ever been. His ears were clogged with sand and his whole body itched from SandWitch bites. But even that didn't bother him. They only had one more Crossing to go, and then the Gatherer would take him to his da. Twig smiled at the thought and stopped to check the atlas again.

'*The Map of the Field of Dreams*. The last Crossing is in a cave at the edge of the field, marked *Underworld Cathedral*. The advice pointing to the cave says, *Turn left at each cave tunnel, never turn right. Or risk everwandering in neverending night.* And this one says, *The tenth turn hides the Sentry.* And this one, *Make haste. Don't dawdle. On winged feet go.* And can you make out this word? Something *is a fast-approaching beast.* I think that's a T at the start . . .?'

Krruk looked at the map. 'Forget the clues! Look, boyo! The Field of Dreams is just over the top of this hill!'

Krruk was right. They were nearly there. Twig started to run up the hill, faster and— 'Oh!' He stopped so suddenly that Krruk flew into him, his wing bones exploding and rattling to the ground.

'What in the name of beaks did you do that for?' Krruk pecked angrily, sticking himself back together. 'I mean, re-al-ly— Oh.' Krruk followed Twig's gaze and froze.

They weren't alone.

There, just over the top of the hill, sitting quietly in the orange light of the setting suns and rising moons, was a circle of ragged-looking people, each with their own skeleton Guardian and each wearing a bright brass skeleton key and crawling with meeples.

'For the love of fish, I don't believe it. We actu-a-lly made it, like! We took the stone to the wall, we did! And don't listen to any naysayers. Never you mind about bein' the last of the Keepers to arrive, my boy, slow and steady gets the worm and all that.'

'These are the other Keepers? Where's Da then? Is he here?'

'Ah no, presh. These are not the Keepers from *your* atlas. You've the Lost Soul Atlas of the Outer Wilderlands. This lot here have the Lost Soul Atlases to the rest of the Afterlife. The Sunken Desert, the Older Isles, there are eight territories in all – you see, there have only ever been eight Lost Soul Atlases. Since the beginnin' of time. At first, each atlas was kept with the Keeper in that territory who would guide those who needed to get messages through the Crossin's to their loved ones. And then, when the Gods banished memories and the Crossin's were forgotten and started to close, the Gatherer collected the atlases so their knowin's wouldn't be lost for ever. She used the Keepers to *open* the Crossin's instead. Atlases only get passed down when their Keeper can no longer go on, like. When they've faded too much to attempt another Crossin'. Or been obliterated by Officials, or when they've . . .'

'Unbecome,' Twig said.

Krruk rubbed his beak against Twig's cheek. 'Your da hasn't unbecome though. The Gatherer told you he waits, remember? She looks after those who have come before. She gives them their peace when they say they're done and can no longer journey on.'

Twig nodded and tried to take it all in. He wondered if he looked as exhausted and worn and as faded as the other seven Keepers. Twig looked down at his own body, to where the fading had now spread across his shoulders and edged at his chest.

The Guardians rose and turned to look at him. They were magnificent. There was a giant elk, a panther, or maybe a leopard stalking back and forth, an elephant, a whale that swam joyously through the sky, a bear, a fox, and what appeared to be a dragon.

Twig looked at Krruk. Krruk looked at Twig. 'I told you, didn't I? You sure were lucky you got me as your Guardian. Can you imagine puttin' up with one of them giant clodhoppers lookin' out for you? Them other

Keepers will be well jealous.'

Twig walked slowly towards the circle. The other Keepers looked at him curiously. A few reached out to touch his hand and smiled, sad, tired smiles. Twig tried to talk to them, but he couldn't understand the words they said back. None of them seemed able to understand each other's words. But in the middle of the circle were their atlases, laid out neatly together, all of them with their final wedged page unfolded. Laid out together like this, the atlases combined into a rectangle of connecting maps. There was only one wedge missing.

Twig beamed at Krruk. 'We're the last piece of the map!'

Krruk snapped his beak impatiently. 'Well, of course we are. Sometimes I wonder about you, my boy. Now hurry, hurry, put your map down and let's see where we're to.'

Twig turned to the final page of his atlas and placed it down amongst the other atlases. The rectangle was complete.

The Keepers cheered and the Guardians stomped and the meeples meeped. They all leaned over the connected map, showing the eight territories of the Afterlife stretching out before them. Twig ran his finger along the parchment, tracing over the river that flowed across each map. *The River of Shadows and Mists*. It circled up and around and there was something about it that tugged at Twig, something he couldn't quite place.

Meeples dropped from clothes and fell from pockets, swarming on to the maps, marching in a long line along the river, meeping a slow, low meep that sounded like a strange sort of summoning chant.

Twig wondered how many more Crossings the others had left to open. Were they all on their last bone? Was the final Crossing the same for them all? Did they need to go into the Underworld Cathedral together? Twig pointed at the cave, and then at the Gatherer's bundle tied around his waist. He flipped the pages of the atlas to the map that showed the final uncircled key and tapped it with his finger.

The other Keepers stared. They smiled. They shouted. They grabbed their own bundles and threw them in the air, and the bundles floated gently downwards. Each one, empty. They cheered and grabbed Twig, hoisting him on to their shoulders and parading in joy.

'Krruk!' Twig called.

'Oh my goodness! You said Krruk! You actually said it right! Well done, boyo!' And Krruk joined in the celebrations. When they put Twig down, the Keepers had tears running down their faces, and they held tight to the keys tied around their necks.

'I think,' Krruk said quietly, 'if I'm not mistaken, like, you have the very final bone. This is the final Crossin' of them all. Once you release your bone, *all* the Crossin's will be open, from *all* the territories.'

Twig looked down the hill. There was the cave. Just

across the Field of Dreams. And suddenly, Twig was buzzing and burning with energy, knowing how close they were to finishing it all.

'Now listen, boyo.' Krruk peered at the field in front of them. 'My advice for the Field of Dreams is to run. Fast. You've no idea what dreams lurk in that verr-rry long grass. So run. And what-ev-er you do, don't turn around.'

Twig gulped. He emptied his pockets of sand and the meeples' stolen treasures. He didn't want anything weighing him down. One bone to go. Just one, and then all the memories would be released. Balance would be restored. And Twig would be with his da.

The other Keepers gathered around and patted Twig on the back. An old man with a back bent with weariness touched Twig's head three times with a small rubber duck, as though giving him some kind of blessing. *He has kind eyes*, Twig thought.

It was then that the sound of bugles rose up. Twig turned. At the bottom of the hill was an army of spiders. The High Official leading the charge sat atop the largest spider in a cape of brilliant blue that flew out behind him, holding what appeared to be a cup of coffee.

An ominous cackle writhed through Twig's mind, eating into his skull. 'HA HA. HA HA. WE TOLD YOU WE WOULD WIN. WE GODS NEVER LOSE . . . THANK YOU FOR PLAYING. IT HAS BEEN QUITE ENTERTAINING. BUT NOW THE GAME IS OVER.

WE ARE ALL LOOKING FORWARD TO THIS
PARTICULAR FEAST. CLAP. CLAP. CLAP.'

Chapter 54

The Flying Death

'Agh, scrimpkins! Are you ser-rious? After all that, we're still to get obliterated?' Krruk stamped his clawed feet angrily on the ground.

'We were too slow.' The words caught in Twig's throat.

The spiders began to scuttle up the hill towards them.

The man with the duck grabbed Twig's shoulders. He looked deep into Twig's eyes and smiled. Then he pointed to the caves.

'He's right!' Krruk pecked at Twig's ear. 'We do still have time. YOU still have time. They'll hold off the Officials for you. We can't give up now! Once the memories are released, everyone will be free, and them Officials won't stand a snowflake's chance in the fire pit. There is still time, boyo! Go!' Krruk crowed.

Twig didn't stop to think. He ran. Across the field, through the long grass, the meeples cheering him on, arms and legs flailing as they struggled to hold on, and Krruk flapping low near his head.

'Don't turn around! Oh my bones! What is— Well, that was a little close. Good thing you didn't see it. It would have turned your hair white and iced the very blood runnin' in your veins. And *what* is that . . . ? Best up the pace a little now!' Krruk cawed in his ear. 'Now don't panic, but can you hear that far-off high-pitched buzzin' sound, that is growin' steadily louder?'

'Yes?' Twig thought of the giant spiders and knew that somehow, whatever *that* was was worse. He didn't turn around.

'Well, that is, without a doubt, the sound of a rather large swarm of Beelzebubs, otherwise known as *the flying death*. I would say we have about eighty-nine seconds to get to that cave before we, or really before you, are stung by the ginormous stingers, paralysed, and taken back to the hive where the queen will then lay her eggs inside your abdomen, and when they hatch, the little babbies will eat you from the inside out and leave your carcass to rot, slowly, and for all of eternity. It's quite a fascinatin' process when you think about it. And at least you wouldn't be obliterated, so that's somethin'.'

Twig ran faster. He used the fear, pushed harder, head-on towards the dark mouth of the cave. He didn't think about Krruk or the Keepers or anything except getting undercover. He reached the cave and kept running, the thumping of the Beelzebub bodies hitting the rock face echoing around him. He heard their angry buzzing loud in his ears and he twisted deeper and deeper into the tunnels of the cliff, turning left at every tunnel, counting each one, until there was nothing but his own breathing heavy in his ears and only one turn to go.

'That was too close,' he panted. 'Krruk?'

There was no answer.

'Krruk?'

But Krruk was not there. A quiet 'meep' emerged from his pocket, and he felt tiny hands gripping the hair on his arms and climbing up and on to his shoulders and settling in his hair. He was glad the meeples were with him.

Twig paused to catch his breath. He realised then that he had left the atlas back in the circle of maps, but he knew it would be all right. He didn't feel frightened in here, despite the dark and the being lost and mostly alone. He felt held by the dark, as though it were a cloak wrapping him tight.

This was it. He could do this. He could face the Sentry. He could answer the riddle. He turned the final corner.

In the thick dark, Twig couldn't make out what the Sentry looked like. But he could feel it. It spun around him, faster and faster, whispering, licking, tasting. Cold scales scraped past his leg, and the chilled voice seemed to fill the entire cave. Twig wished he could face the Sentry in the light. He couldn't concentrate. Couldn't even make out the words in the echoing hiss that

303

surrounded him. He felt his breath slow. Felt the suck of the Sentry, close to his own lips . . .

There was a sharp pinprick of pain on the back of his neck and an angry 'meep'. Twig pulled his head away. He focused on the voice and felt his mind clear. He could hear the words now.

'I fly without wings, with no legs I crawl.
I'm beholden to none, and destroyer of all.
I'm wasted and killed and still I slip away.
I heal the wounds that haunt, and turn the night to day.
In hills of sand I will run out, and yet I never walk.
Only I can tell, but I will never talk.'

Twig's mind raced. He tried to remember the clues from the atlas. *Make haste* . . . The Sentry clawed closer. Twig was trying, but he couldn't think of what else had been scribbled in the atlas. He heard the scrape of the Sentry slide nearer still . . . there was something the librarians had said . . . something that – he scurried backwards, away from the approaching beast. If only he could think . . .

What was that word in the atlas? *T* something is *a fast-approaching beast.*

T . . . *T* . . . If only he had more time. Twig stopped. That was it. He went through the riddle in his mind. He couldn't be mistaken. The answer had to be time. Time flies. Time crawls. Time destroys all things. Time is wasted. And killed. It slips away and heals all wounds. Hills of sand could be a sand timer maybe? Time runs out and, Twig smiled, only time will tell.

The Sentry was on top of him now. Twig felt its lips sucking, felt his breath get thinner, harder to hold.

'Time,' he whispered.

The Sentry stopped. It sighed, a sigh full of longing, and Twig felt it shrink away, growing smaller and smaller until it was little more than a dark presence in the corner of the cave.

He was glad that after this, there would be no more riddles. No more Sentries. After this, there would only be his da.

Twig reached into the bundle, his fingers reaching for the final bone . . . but there was nothing there. The bundle was completely and utterly empty.

Chapter 55
Fog of Forgetting

Twig had failed. All he had to do was this one last thing and he had failed. The bone was gone.

The Keepers wouldn't be able to hold the Officials back. They would all be obliterated. He would never again see his da. The final Crossing would never be opened. The memories would never be released back into the world and the knowings of everyone who had come before would be lost. All those connections, song lines and story lines, gone. Twig thought of the despair with which the Gatherer had spoken when she told of them being lost for ever to the world.

There was a questioning 'meep' from his shoulder. 'I'm sorry,' Twig whispered. 'I can't fix this.' And then he remembered sitting on his da's lap, crying at something or other he had done, and his da's hand heavy on his head, his voice soft and whispering—

'Listen, love. You can't change what you've done. You can only change what you haven't done. So go, fix it as best you can. It's all anyone can do.'

And in that moment, Twig knew exactly what he had to do. It was the only thing he could do. He didn't know if it would work, but he knew he had to at least try. He could only change what he hadn't done. He had to choose to do *something*.

With trembling hands, Twig gripped tight to the only thing he had left. It was, after all, a *skeleton* key. Surely it could open a Crossing as good as any Bone of Lost Wonders? Surely it was a kind of Lost Wonder too? There was only one way to find out.

Twig untied the key from around his neck and squeezed it tight against his palm. He tipped back his head and howled every true thing into the cave, then he sat in the dark and waited.

The fog of forgetting came slowly. Twig got the sense that some part of him was leaving his body and spreading out around him, reaching out, calling, and in that dark, the wild shadows came for him.

Silver. Shining. Eyes.

Clap.

Clap.

Clap.

Twig falls into them, tumbling, faster and more furious than ever before, and suddenly he is caught, tugged towards a tune ringing in his ears, soft snippets calling him forward.

Here comes a

to bed,

And here

　　　　　　　　a

last man

　　Twig lets himself fall—

　　　　　　And the whole world exploded.

Chapter 56

Twist into Being

The Hoblin lady is looking for Flea. She's set traps. No one can get out of a trap set by a Hoblin. *I will not abide rats in my city.*

I need to find Flea. I hold the walkie-talkie up to my ear. There's nothing but static. 'Flea? If you're there – meet me at the gargoyle. Please. Today. Then you never have to see me again. I promise.' I can't say more than that, not knowing whose ears could be listening. I walk the whole city, looking for Flea, and I whisper my message into the static again and again. Then I go to the Boneyard to wait.

But Flea doesn't come. It's then that I see I'm not wearing my memory bracelet. Somewhere, it has come loose and fallen off. All those memories, all those wishes. All those moments, gone. And the ache of losing that is so strong I don't even try to stop the tears shaking my body and catching my breath.

I lie on the step of the gargoyle's tomb and watch the sun going down and wait and wait and I look up at those stars just starting to shine and I start to wish on every one that Flea will make it, will meet me here so I can warn them and so we can all get away. But then I remember that wishing is nothing but a waste of time. I save my breath.

I remember how we used to race to climb to the top of this tomb and how we'd leapfrog the headstones and make bonfires and how we pretended at being superheroes and argued about if it is better to be invisible or to fly and in the end we decided that the best superpower of all would be to twist into any animal we wanted to, whenever we wanted to, and we would hold our arms high in the air and close our eyes and twist and turn ourselves into being. I wonder if I held my arms high now and closed my eyes if I could twist myself into unbeing and disappear from this world for ever.

There is a soft click behind me. It is the click of someone watching, ready and waiting. Every hair on the back of my neck stands on end. I think of Hoblin Lady. And BigMan. My face turns like Dog Growl Man when he knew the game was up. I wonder what he was planning on doing with all that truth he found. Who he would tell. Who would listen. But maybe it doesn't matter who listens. Maybe telling is just the first step. Telling, so people know the truth cannot be swept away and cleaned up. *A single voice*. I think of his map still in my pocket and am sad that I never did give it to Flea.

'Are you alone?' And it isn't the voice of the Hoblin.

Or BigMan. Or Scarface. And my whole body trembles with happiness.

'You came!' I turn and ignore the slingshot cocked and ready to fire that is aimed at my head, and I whoop and fill with fire hearing Flea's voice again. I squeeze Flea to me, but Flea pulls back and puts the slingshot back into their belt.

'Here.' Flea throws a bundle at me. I know what it is even before my hands grab it from the air. My da's coat. Saved. I hold it to my nose and breathe in the smell of the Heavens. 'How did you—'

'How didn't *you* is the question.' Flea spits on the ground and I feel the shame heavy and hard on my chest.

I want to say – but there's no time. 'Flea, you've got to go. The Hoblin is setting traps all over the place. Her packages, her meetings, they're all traps to catch you. She'll kill you, for real.'

Flea looks at me. 'What do you take me for? I'm the best thief this city has to offer, remember? No one can catch me. I'm too clever for traps. I'm too clever for your stupid Hoblin lady, don't you know anything?'

'She isn't *mine*, squirt. I'm not going back. Not ever. We'll go. We'll find some other city. We can make money some other way—'

'You think this is about money?'

And I'm shaking my head and trying to get Flea to listen because Hoblin Lady might be scared but she won't be beaten. You can't beat a Hoblin. Not any way.

311

'May a million bullet ants nest in your brain. It was never about money. This is about Squizzy. It's about the Boneyard. It's about all of them, every sniffer, every street rat, every thief and thug and hooligan. It's about . . .' And Flea looks away. 'Twig, she had you in her claws and wouldn't let go. I had to do something, didn't I? Just like Robin Hood.' Flea smiles and seeing that smile I'm suddenly back, just a little kid leaving the Fruit of the Gods wrapped tight in its paper and yelling, '*For you, squirt!*' and not knowing a thing of the world.

'She's scared and people know it. I'm winning, Twig.'

'You've won already. I'm back, Flea. I was never gone. Every day I waited for you.'

'And every day I came, Twig.'

And my throat aches, knowing that Flea was there, so close, all that time. 'But why didn't you—'

'Because every day, I watched you go back to her.'

But it was never like that. 'Flea, please, let's just get the others and go.'

The smile falls from Flea's face and they shrug, slow, like their shoulders are too heavy to lift. 'There's not so many of us left,' they say softly.

'What do you mean?'

Flea takes another deep breath. 'The others . . . some of us were rounded up by Border Protection and bussed out. We were easy pickings sleeping on the streets. Some left the city searching for some better place to live, others found different crews. Some moved in down Riverside.'

312

'Riverside?'

Flea draws in a long breath. 'We're all just people, Twig.' I think how Da used to say that, and I know with every part of my soul that he did not run away. That he never ran away. That he never even got on the bus. That he never even made it out of that alley. He was killed by the Hoblin all those years back. I guess I've known all along. I guess I just didn't want to know it for sure. 'All just people,' Flea says again. 'Just lost souls trying to find our way.' Flea shrugs, like it doesn't really matter. But it does matter. It matters so much.

'Preacher? Where's Preacher?'

Flea turns away and their voice cracks. 'She moved down the station.'

'The station? With the sniffers? Is she . . .'

'I think it just got too hard. She and Squizzy, they were close, you know? Even though he gave her hell . . . I don't know she ever got over it. Sniffing made it all go away. All the cold and the hunger and . . . the memories. I guess there is a kind of bliss in forgetting. I tried to get her to come back, but it was like I wasn't even there. She was looking all over and yelling something in gibberish. I tried again and again but then one day she was gone.' Flea looks at me and then away. 'One of the other kids said she left with a woman who said she was her mum. Maybe that's true. Or maybe the other kid just hoped, you know? I like to think it's true though. That Preacher found her little bit of happy, and that she still thinks of

313

us sometimes. I like to think Squizzy ran too. That he turned to The Flash and made it out and that he still thinks of us, wherever he is now.'

I think of all of them. Of Squizzy. Of Preacher. Of the little ones, being bussed out and finding new crews, new families to be part of. Of Flea being all alone in that sadness. 'I didn't know.' And now a cold is eating at my skin. I should have been there. And suddenly I am remembering our hands holding together, our blood dripping into the earth, our spit in the dirt, *Blood Family for ever!* But it wasn't.

From the tree above, a raven calls out loud and strong. Flea looks at me and reaches out to wipe the wet from my eyes. 'We are all connected. To each other. To this world,' Flea whispers. 'Do you remember?'

'To everything that ever was.' Of course I remember.

'And everything that ever will be.'

'So whoever you are,'

'and wherever you are,'

'you are never alone.'

'Because we are all made of—' we say together. And then Flea stops. Their eyes grow wide. Their head shakes faster and faster and, and, and Flea is looking at me now like they don't know me and they whip their slingshot furious fast from their belt, steady, sure, marble cocked and readied to shoot. I look at the silver of the piping. I made Flea that shooter.

Behind me I hear a soft laugh. *Clap. Clap. Clap.*

314

Chapter 57
Trapped

Clap. Clap. Clap.

I know without turning that Hoblin Lady is standing there, smiling her iced smile and looking at us with those blazing hot eyes that have no spirit in them at all. Maybe she isn't a Hoblin. Maybe Hoblins are for babies and not for real. But whatever she is, she has no soul.

'No,' I tell Flea but their head is still shaking, slower now, and I turn to Hoblin Lady. 'Please.' But my voice is nothing but a whisper.

'Well done, Little Mouse, well done. I knew you would trap this thief. Just like you promised. Well done indeed.' Hoblin Lady laughs, soft in her throat and the whole world jumps and time stops and I see exactly what it is I've done. I haven't warned Flea. I haven't saved them. I've led Flea right up and into the crocodile's jaws.

I shake my head at Flea. 'I didn't . . .' I say. But then I hear my voice, tinned and echoey, coming out of the Hoblin's phone. *'I'll find out for you. I'll find out who*

is stealing from you. I'll bring them to you. Trust me.
I can get anyone to tell me anything. No problem.' The
Hoblin laughs and her eyes are bright with victory.
She recorded me. She knew already what I would do.
I thought I had the game worked out, when I was the
one being fooled all along. 'No,' I say. But the sound
doesn't even leave my lips.

'I should have listened to Preacher,' Flea says, their
voice thin and breaking. 'She said you'd turn. She said
everyone turns once they're owned. She said you
wouldn't be able to help it. That it wasn't your fault. I
said nothing in the whole of this world could ever turn
you. Not even the magic of a Hoblin.' Flea's voice shakes
and trembles and all the Gods and angels and stars and
wishes and every good thing in the whole world shake
and tremble with them. 'Blood Family for ever,
remember? Or did you never really mean it? Did you
ever really mean any of it?' Flea turns from me.

'Oh, now,' Hoblin Lady says, 'don't be too hard on
him. Blood is thicker than water, you know. Family love
is stronger than anything.'

Flea looks at me and I can see they don't understand
what the Hoblin is saying. The Hoblin can see it too.
'Oh, my. Didn't he tell you? My, my, Little Mouse.
Keeping secrets. Tut tut.' She smiles and leans in close;
her hand comes up to her mouth as though she is telling
a great secret. 'Hasn't he told you who I am? Don't you
know? I am his grandmother.'

Flea pulls back as if they have been hit in the stomach.

'Squirt,' I whisper, and Flea doesn't even blink. All the hurt in the world is aching out of those eyes and I can't look.

'I was wrong,' Flea says.

All I can see now is the silver of the slingshot, the shine of the metal calling to me to hurry up and finish it now before my chest bursts to pieces. That arm. It isn't even trembling. Not even a bit.

I'm not trembling either. I watch the raven disappear into the sky and see now what he was warning about.

I look at those eyes. There are no eyes like those, no eyes that stole the colour from the sun and made it their own. I wish it would end now. I wish it would all be over so I don't have to feel my heart cracking in two any more.

I wish I never, ever existed.

'Go on.' Run rabbit, run rabbit, run run run. 'Do it then.' And I say the words I know Flea can't ever resist. Not ever. 'I dare you.'

Twig is gasping, all the air is being sucked harder and faster and the shadows are disappearing from around him and he tries to grasp hold of them. Tries to find the eyes of the one waiting, tries to become, he is the rain falling, wind howling, dirt pressing under nails, he is pushing the key upwards, forwards to a boy waiting, crouched behind a bush, watching with wild eyes . . . but the shadows have left him. They have no need for him any more.

Twig leaves the dirt, twists into rock, into sand and water, drifts for a moment, feeling himself unthread . . . and just as he is about to let go, to embrace the unbecoming, to cease to have *ever* existed, a thin black shadow snakes across the sky, searching, calling, finding him, wrapping, winding, binding, meeping, clutching, dragging, biting and he is pulled back into the cave by the chain of meeples.

Twig gasps for air. He sees one last glimpse of a face, hears the song ring again through his head—

'Here comes a candle to light you to bed,
And here comes a chopper to chop off your head!
Chip chop chip chop the last man is dead.'

Chapter 58

The Eternal Hereafter

It was Krruk that found Twig, deep in the bowels of the cave, the ache leaking from him in a thin wail that vibrated through the cave and sent creatures running. It was Krruk that led him out and down the long path, through the Field of Dreams which now stood empty and dusty and barren. And it was Krruk that took him back to where the Gatherer was waiting, her wolves surrounding her in a solemn pack.

Twig thought perhaps he should be remembering something. He thought there should be people here. Weren't there other people here? It looked as though a great battle had been waged . . . He remembered then the Keepers and the Officials and . . .

'What happened?' He turned to Krruk.

'Never you mind, presh. Most would have hung the fiddle in the roof long ago, but you fought on. You did what you could. The other Keepers fought on, too. They did what they could. Some fights are older and will live longer than them fighting. All you can do is

319

carry the torch for a bit. It's all anyone can do, isn't it? And anyway, a few of us managed to get away. It seems the Officials don't like the Field of Dreams neither. They'll be back, of course. But you don't need to worry about any of that now. You is done, boyo.'

The Keeper with the rubber duck emerged from behind a rock, picking up pieces of torn and destroyed atlases as he came. He walked slowly to Twig and handed him an old tin whistle. Twig couldn't for the life of him think why. The old man touched the place on Twig's neck where the skeleton key used to hang, and tears ran down his cheek and he held Twig's face in his hands and kissed his head so gently that Twig felt his knees give way beneath him.

'I tried . . .' Twig said. 'But the . . . what was it? Something I had to do and couldn't. I couldn't find something. Which means that . . .' He struggled to remember what it was he had to do. And why this rag-tag man and strange skeleton whale were looking at him with such pity. A teardrop ran from the whale's eye and fell into the dirt next to Twig. And for a moment, he remembered again the shadows, looked for a sign that they had been released, then shook his head. 'Oh. It didn't work,' he whispered to the Gatherer. 'I'm sorry. I thought the skeleton key might be a kind of Lost Wonder. I followed the shadows, and left the key, but . . .'

The Gatherer peered at him with burning bright eyes.

'Quickly now.' Krruk turned to the Gatherer.

320

'Quickly, before he forgets too much of himself. Take him to his da. Please. He's done.'

The Gatherer leaned down close to Twig and ran her clawed fingers over his face, as though she was seeing him through her hands. 'Tell me again, boy, what is it you desire?'

'I don't know . . .' he said. What had the skeleton bird said? 'I want to be with my da. I want to be done.'

She looked at him a while longer, sniffing at the air, staring into his eyes, then she grabbed at a half-burnt map drifting through the air. *The Isle of the Eternal Hereafter*. 'This is where he waits,' she said. 'It's where all the old Keepers wait. The Forgetting is weak there.' And without looking at Twig again, she turned and disappeared with her pack of wolves, back into the wilds.

Twig looked at the map stretching across the page, of an evening sun looking down over a kingdom, the faint outline of stars glowing from the black at the edge of the map, and a land rich with hills and streams and forests and fields, and where the water touched the land, golden sparks floated into the sky.

The Eternal Hereafter and Surrounds

And there was something so brilliant and so right about that picture, as though it was a picture he had almost seen before somehow. As though he had already

321

dreamt it, already imagined it, already seen himself there, inside of it. It made him feel happy, this picture. Safe. And he ached to be already in that safety and warmth. He smiled.

'Come now, boyo,' Krruk said gently. 'The river crossing isn't far. Just down the hill to Ferryman's Cove. I'll take you there.'

Twig nodded and stood. He looked around. Who was that old man again? 'Here,' Twig said and handed the man the whistle in his hand. 'I think this is yours.' The man took the whistle and walked slowly away, and his whale began to sing, a low and mournful song to the moon.

Now what was it Twig was supposed to be doing . . . and what was with the strange skeleton bird?

'Come now, follow me. I am Krruk, your Guardian, remember? I'll look after you.'

'Krruk?'

'No. Krruk. You've to roll the tongue like . . .' And Twig wondered what on earth had made the strange crow start to cry.

They walked in silence to the edge of a raging black river and watched a gaggle of gargoyles leaping in and out of the flaming black waves. 'We'll just wait here for the canoe to come. It shouldn't take long now . . .'

Twig sat down and started drawing in the dirt, his finger moving back and forth on the ground. A speck of white in the dirt caught the sun and Twig thought of

322

stardust falling from the sky . . . Suddenly he remembered again, felt the fog retreat, just a bit. 'I remembered how I died. I remembered who . . . who killed me.'

'That old elevator music? What are you doin' bothering with that for?' The raven eyed the ground, where Twig had drawn a large pair of wings, scratched so deep into the ground that they almost looked like they had cracked through the earth. Twig's finger reached out and scratched at the surface again, his hand feeling the invisible push back and forward of another hand, a smaller hand, showing him again the shape and movement of the letters. TWIG AND FLEA. And he smiled. The raven used his claw to add KRRUK. 'You forgot,' he said.

'And Da?' Twig looked at Krruk. 'Will I remember him?'

'As soon as you see him. The Gatherer will have made sure of it. She's not an Olds for nothin', you know. That's the thing with love. It's stronger than any law, any force. Your love for each other can't ever be forgotten. And like she said, the Forgettin' is weaker out on the Isles. You'll remember all you need to.'

'I'm really going to be with him?'

'For all of eternity. You'll love it, you will. The Isle of the Eternal Hereafter is the absolute best. Like all the greatest summer holiday moments rolled into one, there to enjoy for the rest of eternity.' The raven smiled and pecked Twig gently on the cheek. 'Now listen, presh,

I'm not comin' with you. When you get on that canoe, that is goodbye, like.'

'For ever? Where will you go?'

'Well, I won't lie to you, I am ver-rry popular and there is great demand for a Guardian such as myself. But even so, I was thinking, I might like to carry on where you left off, like. Regroup with the Keepers who got away. Try and get my claws on that last Bone of Lost Wonders and see if I can get things back to the way they were before them Gods got a taste for hoardin' all the memories and feastin' on them themselves. To be honest, I think they've been sellin' them on the black market to the other Spirit Realms . . . but listen, it was a good thing you did. Tryin' to use your key. If you'd have asked me, I would have said it would work, no problemo. You did good, boyo.'

Twig nodded and watched his tears leave marks in the dirt.

Krruk put his claw on Twig's hand. 'Presh, I won't be with you, but that doesn't mean I'm not always there inside of you. I will be. I'm your Guardian. I'm always with you. And no matter what happens, no matter how much you forget, some part of you will always know me. Some very deep part of you will always remember.'

Twig kissed the raven on the head. 'I'll never forget you, Krruk. How could I?' But even as he said it, part of him was wondering who the bird was.

Krruk pulled a feather from inside his ribcage. 'Here, have a raven's feather. They're good luck, you know.'

'Are they? That's nice.' It was nice. The whole place was nice. Everything was just perfect.

'Look now. Here's your canoe. Goodbye, my boy. Have fun, won't you. It's an adventure after all. Embrace the unknown!'

Twig nodded and turned to look at the mountains towering above him. *What a magnificent place*, he thought. *Just lovely. Wonderful.*

Twig looked at the odd scribbles drawn in the dirt, as if from some old, long-forgotten script, and at a pair of large wings, etched deep and waiting. Twig reached out and touched the wings. For a moment there was a jolt inside him, and he heard a muffled cheer. Those wings, those words, there was something . . . something he had lost . . . something he was losing . . . but no. It must simply be a mere shadow of some old dream. Unimportant. Twig wiped them clear with his foot.

A large crowd of strange stick figures had gathered along his arm. He brushed them off into the dirt and told them to shoo. The smallest one gave a sorrowful 'meep' and Twig stood up. He had a canoe to catch. He stepped into the boat and looked around to see if . . . now what was it? No, *who* was it? For a moment, Twig felt as though there was someone that should be with him. He paused, suddenly unsure, and he caught just a flash of memory. Of Flea. Of the slingshot.

'Krruk!' he called and turned back to the shore.

'What is it, my boy?' Krruk cawed, his head cocked to try and hear Twig above the crashing of the water against the shore.

Twig shrugged. 'It's just, I know it's only elevator music, but it was Flea. Did you know? Flea killed me.'

The canoe drifted slowly away from the shore.

'What do you mean Flea killed you?'

'It was Flea. They shot me with their slingshot. The one I made for them,' Twig yelled, holding tight to the memory, knowing with some part of him that he needed Krruk to know, and the river raged angry and loud beneath the canoe.

'Don't be daft,' Krruk called back, his voice almost lost in the noise of the river. 'Flea didn't kill you. You weren't even shot. It was that big fella with the bat—'

'What? Wait.' Twig reached for the key, but his fingers only scrabbled at his bare neck. 'Krruk! I don't want to forg—' The river surged, and the canoe tilted dangerously close to the water. Twig lay low against the bottom of the boat. What was it he was saying? And where exactly was he going? And what . . . ah well. Probably didn't matter much.

Above the canoe, a skeleton raven spun circles in the air. It cawed once, then exploded into a shower of black feathers that rained down upon the boat. *Crow feathers*, Twig thought. *What good luck*. And the canoe drifted further from the shore.

Chapter 59

The End

Twig didn't look down at the dark nothing of the river beneath him, at the way it seethed and broiled and churned with fury or wonder at the ferocity of the tide pulling the boat. He looked instead to the brilliance of the setting sun and gazed steadily towards his future shore.

There was a song, barely audible above the splash of the waves. But it was there. He leaned his head over the boat, trying to find where it was coming from. It rose up from the water, tugging at Twig, calling him—

Bull's eyes and targets, say the
bells of St Margret's

It was becoming clearer the closer Twig leaned down towards the water. The waves crashed hard against the boat and the song stopped, the words turned to bells playing a tune, ringing loud and strong, and Twig could hardly resist reaching into the water to find them.

But then he looked up, and there it was, the Eternal Hereafter, where all his wishes and dreams washed into shore in a blur of colours and sounds that dripped from the sky and clouded gently upwards from the sand. And there, waiting, was his da.

'My boy!' His da, as brilliant and wonderful as he had always been, his arms stretching towards him. Twig could already feel the squeeze of those hands, the safety and love and comfort of being together again, and his heart beat hard against his chest.

'Da!' Twig called, the call of the bells forgotten, and suddenly he was as light as air remembering the pure engulfing joy of being held in his father's arms, the brilliant everything of being again with his da. Fruit of the Gods began to fall from the sky.

There was a crash of thunder from deep in the river and the canoe tipped again towards the raging water. Twig fell backwards, into the canoe. A single black feather dislodged itself from his clothes and floated on to the deck. It was a beautiful feather. All the colours of the rainbow were captured in that black, and then some . . . A crow's feather . . . No, a raven's feather.

And now the river is seething, stronger even than before. There is a quiet 'meeeeeep!' from his pocket and Twig looks down to see a very small stick-figure person emerging from his pocket, one hand holding tight to a rolled-up scroll, and in the other is an old leather bracelet, knotted and tied with bits and pieces. Twig takes the bracelet. He touches a dark knotted rock and somehow knows it is more than just a rock. It is a piece of a star. *We are all made of stardust.* And suddenly Twig knows that this is his. That he needs this, more than anything.

Twig looks at the little stickperson watching him and puts the bracelet on his wrist. The fog around him lifts, just a bit, and Twig feels as though everything is coming slowly back into focus. He touches the little car wheel and remembers. The rock, the stone, the small piece of red bandana. And finally, the twisted silver lock-picking keys. He remembers it all.

The meeple waves the scroll at him and Twig takes it in his hand and lets it unfurl. It's the final map wedges from all the Keepers' atlases, stitched together. The meeple starts walking along the map, its feet leaving behind silvery footprints that shimmer from the page. It walks up and down the river, just like the meeples did back when all the Keepers were together, making the river shine brighter with each step. There is something about the shape of the river on the map . . . it looks familiar somehow. As if Twig should know it. He hears the whispered memory of the Gatherer in his ears, *Key, map, map key, see yourself and be set free!* and there is something . . . Twig takes the map from the meeple and hears the Gatherer again. *Where you see the key, a Crossing will be.* And that is when he understands.

The key. The river. The river *is* the key. He traces the silver line of the river with his finger. He sees how it

329

flows in the shape of the key. The caves weren't the final Crossing after all. Maybe the skeleton key *did* work. Maybe there is just one *more* Crossing that needs to be opened to release the wild shadows and bring back the memories. The river. The *river* is the final Crossing. *Which means*, Twig thinks then, *that somewhere, a Sentry is waiting.*

Twig looks over the edge of the boat. But there is no Sentry. Just his own reflection staring back at him, ragged and tired. The water shimmers, and for a moment, his reflection looks as though it has grown wings, bright white and brilliant. His thoughts run wild, words toppling into each other, over each other, until a single sentence whispers through the noise. *Come with me, I can show you how to fly.* And with absolute certainty, Twig understands that somehow *he* is his own Sentry. That the answer to this riddle is not a thing, or a word or a feeling. The answer is more than that. It is the answer that he has been searching for, for a very long time. The answer is to listen to the whisper of his soul. 'Yes,' he whispers.

'My darling,' his da calls again. 'You are home now. You will never be lost again . . .' And his da holds out his arms and beckons him to hurry.

Twig breathes in the smell of his bracelet. 'But I'm not lost,' he whispers, the sound barely leaving his lips.

And in that moment, he sees with eyes that look for

whispers, and ears wonder-wide, and he understands just what he has to do. It is like Krruk told him. He must embrace the unknown.

On the shore of the Eternal Hereafter, Twig's da is quiet. He watches his son, standing still, and even before Twig places his foot on the edge of the canoe, his da knows, as every father does.

Twig does not turn back to look at him. He does not see him nod. He does not see the kiss blown to him on the wind, or hear his da's whisper, 'So you may always find your happiness, my darling.' But he does raise his hand to his own lips, as though he can feel the feather touch of his da's kiss tingling, for just a moment.

Twig lets himself tip backwards, and into the dark, twirling wild of the raging river of shadows. There is a roar, a great release, and Twig can feel all the memories, the song lines and story lines, the stories told and stories heard, the secrets of the earth, the knowings of everyone who has come before, the wonders and whispers that connect everything surging past him, over him, through him as they erupt from the river and tremble the fabric of everything that has ever been. He hears the triumphant howl of the Gatherer, the curses of the Gods, the meeps of a million meeples, he sees silver heads floating and swirling through the air above him.

The water, dark and flaming black, pulls and tugs, and Twig closes his eyes, twists and turns, and is dragged down, down, deeper and deeper, and then . . .

Then there is nothing, for a
very
long
time.

In a moment, Twig will open his eyes. The black will fade and for just one brilliant moment, everything will be brighter and clearer and sharper and louder and more perfect than it's ever been.

He will be alive inside every tree and rock and trembling cloud. He will burn with whispers, rustling the air. His blood will twist through veins and roots, and dance in the smoke that falls from the sky. His heart will pound in a thousand chests, thrum in a thousand drums, beat in a thousand waves upon a thousand shores. His eyes will burn with the brightnesses of a hundred suns. His skin will crawl across long-forgotten bones and his breath will fill the emptiest, oldest, most ancient lungs. He will see everything that's ever been, and everything that's still to come, dancing and spinning and humming, paper-thin on the wind. He will see the seas swelling and the rivers rising. He will see the moon crumbling and the stars falling from the sky. He will see the footprints left behind and the footsteps not yet taken. He will be the beginning of time, and the end.

In that one moment, he will understand everything.

And after that, nothing will ever be the same again.

Chapter 60

The Beginning

My head is on fire. Everything is spinning and my eyes are burning and scratching and so, so heavy—

You owe me five farthings, say the
bells of St Martin's.

There's a tune ringing out somewhere nearby, from a radio, maybe? And I'm in a cave. No. Not a cave. I'm in a tomb. The gargoyle's tomb, and there are little stick-figure people drawn on the walls. How did they draw them like that? So it looks like the stick figures are riding the shadows on the walls, and how did they make them look so alive that for a second, I think I see them actually move? There's something important about them . . . but everything is so fuzzy and the only thing I can remember is 'meep'. I rub the back of my head and the memory fades.

My da's coat is soft in my arms and I try to still the spinning world. I want to sleep, to let the pain hush and quiet, but there is something about that tune, playing all tinny and far away, calling to me—

Pray when will that be? say the
bells of Stepney.

I try to follow the notes, to remember what it is about the tune – but the song isn't playing any more. Maybe it never was. Maybe it was just playing in my head. Outside, the sky is turning dark and I blink my eyes to try to slow the world from spinning.

I touch the knot on my memory bracelet and bring it to my lips. And when did I find my bracelet? I was sure I'd lost it. I don't remember finding it. I don't remember why I am here . . . There's blood on the floor and scrape marks in the dust by the door and I think it's my blood . . . but it's not my scrape marks. And I remember now. Flea. Flea was here with me. And now they aren't.

There are footsteps, and a shadow tumbles through the door. It's one of the little ones from the Boneyard. What was his name? Silas? He's bigger now, and surer, and he doesn't look at me like I'm a hero any more.

'Come on. Hurry up, will you? They'll be coming back for you.' My legs are only half walking and I'm leaning on Silas, and he's dragging me over the graves and through the trees and the world keeps spinning and the black keeps creeping in from the side and I'm back in the arms of my da, being spun around and around and around and I can smell him, Da, and he smells like cracked rock skin and tunnels through stars and . . .

There's a needle-sharp pain like something has bitten me on the back of my neck and the black fades. I try to focus on Silas. He sits me on a motorbike. I guess he fixed it on his own. But he's too little to be riding a bike. Isn't he? Aren't we all? Too little for any of it. He grabs my shoulders and gives me a shake and the world becomes sharp again.

'You were dead,' he says. 'I was watching from the trees. I saw the whole thing. You and Flea and the Hoblin. And when that big fella snuck up from behind and whacked your head with his bat, I was sure your brain would explode out your nose. You dropped like rocks to the ground, and there was no living in your eyes at all. I know. I've seen dead eyes before and that's what yours were. Dead.'

Blood drips from the back of my head and I feel the swelling, tight against torn skin . . . 'What about Flea? Where are they?'

'The Hoblin took them. Kicking and screaming and fighting like hell—'

And here comes a chopper to chop off your head!
Chip chop chip chop the last man is dead.

'I heard a song. A tune . . .'

Silas nods at my pocket, at the walkie talkie. 'The bells? There were bells ringing a tune through that. Come on, we've got to get from here.'

Bells. Squizzy's voice whispers in my ear, '*Can you hear that tune? My sister and me used to sing along—*'

Oranges and lemons, say the
bells of St Clement's.

'*and their bodies fall, BAM!*' And Squizzy said that water, it sucks you down. It sucks you down and under and into the rock.

'The quarry. They're going to the quarry. We have to get Flea. We have to save them—'

'Don't be stupid. They'll kill us all. And I don't even know where the quarry is.'

For a second I think I hear a small squeak in my ear, and a flash of something like a dream. *Our stories are the maps for how we can be.* And I remember the Dog Growl man's map. Still in my pocket. Still waiting for me to give it to Flea.

I unfold it, trying to make sense of the roads and the rivers and . . . 'There. That's the quarry there.' I touch the map where a mob of red Xs are bunched, and think of Squizzy, trying so hard to get us to believe. He was telling the truth. Those Xs, they didn't mark where anyone keeps their treasure. Those Xs marked where the Hoblin keeps her dead. The quarry *is* a body pit. And now the Hoblin has taken Flea there.

Silas spits on the ground and shakes his head. 'I can't.'

'Just take me, and then go. Please. For Flea.'

He looks again at the map. 'That looks like a shortcut. Look.' Silas grabs the map and points to a thin line cutting the map in two. 'Come on then.'

And all I can think of are those bells ringing, over and over again.

I can hear them. Their voices carrying across the quarry, the wind whipping the words through the trees. I can hear BigMan laughing and the Hoblin asking questions and Flea spitting that a billion spiders would nest in her nose and her nostrils would swell to the size of melons. I hear Silas riding away and am glad he's safe.

A raven lands on a branch in front of me, its wings ruffled from the wind. The bird looks at me with its white-as-light eyes, and takes to the skies with a '*Krrruuuuuk*' and I wish I knew what it was it was trying to say.

The wind howls harder and thunder rolls across the sky. Flea cries out. I run. Deeper and deeper into the forest, over the rocks and through the trees, the wind stirring up leaves and snapping branches and howling in my ears, and I'm running so fast I am the King of Wolves, running with my pack, and all the wild shadows in the forest run with me. I'm almost there. Almost at Flea.

I stop. I can see them through the trees, torch lights flashing in the almost-dark. ScarFace is holding a gun, keeping watch and BigMan has Flea tied up with chains and a lock. He's holding tight to Flea's arm, and they're only steps away from the edge of the quarry cliff. I can't see the water from where I'm hiding, but I can imagine it, deep, dark and cold, and ready to suck Flea in and under the rock. I'm remembering Flea's voice in my ears, '*With my sister's picks, I can whisper open any lock in the world, just like Houdini.*' But Flea doesn't have their sister's picks. I've got them. Bent and twisted out of shape, hanging useless on my bracelet.

I creep, sure and steady, keeping low down behind the bushes, crawling slow so any moving branch could just be the wind. That wind is here to help me. Like the ghosts of all those dead in the body pit are on my side. The Hoblin asks a question, and Flea spits in answer. BigMan shoves Flea towards the edge, and my fingers clench the dirt. And then my finger hits at something wedged under the earth. Something cold and hard. There is the smallest whisper of wonder, pulling at my fingertips, demanding to be heard, and I dig with my nails, the dirt pressing . . .

I edge closer. Flea is right in front of me now. I can feel the warmth of their skin pushing through the bush. All I need to do is reach out my hand and I could touch them. I push my arm slowly, quietly through the bush, only a few leaves separating us. I don't know if Flea knows I'm here, if they can feel the nearness of me, the same way I feel them, but they step back towards the bush, just a step, and now my fingers are gripping tight to Flea's and squeezing, squeezing, letting Flea know that I am here. That I will never leave. That I will never run.

BigMan pulls Flea back again, closer to the edge of the quarry, not seeing the smile on Flea's face, or the old brass key dug from the dirt held tight between their fingers. Not knowing that Flea is Houdini, and doesn't he know anything?

I'm pulling my arm back out of the bush, and I'm thinking of finding a branch big enough to whack ScarFace with, or BigMan even, when the wind stops. It drops from the sky and the whole quarry turns still as death. Nothing moves. Nothing except the bush, its thorns snagged on my da's coat, and the rustle of those leaves is as loud as thunder. The voice in my head cackles loud and long.

ScarFace turns. His gun steady and level in his hand. 'Who's there?' he yells. And BigMan turns. And Hoblin turns. ScarFace clicks the gun.

'Run, Twig! Run!'

But I won't ever run again. I stand up straight and tall, and my eyes lock with Flea's and I am here and Flea is here and we are together and right now, at this exact moment, that is the only thing in the world that matters. The voice in my head stops laughing. It hushes. I won't ever hear that voice again. I know exactly who I am.

And then. The gun fires.

I'm not scared. Not even a bit.

Hoblin Lady yells. Her voice echoing loud and fierce, and she steps. Just one, single step. One step to put herself between me and the bullet. To save *me*. She looks right at me, just before she is hit. There is only soft in her eyes.

And the whole world stops.

Completely. Stops.

When it starts again it is going twice, three times as fast as before.

The Hoblin is falling, her blood spilling. BigMan is pushing towards her. His arms stretched. He's reaching for her. And Flea . . .

I see the flash of their bandana in the torchlight as Flea falls. Tumbling from the quarry cliff. Those chains wrapped tight. I hear the BAM as their body hits the water. I'm at the edge. I'm reaching. I'm screaming—

The police burst from the trees. Hands hold me tight. Pull me back. I'm kicking. I'm fighting. I'm screaming, trying to get to the water to reach Flea. Trying to get them to hear me. To listen. To see . . .

I was expecting for the quarry water to be churning and blood-red with fury. I was expecting fire and destruction and floods of tears to be raining down from the heavens. I was expecting every angel in the sky to weep and every God to fall down dead in horror at what their world has become.

But the quarry is just the quarry. Not a wave. Not a dip to show where Flea could be. The storm has stilled. The moon is shining and the stars are sparkling in the sky.

The coppers pull me away. Put me in an ambulance,

and they're covering me with blankets and telling me I'm safe now, I can trust them, and they aren't the usual city coppers in their usual uniforms. And I think maybe I can trust them and I'm trying to tell them about Flea, and then Silas is there, and he's saying, 'I had to get help or they'd kill you both. I rang the number on the map . . . these coppers aren't from here. The Hoblin doesn't own these ones. They said they would help. Twig? Twig? Where's Flea?' and all I can hear is Squizzy's voice in my ear, telling how that water sucks you down. '*That's how they do.*'

Chapter 61

Life After

Twig is walking. He'll keep walking, past the station, along the canal, over the bridge and beyond the city walls, walking and walking, wherever the world takes him.

His last night in the city had been spent painting. It had taken him a while to find the perfect wall. A wall tall enough to be seen and noticed. A wall that could be added to by people who had their own stories to keep alive. A wall where everyone passing would raise their eyes and see the truth. *A single voice can change the world.* Maybe it won't make a difference. But maybe it will. And that's all that really matters.

Twig had painted a map of the city on the wall, just like Flea had wanted to, all that time ago. '*So hundreds of years from now, people will look at this wall and say "This used to be a City of Beasts. They existed and were true."*'

He drew the Towers. *People were taken from here.* The markets and the station. *Here a mother found their child*, and every place in the city that had once been theirs. *Here lies the death of music. Here a car flew. Here the river gives back the dead. Here sits Squizzy's house. Here waits the Hidden Skeleton.* He drew the Boneyard, *Blood Family for ever*, and thought that even if it hadn't turned out the way they all imagined, there was still a truth in those words. Then he paused, and with shaking hands drew a bright star over the quarry. *Here lies those whose truths were not heard.* And when he was done drawing their story on to the wall, he wrote, in great big white letters that shone from the bricks, *THE LOST SOUL ATLAS*, so everyone, no matter how lost, could tell their story and find their way home. Because stories are the maps for how we can be.

And now Twig is walking. There is only one thing left for him to do. He needs to say goodbye. And then he will leave the city. He knows it will be for ever. And even though there are no stars visible in the sky, and even though he no longer really believes, he wishes all the same. Just in case.

It is morning by the time Twig reaches the park. He stands, looking at the white wings and flecks of stardust faded almost completely into the bricks, then leans his back against the wall for the very last time. He can feel the shadow of a much smaller boy imprinted there on the bricks, can hear the song of a voice, the click of a camera. He closes his eyes and feels his wings hum the air around him. He feels the whole world drop away and the wind carry him high into the sky, higher and higher, until the stars shine beneath his fingertips. He knows, if he were to look through the seeing stone now, he would see his wings, bright white and brilliant, sprouted from his back and trembling in the air. But he doesn't need to see them to know they are there. This time, he just believes.

He's almost smiling when he steps away from the bricks. And as he bends down to leave a single knot against the wall, his tears drip in splotches in the dirt and make a picture of something that looks just a little like a bird. If he had noticed, Twig might have thought it was an omen of sorts.

And then he writes his goodbye on the wall. *We are all made of stardust.* Even though he knows it is too late, Flea would have liked it, he thinks.

'For you, squirt,' Twig says out loud and for a moment he imagines he feels that nearness once again. The feeling of being made whole.

'For always,' comes a voice, and the voice is warm and true and there they are, stepping from the shadows, Flea, with setting-sun eyes and a smile as bright and brilliant as always.

Flea's fingers brush the wet from his cheek. 'You are such a baby. Did you think I couldn't swim? I can swim like a salmon. When you swim, you swim like a chicken. Good thing it was me that thug knocked into the quarry and not you, or you'd be food for the fish no doubt. Did you think that those water spirits would suck me down? That I wouldn't be able to get out of those chains like Houdini? I'm the lock whisperer, don't you know? And thanks for the key.' Flea fingers the brass key hanging from a leather strap around their neck. 'What is it? A skeleton key? I've heard of them but never thought they were real. But this key is the best. It pops locks open like butter. Better even than Maha's lock picks. And what took you so long to get here anyway, squirt? Did you think I wouldn't come?'

'I thought—' But then Twig stops talking, because it doesn't matter what he thought. What matters is now. And Twig has a sudden flash of a memory—

Maha

A *dream*, he thinks, or a memory from so far back it almost isn't real any more. It's a message written on cracked yellow paper—

From: Maha

He smiles.

'Hey, Flea. Why did the chicken go to the séance?'

'Why?

'To get to the Other Side.' And the two of them laugh longer and harder than they have ever laughed at a joke before.

'I waited all these years for that? That's terrible.' Flea stops laughing. 'Thank you, Twig. Now come on.

If we're to visit every single place that exists, we'd better get going. I've made a list. First stop, Disneyland.'

'Disneyland? To hug a giant mouse?'

'Of course. And a giant duck. And a giant elephant. I think they have one giant of everything.'

Flea picks a black feather up from the ground and holds it to the light. 'Look at that. A raven's feather. So beautiful, don't you think?' And they take Twig's wrist and tie the feather on to the bracelet. 'They're good luck, you know.'

'I know,' Twig says. He takes Flea's hand in his own, and their fingers tangle and hold tight and don't let go. Not for a very long time.

High above them, on a branch of a long-dead tree, a raven watches. It calls out once, then takes to the skies. Flying black and beautiful against the bright white, circling higher and higher on the wind, its call trembling through the streets. And when the raven drops feathers all across the city, in plumes of brilliance that rain down on the people and turn the streets black, everyone knows then that it must be some kind of omen. A good omen, for everyone knows that raven feathers are good luck.

But neither Flea nor Twig notice. They are already following the promise of footprints down paths not yet taken. Together. For always.

Author Note

Although the people and places in this book exist only in our imaginations, the circumstances that Twig and the Beasts find themselves in are all inspired by real events. Lack of housing and social support funding, unemployment rates, failing mental health care systems, natural disasters, conflict and war have led to a global homelessness crisis that affects every country in the world. It is estimated that there are approximately 150 million children currently living on the streets. That means there are more children who are homeless than the *entire* populations of Australia, the UK, the Republic of Ireland, New Zealand, Canada and Greece combined.

For many of these children, discrimination, police brutality and corruption, street 'cleansing', death squads, criminal gangs, drug addiction, abduction, abuse and the constant struggle to find food and shelter are all part of their daily lives. And yet, these same young people are still finding the bravery, the determination and the courage to fight injustice. Whether it is through the production of newspapers or pamphlets, street performances, protests, graffiti or other acts of creative resistance and activism, their voices are rising. We just need to listen.

To find out more about homelessness and children living on the streets, a good place to start is Amnesty International or UNICEF. The Consortium for Street Children, and Railway Children also provide a wealth of information and fundraising opportunities for those looking to help.

A single voice really can change the world. No matter how small a person, no matter how small an act, what we do, where we look, what we remember, it all matters.

Fight the forgetting.

Acknowledgements

There is so much blind belief that goes into writing a book. Belief that the small seed of an idea that sidles up to you unexpectedly might just be one worth paying attention to; belief that the characters will reveal themselves, given time; belief that the plot will emerge (or be dragged, biting, scratching and screeching from its burrow . . .); belief that this story will become one worth telling, and the even stronger belief that the story will become one worth reading; belief that you are the only person who can do all these things for this particular story; and the undying belief that someone else out there will believe all of that too.

Without that someone else to believe, this story would never have grown beyond that first seed. And I am ridiculously fortunate to have multiple someones who believe strongly enough in my words to make writing this book possible, and to keep me sane in the process. Without them, this book would not exist.

Thank you to the amazing community of book folk – fellow writers, booksellers, librarians and readers, who have all been so wonderfully supportive, enthusiastic and encouraging, and to all those creators, artists and writers who have come before and so generously feathered my nest.

To my wonderful agent Claire Wilson, who guides me through the publishing realm better than any Afterlife Guardian. Thank you for your calm wisdom, kindness and constant encouragement, even from half a world away.

To the fantastic publishing teams at Hachette – Suzanne O'Sullivan, Helen Thomas, Amina Youssef and Emma Roberts – you are the wizards behind the curtain that brought this all together and made this book so much more than I hoped for. Thank you for your gentle questions, prods, suggestions and comments that always led to bright new flashes of insight.

To the two people I entrusted a ridiculously early draft to – Dani Solomon and Penni Russon – if it wasn't for your early encouragement and guidance throughout, I would have let this story go. Thank you for seeing what it could become and for showing me how to get there. And Dani, an extra thanks for gifting me the genius of Terry Pratchett, so I could hear the susurrus of Granny's wisdom when I most needed it.

They say everyone needs to find their people, and I am so lucky to have found mine. To the Coven – Kate Mildenhall, Penny Harrison, and Penni Russon – brilliant authors and wonderful friends who talked me through every facet of this book, who picked me up and dusted me off, who helped plan, plot, edit, market, create, rejoice and manage all the stuff in between. Thank you for the magic.

And to my amazing children, Mani, Mischa and Luca, who showed me what it means to have eyes that look for whispers and ears that are wonder-wide. Thank you for the meeples, monsters, riddles and maps; for songs and stardust, plot twists and logic loops; for the endless throwing around of ideas and for rescuing me from my moments of despair; for the cups of tea when I needed them; for the cooked dinners and walked dogs; for the washed clothes and cleaned house; and for giving me all the time I need. Thank you for believing I could.

And finally, to Jugs. For absolutely everything. For always.

About the Author

Zana Fraillon is a multi-award-winning author of highly acclaimed books for children and young adults, including *The Bone Sparrow* and *The Ones That Disappeared*. *The Bone Sparrow* won the Amnesty CILIP Honour 2017, and the Book of the Year for Older Children 2017 at the Australia Book Industry Awards. It was also shortlisted for the *Guardian* Children's Fiction Prize 2016 and the CILIP Carnegie Medal 2017. *The Ones That Disappeared* won the 2018 New South Wales Premier's Award for Young People's Literature. Zana lives in Victoria, Australia with her husband and three children.

Zana was once told to 'shine a light in all the dark places'. Through her writing, she hopes to bridge the walls that divide us. To give voice to those who have been silenced, and enable us to see those who are hidden, balancing the realities of their situation with the power of hope and the strength of the human spirit.

You can follow her on Twitter and Instagram @ZanaFraillon and visit her website to see even more content at www.zanafraillon.com

OTHER AWARD-WINNING TITLES BY
ZANA FRAILLON

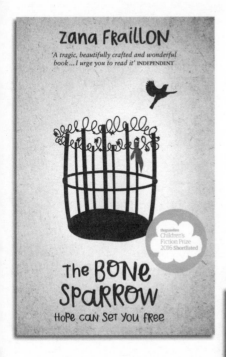

'Think of it as a powerful polemic, yes, but also think of it as a story of the redeeming power of friendship and the vital nature of storytelling'

THE BOOKBAG BLOG

'By turns harrowing, heart-wrenching, and magical, this is an incredibly powerful – and incredibly important – novel'

LOVEREADING4KIDS